Ciao Bella

**Center Point
Large Print**

**This Large Print Book carries the
Seal of Approval of N.A.V.H.**

Ciao Bella

Gina Buonaguro and Janice Kirk

CENTER POINT PUBLISHING
THORNDIKE, MAINE

F
L P E

This Center Point Large Print edition
is published in the year 2010 by arrangement with
St. Martin's Press.

Copyright © 2009 by Gina Buonaguro and Janice Kirk.

All rights reserved.

This is a work of fiction. All of the characters,
organizations, and events portrayed in this novel
are either products of the authors' imaginations
or are used fictitiously.

The text of this Large Print edition is unabridged.
In other aspects, this book may vary
from the original edition.
Printed in the United States of America
on permanent paper.
Set in 16-point Times New Roman type.

ISBN: 978-1-60285-689-9

Library of Congress Cataloging-in-Publication Data

Buonaguro, Gina.
  Ciao bella / Gina Buonaguro and Janice Kirk.
    p. cm.
  ISBN 978-1-60285-689-9 (library binding : alk. paper)
  1. Married women--Italy--Fiction.
    2. Italy--History--Allied occupation, 1943-1947--Fiction.
    3. Americans--Italy--Fiction. 4. Large type books. I. Kirk, Janice. II. Title.
  PR9199.4.B86C53 2010
  813'.6--dc22
  2009039926

For Uncle Bud and Grandpa Gaspare

And in memory of Frances Daunt

And thus, without a Wing,
Or service of a Keel,
Our Summer made her light escape
Into the Beautiful.

EMILY DICKINSON,
"As imperceptibly as Grief"

Do good whenever you can,
love freedom above all,
never renounce the truth.

LUDWIG VAN BEETHOVEN

Ciao Bella

Prologue

July 1945

Rumor of the American soldier blew through the mountains and valleys with all the swiftness of an incoming summer storm. It had been more than two months since Liberation, when the residents of Italy's Euganean Hills had cheered on the Allied troops as they swept northward on the Germans' heels. Relieved that five long years of war and occupation were finally behind them, the locals had waved from their windows, their fields, the sides of the roads. The soldiers had returned their waves, stopping just long enough to hand out candy to the children and kisses to the girls before continuing on to Venice only sixty kilometers away. No one in the Hills ever expected to see the soldiers again until now, when word came one was staying at the Nevicato farm.

Father Paolo Archangelo was the first to meet him. He was on his way to eat dinner with the old man Giovanni and his daughter-in-law, Graziella, as he did every other Friday. His Church of Santa Maria was only five hundred meters above the Nevicatos' on the steepest road in the Euganean Hills. In his tiny church, Father Paolo diligently served the families who peppered the mountain, but he often daydreamed of delivering the Eucharist in the cathedrals of Milan, Venice, and Rome.

Indeed, he was doing just that when he saw the American splitting wood in the yard without his shirt on. Although he paused from his work to shake the priest's hand, he did not join them for dinner, and Graziella would only say he was there helping until he fixed his motorcycle. She carried out a plate of food to the soldier, and while she was away, Giovanni, whom the priest knew disliked him, complained that those Americans would soon be everywhere. They did not talk about Giovanni's missing son, Ugo.

So Father Paolo, having learned not much more than a name, went home and told his housekeeper, a middle-aged woman by the name of Annunziata whose chances of ever procuring a husband had been ruined by a harelip and a lazy eye that nonetheless never missed a thing. *What did he look like?* she demanded. *What's his name? Is it proper he stay at the house with Ugo's wife, even if Giovanni is there?*

She didn't think it was proper at all and said so to Ugo's eldest sister, Maria Serena, the next day, having stolen away to her house after making Father Paolo his breakfast. She took the wooded path behind the Nevicato farm although it was longer for her. The shutters were closed, and no one was in the yard. Not even the old man, who often sat out there with a blanket over his lap. The only thing out of the ordinary was the motorcycle, still lying on its side by the road.

Maria Serena, a solid tank of a woman with a prominent purple birthmark on her right cheek, said she'd been meaning to call on Graziella anyway. She was having female troubles, and Graziella had once cured her younger sister, Maria Valentina, now seven months pregnant with her seventh child, with tea made of motherwort.

And so Maria Serena took a crock of milk to pay for the herbal tea and, dragging her eldest daughter, Enza, behind her, retraced the route Annunziata had just taken. She crossed herself when she hurried by what used to be her youngest sister's home. It had been less than a year, and her heart still pounded whenever she passed it. Maria Lisabetta and four of her five children—all burned alive in revenge after her husband, Lorenzo, had shot a German officer in the shoulder. Maria Serena could not bear the empty windows like staring eyes, and although she would never admit it, she still had nightmares of their screams piercing the autumn night.

The American was drawing water from the well when Maria Serena and Enza arrived. He was wearing his shirt. He said hello to them and held out his hand. Maria Serena had never shaken anyone's hand before, and she wished she'd worn

13

her good dress. His hair was in need of a comb, and she resisted the temptation to smooth the blond waves. He smiled at them, revealing bright, straight teeth. His nose, though, was crooked as if once upon a time it had been broken. He was much taller than they were. Maria Serena wished Enza could at least manage a smile in return.

He's staying in the loft over the barn, she told her husband, Nino, when they returned home. *And helping out on the farm while waiting for his ship to leave. Not that Graziella told me any of this— she was still sleeping! Can you imagine? God knows, though, she needs the help. I wouldn't be surprised if that barn fell down around his ears. And the grapes—they're ruined! What will Ugo think when he comes back? No, not of the grapes—of the soldier! I mean, it's not the same as you or your brothers going over to lend a hand.*

Nino was convinced Ugo was dead, or surely he'd have come home by now. Everyone else was back from the war, including their own son, Tazio, who had also been a partisan and fought with the Resistance in Venice. And while Ugo had been gone for most of the war, he'd still managed to come home periodically, working the family farm for a few days before disappearing again. But they hadn't seen him since this past winter, when the fighting was at its worst. Still, even if Ugo was dead, he wouldn't be happy knowing his wife had an American soldier working in their yard without his shirt. Nino was not an educated man, but he knew about Americans, having seen a movie once in Padua. All they had to do was smile and the women were helpless.

That afternoon, while Nino was building a new bed for his cart, he decided to borrow a plane from his cousin who worked at the mill by the train station in Il Paesino. He could've sent one of his sons, but he was curious. The way down the mountain to the village took Nino past Graziella's. The American was standing on a ladder fixing a broken shutter. He climbed down, shook Nino's hand, showed him the motorcycle, and offered him a Lucky Strike, which Nino took gladly. *An American cigarette! Like heaven.* The American talked and talked and Nino nodded. He didn't understand a word, but he liked the motorcycle. The American climbed on, gripping the handlebars and making *vroom, vroom* sounds, then gestured for Nino to do the same. Nino sat on the motorcycle but didn't make the *vroom, vroom* sounds. He wanted to ask questions, but of course couldn't.

Graziella came out of the henhouse, and Nino explained he was going to Il Paesino. She said a few words to the American. Although Nino knew that Graziella's first language was English, he'd rarely heard her speak it. He wanted her to ask about the motorcycle, but when it came to Graziella, he was too shy to say much of anything.

She fetched some herbs bundled in a piece of cloth for him to give to Maria Serena. That night before bed, Maria Serena would make tea with them and the cramps would stop.

And so Nino took the news the rest of the way down the hill to his cousin, whose wife immediately passed it along to the pregnant Maria Valentina, who in turn told another of Ugo's sisters, Maria Benedetta. Maria Valentina, who delighted in any gossip, especially where her sister-in-law was concerned, said this was the inevitable result of their little brother marrying a foreigner, and Maria Benedetta, a thin, nervous woman who lived in mortal fear of her sisters despite being the second eldest, could only agree. There was no point in telling Ugo's one remaining sister, Maria Teresa, who lived in a convent in Padua and was rather peculiar anyway. But could they have told her, she too would have agreed and prayed to the Baby Jesus for Ugo to come back and save them all from disgrace.

1

When Graziella heard the motorcycle laboring up the hill, her first thought was the Germans were back. She stopped to listen, the wet sheet she was hanging on the line poised above her in midair. No, not Germans. Of course not. It was Ugo. It had to be. Ugo back at last! She dropped the sheet back into the metal tub, letting the clothes-peg fall to the ground, her hands flying up to smooth her hair as she ran around the house toward the road.

"Cossa xe?" Giovanni called from his chair in the open doorway. Graziella heard the fear in his voice and knew he too was thinking of Nazis. But then he never quite believed the war was over and dreaded with every nightfall the air-raid sirens followed by the whine of the mysterious plane they called Pippo. He fumbled for his cane and attempted to rise from the chair, nearly knocking over the potted lemon trees that flanked the front door.

"It's okay, Papà. The war's over." She picked up the blanket he insisted on despite the heat and placed it back over his thin, arthritic legs. "I'm going to see. Don't worry—it's just a motorcycle." She didn't tell him it might be Ugo, knowing he would be almost as disappointed as herself if it wasn't. But nobody around here owned a motorcycle. The doctor down in Il Paesino had a car, as did the Zizzo family, who owned the biggest farm in the valley, but they never came up here, so who else could it be?

She stood by the road and watched as the motorcycle appeared around the bend, the engine sounding as if it were choking on dust. But there was no identifying the rider. Helmet, jacket, goggles, scarf, face—everything as gray as the road. The motorcycle roared and swerved, fighting to stay upright as it climbed the steep hill. Its front wheel dug into the dusty road, trying to find enough grip to keep its forward momentum. *Please God, please God,* she prayed as she watched the motorcycle's painful progress. *Let it be Ugo.*

Whether in answer to her prayers or not, the motorcycle sputtered and died, collapsing in a cloud of steam and smoke on the grassy roadside. She jumped out of the way as the rider staggered free, peeling away helmet, scarf, and finally goggles, revealing bright blue eyes ringed with clean skin, like an inverse raccoon.

It wasn't Ugo. Of course not. She already knew that even as her lips formed his name again. Though it *could* have been him and any day now it *would* be him.

The man looked at her and held out his hand, but

the moment he tried to speak, he was overcome with a fit of coughing. He doubled over, coughs racking his entire body. Graziella was sure she could see dust billowing from his mouth like smoke, and for one strange moment she thought it might even be coming from his ears.

When the coughs at last subsided, he straightened up, brushing at the dirt on his sleeves. It rose in little clouds before settling back into place as if comfortable to stay where it was. "I'm sorry. My name's Frank and . . . I mean, *mi dispiace. . . .*" He stopped and she could see him searching for what to say, looking over her shoulder and studying the side of the house as if he would find the words written there across the gray stone and crumbling masonry. But Graziella knew even if he found the words, they were sure to be in Italian and not Venetian, the provincial dialect that still caused her trouble.

"It's okay. I speak English. Let me get you a cup of water." How easily the words came out! It was her native language, but for so long now it was only spoken in her dreams.

"Thank you. That's very kind of you, ma'am," he said, wiping his palm on his dusty pants and shaking her hand. "Frank Austen. Eighty-eighth Division. Pleased to meet you and especially pleased you speak English. They taught us some Italian on the boat on the way over. Things like 'Can you direct me to the Red Cross, please?' and

'The weather is beautiful and all the girls in the town are pretty.' They didn't seem to know there were a million different dialects. I tried to get directions this morning from an old man, but I couldn't make heads or tails of what he said."

He smiled as he spoke, and she decided it was a very nice smile, its generosity reflected in his blue eyes and the warm hints of an American accent. She noticed too the slightest bend in his nose, but far from being a defect, it added charm to his already handsome face. She wished though he hadn't called her *ma'am*—it made her feel much older than twenty-five. Except in her worn brown dress with her blackened feet and dirty hair she probably looked older. And him? Twenty-one or twenty-two? Not much younger than she was.

"You're lost then?" she asked him.

"No, I'm not lost. . . ." He broke off in another fit of coughing.

"Let's get you that cup of water," she said, and he followed her, still coughing, to the well in front of the house. She lowered the wooden bucket by the rope, and it landed with a muted splash.

"Here. Let me do that," he said, taking the rope from her and hauling it back up, the pulley creaking in rusty protest. "It must be heavy." It wasn't, as the pulley bore most of the weight, but she didn't object. He set the pail on the ground, and she handed him the dipper.

"Don't drink too quickly," she said. "It's very cold."

He ignored her advice, watching her over the dipper as he took gulp after gulp. When his thirst was finally quenched, he put down the dipper and walked over to where the land suddenly stopped, ending in a jagged cliff face that dropped at least ten meters to rocks and shrubs below. Graziella knew the terraces had been built in ancient times, carved out of the steep hillsides to create flat areas for planting, like the steps of a giant's staircase. The house itself stood about ten meters from the edge of this cliff, facing west to the sunsets and the snowcapped Alps in the distance. Behind the house, a wooded path led to the rest of the family's homes, their farms forming a belt that wrapped halfway around the mountain. On the other side of the path, the hill rose sharply again to another terrace planted with grapes and olives. To the north of the house was her garden, the chicken coop, the barn, the woodshed, and the outhouse. Beyond that were the fruit trees: cherry, jujube, apricot, plum, apple. The cherries were long finished now, and the apricots and plums were already ripening.

"Nice view you have here," Frank said. "It's like the paintings my little sister makes at school. Perfect green triangle hills, the blue sky overhead. All that's missing is a big smiling face on the sun."

She laughed, telling him the hills were actually extinct volcanoes.

"It reminds me of Vermont," he said. "Though I don't know if the mountains near me were ever volcanoes." She could hear the homesickness in his voice, and suddenly he seemed less a stranger.

"You're from Vermont? I'm from Toronto."

"And you asked me if *I* was lost? What brought you all this way?"

"This is my husband's family farm. He's out helping a neighbor now." She wasn't afraid of this soldier, but it probably wasn't a good idea to let him know she was alone except for her helpless father-in-law.

Right then, Giovanni called out from the doorway. *"Chi xe? Chi xe?"*

"Just an American traveler, Papà," she called back in Venetian. "His motorcycle broke down. I got him some water."

"My father-in-law, Signor Nevicato," she explained, turning back to the soldier. "He was worried the Germans were back."

Now it was his turn to look a little worried. "Does your father-in-law like Americans?"

She laughed. "Better than Germans. Although he says the Americans will be the next to try and take over the world. And don't get him started on the subject of Allied bombing raids." She regretted the words as soon as they were out of her mouth. This was not something to joke about.

Besides, she liked him already, and she didn't want him to change that by giving some oversimplified justification about it all being necessary to win the war. She didn't want to offend him either. She just wanted someone to talk to in English for a while, to pretend as if none of this had ever happened and they were just two travelers whose paths had crossed in a distant land. And so she smiled again as if the war had been of little importance and suggested he meet her father-in-law.

As they passed the well again, Frank splashed water from the pail onto his face, smearing the dust into muddy streaks. He dried his hands on his pants before approaching Giovanni, who had knocked the rug from his knees again. Graziella thought he did it deliberately, so she would have to pick it up for him. She did so now, ashamed that he was in need of a good shave and a haircut. A bath wouldn't have hurt either, something she relied on her brother-in-law Nino to help her with, as the old man shook his cane at her every time she came near him with a bar of soap.

"Hello, sir. Pleased to meet you. My name's Frank Austen," he said, holding out his hand. Giovanni didn't take it, though Graziella knew he probably saw it. But Frank didn't seem to mind and instead stuck his hands in his pockets. "Sorry to bother you," he said, looking to Graziella to translate. "I'm with the Eighty-eighth Division— or was. Infantry. Most of my buddies are still guarding German soldiers back at Lake Garda." As he talked, Giovanni's rug fell from his knees again, but before Graziella could bend down to retrieve it, Frank scooped it up and placed it back on the old man's lap. "A lot of guys have already gone home, but I missed that boat, so I have to wait until the end of August. . . ." His voice trailed off, and Graziella used this moment to translate, knowing Giovanni would forget it all in the next ten minutes and for the next week would be asking her a hundred times a day who that American was and what division was he with. She gave a simplified version, less for him to forget.

"But it's okay," the soldier went on. "I get to see a bit of the countryside. And these hills remind me of home. My family has a dairy farm in northern Vermont." He pulled his wallet from his back pocket and removed a photograph, badly creased from being folded. Graziella told him Giovanni had bad eyesight, and so she described the photo-graph for her father-in-law. It showed a frame farmhouse with a porch along the front and a hill rising behind it. Under a tree, a little girl with fair curls and a big smile sat on a swing. "That's my little sister, Clara," he said. "She was six then. Now she's ten." He returned the photo to his wallet. "You've got a really nice place here, sir."

"Falling to pieces is more like it," Giovanni answered irritably. "You should stop babbling like a nervous schoolgirl and help my daughter-in-law before she destroys the grapes completely." This Graziella translated as: "It has been in the Nevicato family for hundreds of years and will soon be my son's."

"When will your husband be home?" Frank asked as they walked to the edge of the road where the motorcycle still steamed.

"Later," she said, avoiding his eyes and looking instead to the motorcycle. "Can you fix it?"

"I don't know. Does your husband have any tools?"

She pointed to the barn and told him he was welcome to whatever he found. They didn't have any machinery, as first the Italian Fascists and then the Nazis had made off with just about everything made of metal, so she doubted he'd find anything useful. She still had her cooking pots only because she'd hidden them in the cellar.

"I'll look. Maybe she just needs to cool down a bit." He stared down at the motorcycle for what seemed like a long time. Finally he shook his head and let out a long sigh. "I'm not really sure what to do." He looked at Graziella with troubled eyes as if she might have the answer. He certainly wasn't all swagger and confidence as she imagined American soldiers to be.

She pretended to study the motorcycle, at a loss as to what to do herself. She wasn't in a hurry for him to leave, though she wished she hadn't lied about Ugo's whereabouts since it would be awkward to explain the truth. But as Frank wouldn't be around long, it probably wouldn't matter, and so instead she asked him if he'd like something to eat.

"Only if you can spare it," he said very seriously, and Graziella was suddenly embarrassed by their obvious poverty. Everybody on this mountain was struggling—the war had taken its toll on them all—and Giovanni was right. The place did look like it was falling apart, and the grapes were a sprawling unpruned mess, with weeds growing up between the rows. They hadn't been sprayed either, as no one had any copper sulfate to protect against fungus, though luckily the season had been mostly dry. Really, only her garden looked cared for, and Frank hadn't seen that yet.

"Come into the kitchen. I'll give you some bread and wine."

"Thank you. You've been very kind . . . ma'am."

She knew she should tell him her name was Signora Nevicato. But it came out so easily, her name from before she knew Ugo, before he had brought her here. A name no one had called her since her brother, Westley, had died nearly seven years ago. "You can call me Grace."

Sometime in the early afternoon, Graziella remembered it was her day to feed Father Paolo. She busied herself in the kitchen, a warm breeze wafting through the front door and out the back, the room redolent with the scent of herbs hanging from the ceiling beams. Every five minutes she found herself checking at the window to see if Frank was making any progress on the motorcycle. Not that she would know what progress looked like, but the bits and pieces laid out on the grass did not look encouraging, and she took heart from this.

Father Paolo, she knew, would go home and give a full report to that horrible housekeeper of his, who wouldn't be able to sleep in anticipation of passing on the news of an American soldier to one of Ugo's sisters. No doubt by the end of tomorrow they would all know. She could almost hear them clucking: *That's what he gets for marrying a foreigner.*

Graziella did her best to understand them. Their lives hadn't been easy. She knew their mother had died giving birth to Ugo, leaving the then fourteen-year-old Maria Serena to raise four younger sisters and an infant brother. At sixteen, Maria Serena married Nino Zampollo and started having children of her own, leaving Maria Benedetta, the next oldest, in charge. All the Marias had cared for Ugo with no less concern than if he'd been the Baby Jesus himself, no doubt adding to Ugo's indulgent view of them even after Graziella complained about how much they hated her.

Of course they do not hate you, he protested. *It is just that I am their only brother, and they are*

27

overprotective sometimes. And whether or not they like my choice of wife, you are family now, and they will defend you. Do not let them upset you.

And so she tried to ignore their criticisms and unkind remarks, in time earning at least the respect of the youngest sister, Maria Lisabetta, in whom she sensed a deep-seated unhappiness. While she wasn't to learn for some time the reasons for that unhappiness, Graziella could already see the tension between her and her husband, Lorenzo. Looking back, it was hard not to wonder if their strained home life had been a contributing factor in their deaths.

Except for Maria Teresa, who'd been sent to the convent as a child, Ugo's sisters had all married into the same family, trading the last name of Nevicato for Zampollo. With Maria Teresa out of the picture, there were just enough brothers to go around. But there were the twin Zampollo girls as well, and it was the belief of Ugo's sisters that their brother should have married one of them. Which one, Graziella didn't know, but the two girls also seemed to believe she had stolen their husband from them, and Graziella wondered if they'd thought he would marry them both. Moreover, everybody seemed to have forgotten that Ugo had never intended on marrying at all, instead planning to join the Benedictine monastery of Montserrat in Spain. It was the church she had stolen him from, not the Zampollo twins.

Of course, none of them had any problem getting her up in the night if someone was giving birth. Nor did they seem to worry about whether she kept their secrets. What would Nino say if he knew she'd given his daughter Enza an herb to end a pregnancy, even if she had been raped? Maria Serena had sworn Graziella to secrecy. She'd been grateful too. But she still didn't like Graziella as her sister-in-law.

Outside, Graziella picked up the axe from the woodshed and went to the henhouse to sacrifice one of her chickens for the priest's dinner. To keep the house cool in the summer, she cooked outdoors, and so now she built a small fire in the pit beside the woodshed, set the iron rack over it, and on top of that placed a cast-iron kettle of water. When it was hot, she dropped the now headless chicken into the pot to loosen the feathers. After changing the water and putting it back on to boil, she then cleaned and plucked the chicken, setting aside the liver, which she'd cook in the morning for Giovanni's breakfast. It was a small hen, and Graziella knew if any of her sisters-in-law were to cook it, it would be tough and stringy. But it wouldn't be when she was finished, and she took some satisfaction in knowing that Father Paolo preferred her cooking to any of the Marias'.

After replacing the hen in the pot, she drew

more water from the well, heated it, and carried it up to her room. As she poured the warm water into the basin on the washstand, she caught her reflection in the badly tarnished mirror. She'd told the American her name was Grace, but it was Graziella, not Grace, who looked back at her now. They both had the same violet eyes, but Grace had lived a long time ago in Toronto. She had worn her hair in a neat, clean bob and had owned lovely clothes, shoes, stockings, even lipstick, all Christmas presents from her aunt Beth. By contrast, Graziella was sunburned, her brown hair long and dirty. Her shoes she kept for Sundays, while stockings and lipstick were as unattainable as the moon. She was too thin from too little food and too much worry. *After the war, I promise,* Ugo had said, *we will return to Venice. You will continue your studies, and I will play with the best musicians in Europe.* They should be in Venice now, in their little apartment in the square. *Please, Ugo, hurry back. I can't take this much longer.*

The soap made of pork fat and lye was strong and stung her eyes, but it worked, and she rinsed her hair until it squeaked, as she'd learned to do as a child. She washed every inch of herself, finishing with her feet, which turned the water black. After drying herself with the thin towel, she took down her Sunday dress from the back of the door. It was still brown, but the floral pattern at least attempted to be cheerful. She pulled it over her head, and in the darkness of its folds was the memory of putting on another dress, the one now lying wrapped in tissue paper at the bottom of the armoire. Of the brightest yellow, it was as light and soft as a summer breeze. Ugo had bought it for her in Venice to wear at his performance of Beethoven's Violin Concerto. She had danced around their apartment, the skirt swirling around her, and later at the concert, when her own applause had been drowned out by the calls of *bravo* and *encore,* she had turned to the stranger beside her and said in her best Italian, *Ecco, lui è mio marito—that's my husband.*

It wasn't until they read the review in the paper the next day that Graziella learned the identity of the stranger beside her. *Ugo Nevicato was born to play Beethoven. Nobody else can capture that soaring passion for freedom in the same way. . . . And may I add,* the reviewer concluded after another column of praise, *he has a most charming and beautiful Canadian wife.* Ugo had laughed. *I will have to become accustomed to being upstaged by you!*

She emerged now from the folds of the brown dress and, avoiding her own eyes in the mirror, combed out her tangled hair, pressing it into waves over each ear and securing them with a couple of bobby pins. She hadn't taken this much care with her appearance for a long time, and she knew it wasn't for Father Paolo's benefit. It

31

wasn't entirely for the soldier's either. From her dresser lined with books, she picked up a photograph of herself and Ugo standing outside the music conservatory in Venice. What if Ugo had been on that motorcycle, returning home and finding her in such disarray?

She set the photo down again, using the damp towel to wipe away the dust that had collected around the books. Ugo had given her most of them: Engels's *The Condition of the Working Class in England,* Forster's *Where Angels Fear to Tread,* a volume of Emily Dickinson's poetry, and Dickens's *Oliver Twist.* He'd been pleased to find her these books in English, and she never had the heart to tell him the last few chapters of *Oliver Twist* had been torn out, leaving her to imagine her own happy ending.

The other books had been shipped to her by Aunt Beth and included her mother's copies of *A Vindication of the Rights of Woman* and *Anne of Green Gables.* Aunt Beth had also sent a hundred American dollars as a wedding gift, though she wrote it pained her to know her only brother's daughter had married a Catholic, and an Italian at that.

So used to Aunt Beth's criticisms, Graziella had barely registered the insult. The widow of a wealthy shipping magnate, Aunt Beth had felt it her Christian duty to make the 150-mile trip from Kingston to Toronto on a semiannual basis to give advice on everything from her brother's inability to manage his finances to her niece's appearance. *Why aren't you wearing that lipstick I sent you for Christmas? Your lips are far too thin. And don't ruin your eyes with all that reading—they're your only nice feature.* Aunt Beth's own eyes were as black and beady as those of her fox stole, and she smelled of peppermint and mothballs.

It is so much, Ugo said when Graziella showed him the one-hundred-dollar bill. *Should we accept it? Of course,* Graziella said. *Believe me, she'd rather I was married to you than living with her.*

She and Ugo had used the money to secure the lease on their apartment in Venice, and Ugo had toasted her aunt at the kitchen table. *How does she have so much money if everyone lost it during the Depression?* he asked. Graziella had shrugged. *Deals with the Devil, my father always said.*

She picked up the washbasin now and took it downstairs, emptying the dirty water on the holly-hocks beside the back door before going to see if the motorcycle was still in pieces. It wasn't, but it wasn't running either, and Frank was sitting on the ground, knees drawn up to his chin, contemplating it.

"I don't know what to do, Grace." He got to his feet and turned to face her, pausing for a moment. While he didn't comment on it, she knew he was registering the change in her appearance. "How about your husband? Does he know anything about mechanics? Maybe he can help when he gets home."

Graziella could hear her mother's voice from what seemed like a hundred lifetimes ago: *Oh what a tangled web we weave, when at first we practice to deceive.* She wished he'd stop asking her about Ugo. "My husband's been delayed. He won't be home tonight." Why not tell Frank the truth—that she didn't know when Ugo was coming home? Refusing to contemplate *if* rather than *when,* she looked at the motorcycle again. "Maybe tomorrow Ugo will be home. Or the day after that."

"Ugo's your husband then? And he's coming home tomorrow or the next day for sure?"

"I think so," she said hastily before changing the subject. "You'd better sleep in the barn tonight." She could suggest he walk to the Zizzo farm in the valley, as they had a car, a truck, and a tractor. But even though Father Paolo preached it was time to forgive and forget, she wasn't about to send an American soldier to known Fascists, even if those same Fascists were now advertising themselves as committed democrats. Still, if she were honest with herself, the fact that the Zizzos had once been Fascists was only an excuse, as she was in no hurry for him to fix the motorcycle and leave. If only he'd stop asking her about Ugo.

"Thank you, ma'am . . . I mean, Grace. I appreciate the offer."

"Good, that's settled. But I hope you don't mind eating your dinner outside tonight. The priest is coming, and it wouldn't take much for a rumor to start that I'm entertaining American soldiers while my husband's away."

"I understand," he said, looking a little embarrassed now. "I don't want to cause any trouble. And look, I can help out in exchange for my room and board. I'm sure your husband will understand. I'm looking forward to seeing him."

Graziella wondered what kind of husband Frank thought she had. At best a lazy one, to leave everything in such obvious disrepair. "Thank you. There's wood to be split by the barn." Nino had taken down an old oak that had been struck by lightning, and while she'd been able to deal with the smaller branches, the trunk was more than she could cope with. She turned to go, then stopped. "I have a fire lit by the woodshed, and there's a washtub on the woodshed wall. You can heat water in it. And if you leave me your dirty clothes, I'll wash them for you."

"Thanks, but I can do my own laundry."

She nodded in response and returned to the kitchen to get the last of the salt for the chicken. "That American still here?" Giovanni asked. He'd been napping in his chair the entire afternoon.

"Yes, Papà. His motorcycle's still broken. He'll be staying in the loft over the barn tonight. He's going to split some wood for us."

"Watch he doesn't rob us blind."

She sighed. "Except for this salt, we have nothing worth stealing. And it's going into the priest's dinner."

"Oh, is that old hypocrite coming for dinner? He supported the disarmament of the partisans. Afraid of the Communists coming to power. He'd rather bring Mussolini back from the dead than let that happen." He banged his cane on the floor. "Where's Ugo? He'd have something to say about this."

"Ugo isn't home yet. And you know we have Father Paolo to dinner every other Friday. Maybe he'll play chess with you. Although I don't know why he does since you're so mean to him. You know very well he wouldn't bring back Mussolini. He supported the Resistance just like everyone else on this mountain. Besides, I'm not so sure you want a Communist government anyway. Afraid they might take your land away."

Giovanni grumbled about her lack of respect and what kind of a name was Paolo Archangelo for a priest anyway? "Might as well just call him Lucifer and be done with it." As she went to check on the chicken, she worried the priest would be in for an earful tonight if Giovanni's mood didn't improve. Giovanni couldn't remember what he'd just eaten for dinner, but when it came to chess and politics, he liked to think he could dance circles around the priest. He led the priest on too, trying to make him believe he was blinder than he really was, pretending he couldn't make out the pieces on the board. But Father Paolo knew just how much glee Giovanni got out of playing him for a fool and cheerfully threw the game every time.

She set down the plate she'd brought from the kitchen on a big round of oak. Pulling the chicken from the pot, she rubbed the inside with salt before stuffing the cavity with cloves of garlic, onions, and chopped herbs. Chives, basil, tarragon. She poured off most of the water to thicken later with flour. After rubbing the outside of the chicken with pork fat, she placed it back in the pot. Around the bird she arranged some newly dug potatoes and the first apricots from the tree. Then she banked the pot with coals.

"That smells awfully good, Grace," Frank said from behind her. She straightened up, checking without thinking the bobby pins that held the new waves. He had his big pack on and was holding the saddlebags from the motorcycle. "If you could just show me where to put these, I'll heat up that water. And afterward I'll split these rounds. When it's done, there'll be enough for a whole winter."

"Maybe," she said as she led the way to the barn, not wanting to think of another winter here. The barn was small, built from stone like the house and shaded by an enormous chestnut tree that kept it cool even in the hottest weather. Inside was room for a pig and a cow if she'd been lucky enough to have either, and over it was a small loft for hay. She led him up the steep stairs through the darkness to the window, pushing open the shutters to let the leaf-filtered light in through the glassless opening. "You can bring out a mattress from the spare room. And a blanket too."

"Thank you," Frank said, setting the pack down next to the saddlebags. "I'll get them later. It's nice of you to let me stay. I know it's been tough for you." He sat down on his pack, pulled out a packet of cigarettes, and offered her one, but she shook her head. "Somehow I think you got the lousiest deal up here. You get rid of Mussolini and join the Allies only to have Hitler spring him from prison and set him up as leader while the Germans occupy northern Italy. Nazis and Fascists. A double whammy, I'd say. Bet you're glad it's all over."

It wasn't all over for her, though, at least not until Ugo was back, but she agreed anyway and left Frank unrolling his sleeping bag, the tune he whistled following her out into the yard where her chicken bubbled away.

As she lifted the lid on the pot, she marveled how only a few short months ago letting Frank stay in the barn could have resulted in both of them being shot. The winter before, she'd discovered a British soldier hiding there. Already imagining their fates, she'd yelled at him, but he'd been so young and frightened she hadn't stayed angry for very long. After giving him some of their dinner, she had taken him to Father Paolo, who'd hidden him in the short tunnel that connected the cellar of his house to that of the church. As much as Giovanni hated giving Father Paolo any credit, the priest had risked his life more than once harboring strangers. Partisans, fleeing Jews, refugees from the cities, Allied soldiers separated from their regiments, even a deserting German—all could count on his hospitality until false documents and a safe passage out could be found.

And it wasn't just strangers who had to hide but family members too. Excepting Maria Lisabetta's husband, Lorenzo, the Zampollo brothers were too old to be drafted by the Fascists, but when the Germans invaded, they wouldn't have been considered too old to be sent to Nazi labor camps. The brothers had aided the local Resistance, working on their farms while carrying out acts of sabotage. It was dangerous, and so the family and the priest devised a chain of hiding places: a trapdoor camouflaged with sod, a hollowed-out haystack, a cave carved into a terrace, its opening disguised with branches. Children and wives were the lookouts, and at the agreed-upon signal, the brothers and Nino's older boys would suddenly disappear.

The women became very adept at fabricating stories for the patrols. Their husbands and sons, they'd say, were on top of the mountain cutting wood or hunting wild boar. Other times they were in Este, Cinto Euganeo, Arquà Petrarca—anywhere but home. And they couldn't possibly have spiked the road and destroyed any tires, the women would say with the sincerest of smiles, as they'd been gone for days. Father Paolo liked to invent passing groups of banditos who'd been seen heading north and lay the blame on them. His baby-faced, earnest appearance worked to his benefit, and the Nazis always believed him—a good thing, as they didn't hesitate to arrest, torture, and kill any priest suspected of anti-German activity. When Graziella told him she found it ironic that the best liar she'd ever met was a priest, he'd laughed. *It's a gift from God, my dear Graziella. You have your gift for plants and healing, and I have one for lying to the enemy. Who am I to question God's ways?*

For the rest of the afternoon, Graziella continued to check at the window. She watched as Frank took down the tub from the woodshed wall and filled it from the well. It slopped water all the way back, and she was tempted to go out and tell him it was easier to place it on the fire and then carry pails from the well. No doubt he, like herself, was used to tiled bathrooms and water that ran hot from the tap. He dragged the tub off the fire, using his shirt to protect his hands from the hot metal before carrying it behind the shed. She should've told him to take it into the barn. *Please God, don't let Ugo's sisters see him.*

That night, after the priest left, Graziella dreamed of the war and Pippo flying somewhere above them in the night sky, only his menacing drone giving him away. In her dream Giovanni insisted she take him down to the root cellar beneath the kitchen. *We'll be safer down there, you know that!* he shouted, his eyes wild. But she didn't want to go, couldn't contemplate another long, cold night spent in the dark hole among the shelves of squash, onions, and potatoes. And getting Giovanni down the cellar stairs with his bad legs—why, the fear of them both falling down the steps was almost as great as her fear of Pippo. Besides, what was the chance of Pippo bombing their house on that particular night? It was a risk she was willing to take, to stay under the covers, pretending to sleep. But Giovanni wasn't, and he kept shouting at her to get moving before it was too late.

So she got him down the stairs, settling him on an overturned crate while he ranted that Pippo was going to hunt them down. *It's me he wants,* he kept insisting, his paranoia instilling more fear in her with every passing minute. She counted the bottles of wine in the flickering light of the single candle, worrying there would never be more to replace them, then poured off two cups, hoping to calm them both. They strained their ears for the whine of falling bombs. Their house was in darkness, she was sure of that, the only light this candle beneath the kitchen floor. But bombs had been known to fall where there was no light, the destruction of the barn belonging to Maria Serena and Nino being one case. The pig had been inside, the family's meat for the rest of the winter. It had nearly been the end of Maria Serena. She had taken to her bed and cried for days, the only weakness Graziella had ever seen her display. Nino too was shocked by his wife's response and had come to see Graziella. *Is there something you can give her?* He looked ready to crack himself. It almost seemed as if the pig's death had been more tragic than the death of their eldest son, Dario, who had been killed in the Russian campaign. But that had been early days, before they knew how long they would have to endure, how hungry and cold a winter could be. Before their sister, nieces, and nephews were incinerated in their own home, before their brother was hanged from a tree, before the rape of their daughter. They were weary, and the loss of the pig was more than God should have expected them to handle. Graziella gave Nino some valerian root, and although Maria Serena cried in her sleep, at least she slept.

But Maria Serena's despair did not make it into Graziella's dream, only her own despair as she spent another night in the cellar. Tired, hungry, scared, knowing the trip back up the stairs with Giovanni would be as treacherous as the trip down, she was angry now in her dream. Angry at Ugo. *I could take this, Ugo, if you were here. Your sisters hate me. Your father hates me. How could you leave me here?*

And then suddenly she was awake, and Ugo stood at the foot of the bed as if she had conjured him up with her dream. She couldn't believe it. He was so real. Solid, tall, strong. Thinner maybe, his clothes worn and ragged. But he was every bit as beautiful as when she had fallen in love with him that night in Spain during those final terrible days of the civil war, when the snow had floated down like tiny lights in the darkness. She and Ugo had stood on the steps of the burned-out stone house that served as the field hospital and watched as the flakes collected on the dark cloth of their coats. In school she had been told no two snowflakes were alike, and looking at them then, so perfect on their sleeves, this struck her as miraculous even though she had long stopped believing in miracles. *Neve,* he'd said. *Snow,* she'd answered, even though he already knew the word. How long ago that was.

She held out her arms to him now. "I was having a terrible dream about the war. Oh Ugo, I can't believe you're finally home. Where have you been? Almost everyone thinks you're dead. They don't say it to me, but I know they're thinking it."

He smiled at her and sat down on the edge of the bed. "Do not forget how much I love you," he said as he leaned over and kissed her.

"Please don't go again. Please stay here with me." But when she reached out, there was only darkness.

She was awake for real now, her cheeks wet with tears and Ugo gone. *Only a dream,* she told herself. That was all. He wasn't here with her. She'd been asleep. But how could a dream be so real she could feel the touch of his lips on hers? Could feel it even now?

The silence of the house was more than she could bear. So she got up and, despite the closeness of the night, pulled Ugo's flannel shirt over her old nightgown and found her way through the darkness to the hall, her bare feet moving silently over the wooden floorboards. She edged down the stairs and crossed the stone tiles of the kitchen.

She stepped out into the front yard where all around her was fog, an iridescent watery green in the light of the hazy moon. It confused her. *It was all a dream and I'm still dreaming. I'm still dreaming and I'm walking in a cloud.* She crossed the dusty yard past the well to where the land fell away to the valley below. But tonight the valley was full of this same dense fog, and she had the strange urge to put one foot out to test its strength, to see if it would hold her weight. She looked down at her foot and felt unconnected to it, as if it belonged to someone else. She was about to lift it when she heard her name.

"Grace?" Not Graziella but Grace. Softly. She

didn't turn, didn't really comprehend this voice. Nobody called her Grace anymore. "You all right? You look like a ghost."

It was Frank, the American. She turned around, strangely relieved to see his figure emerging from the fog. She sensed he might have saved her from something, although she couldn't say what it was. "I'm okay." She didn't want to tell him about her dream. "I couldn't sleep." She took a few steps toward him and away from the edge. He too looked ghostly in the fog as it entwined itself around them. Not even the house or barn was visible. He was still dressed, although his shirt hung open as if pulled on hastily, and his feet were bare too. She held together the edges of Ugo's shirt over her nightgown.

"I couldn't sleep either," he said.

She nodded. Earlier, after Father Paolo had left, she had gone outside to look for him. His plate was on the front step, a Hershey's Bar beside it, but he was nowhere in sight. There was already a pile of chips where one of the rounds had sat, and inside the woodshed was a neatly stacked row of pale split wood. Disappointed, she'd fed her hens and returned to the house. She'd hoped then that she and Frank might talk, but now she couldn't think of anything to say. "Thank you for cutting the wood," she said finally. "And for the chocolate bar."

"Thank you for dinner. It was delicious." He

looked past her at the cloud filling the valley. "You should be careful standing so close to the edge in this fog. It's steep. You could get hurt."

She nodded.

"You sure you're okay? Is there anything I can do to help?"

Bring Ugo back. Take me away from here. These were things he couldn't help her with. "No, I'm okay. I better go back inside." It felt too strange being out here with him.

"I'll chop more wood in the morning," he said. "I can do that much for you."

"Thank you," she said. He kept looking at her as if he wanted to add something, but he didn't, so finally she murmured goodnight and went back to the house.

2

When Graziella woke up, sunlight was streaming around the edges of the broken shutter, and she could hear the steady sound of someone chopping wood. She was confused for a second before remembering the American. He'd told her he'd chop more wood today. They'd been standing in the mist in their bare feet. How strange that Ugo's kiss that had seemed so real was a dream, while the fog in the valley that had seemed like a dream was in fact real. She closed her eyes and tried to recapture his kiss, but she couldn't— the moment was gone.

Nor could she remember the last time she'd overslept. Giovanni should've been calling for her to help him out of bed. It didn't matter he no longer worked and slept most of each day in his chair. He was still up at dawn and expected Graziella to be up too.

She was tempted to lie here all morning, doing nothing except watching the light as it moved along the whitewashed walls, marking time, lazing around as she used to with Ugo after late nights of listening to him play. *There is a legend,* he'd told her, *that I picked up the violin for the very first time and played so beautifully that the teacher handed me his violin and vowed he him-self would never play again.*

Is it true?

He had laughed. *Yes, or part of it anyway, for it is still his Stradivarius I play to this day. But I do not think I could have played so beautifully if I needed to practice so many hours a day.*

Whether true or not, even she, with her limited knowledge of music, knew he was exceptional. She had gone everywhere to hear him, rehearsals, concerts, but best of all were the evenings spent in the cigarette-smoke-filled apartments of his musical friends, where one by one they would put down their instruments until only Ugo was left playing, filling the night with music that made them forget everything else. Outside, under the windows, passersby stopped in the street, unable to keep going, forgetting dinners, appointments, lovers, everything but the notes that floated down to them. *What was that? Brahms? Paganini? Beethoven?* new friends would sometimes ask when they could find their voices again.

I do not know. The music just comes to me.

You should write it down.

I cannot. It is gone. It was written for the moment and, as there can never be another moment like the last, the music can never be the same either.

Once an American poet, whom Ugo liked despite his Fascist sympathies, asked to record one of these improvisations. It took him weeks to convince Ugo, but when at last he relented, the recorded disc would play back only silence. *You see, I was right,* Ugo had said. *It cannot be recorded. It was never meant to be heard again.* And brushing aside any mundane technical explanation for this strange phenomenon, he went back to arguing politics with the puzzled poet until the small hours of the morning.

In the first light of dawn, he and Graziella would walk home from these gatherings arm in arm through the maze of streets, a little drunk perhaps, stopping on bridges to kiss before climbing the stairs to their apartment with its view of the Church of the Angelo Raffaele.

Those were great lazy mornings of lovemaking and talking and reading, windows open to the sounds so unlike any other city: the buzz of a motorboat on the canal, the dip of a paddle, the lap of a wave, the laughter of children playing soccer in the square, the church bells that every hour chimed out new works. Ugo could identify them all. *Those are the bells of San Sebastiano, those are from San Nicolò dei Mendicoli, and those are from Santa Maria dei Carmini. . . .* And to their accompaniment, she would practice conjugating verbs in both Italian and Venetian: *I love you. I loved you. I have always loved you. I will always love you.*

They had their disagreements, of course, usually

regarding money. Ugo gave violin lessons regardless of a student's ability to pay, and she, growing frustrated, argued with him to leave at least some time for paying students—they did have to eat. But those arguments had faded with time, while those mornings full of light and sound retained all their vividness.

The crack of splitting wood from the yard brought her back to the present, and she threw off the blanket, refusing to indulge in any more memories. It only made things harder. Better to concentrate on what needed to be done. And that first meant getting Giovanni up. She was starting to worry. Even though Giovanni hadn't worked in several years, he still woke at dawn and expected her to be up too. Why hadn't he called for her?

She was still wearing Ugo's shirt. She took it off and hung it over the back of the wooden chair next to what was still technically a blanket box, though its contents were long gone, given to Resistance fighters and deserters. She'd even turned Ugo's mother's tablecloths into undershirts. Ugo had told her his comrades had laughed as they modeled their new undershirts embroidered with colorful flowers and butterflies. He had buried two of those comrades only a week later, and while he hadn't given her details, she knew somehow they'd still been wearing the undershirts, those same flowers and butterflies that had made them laugh now stained with their own blood.

Wearing her brown-flowered Sunday dress again, she went down to the kitchen where the door to the front yard stood open. She was sure she'd closed it the night before, but perhaps she was mistaken. She went to shut it now and was surprised to see Giovanni sitting in his chair under the chestnut tree, his cane propped up against his blanket-covered knees, looking happier than he'd been in a very long time. He was chewing on a piece of bread, crumbs collecting on his unshaven chin before dropping to the ground where a dozen or so sparrows waited.

"How did you get here?" she asked. Frank had his back to her, working on the next round of wood. A small fire burned in the pit, a pot resting on the grate.

"Well, you weren't in any hurry to get me up, but the American heard me. Came bursting in as if he thought I was being murdered in my bed." He chuckled. "But he figured it out and helped me with my pants. Got me some bread too. And look—real coffee." Giovanni took the tiniest sip before putting the cup back on his knee. "He's a good worker, that boy. What's his name again?"

"Frank," she said, hoping there was some coffee left for her. She wondered how she should broach the subject.

But she didn't have to, as Frank had put down his axe and was wiping his forehead with the hem of his shirt. "Morning," he said. "Would you like a cup of coffee?"

"It's been so long since we had real coffee," she said. "We only have chicory, and it tastes awful. Where'd you get it?"

"American army issue. Not bad either."

"Thanks for helping my father-in-law. I can't believe I didn't hear him," she said. Just as she was wishing for sugar, he scooped a spoonful out of a thick brown paper bag.

"You must've needed your sleep," he said, stirring in the sugar and handing her the cup. "Are you feeling better this morning?"

"Yes," she said quietly. "I'm sorry about that. It's been hard, even though the war's ended." A little embarrassed he'd seen her like that, she took a sip of coffee. It was delicious. Sweet and strong, it flooded her with something close to happiness. "Anyway, thanks for the coffee, and thanks too for getting my father-in-law his breakfast. I hope you took some bread for yourself."

"Just a little," he said, and she said she would make him an egg as soon as she finished her coffee.

"A woman came by earlier," he said. "She had a pretty girl with her. Her daughter maybe? She talked to Signor Nevicato. I introduced myself, but I'm afraid our conversation was pretty limited. Maria something."

Graziella laughed. "One of my sisters-in-law.

They're all Maria something." And she listed them, starting with the eldest. "Maria Serena, Maria Benedetta, Maria Valentina, Maria Teresa."

"She had a big birthmark on her cheek."

"That would be Maria Serena. She—"

"Maria Serena stopped by," Giovanni interrupted, evidently having picked out his daughter's name in the flow of English. "She brought milk and that strange girl of hers, the one who doesn't say anything, the one she's so desperate to marry off. What's her name again?"

"Enza," Graziella said.

"That's right. Anyway, she wanted one of your herbal concoctions. I told her you were still in bed. She's going to send Nino around later."

No doubt to spy on me some more, she thought. Graziella could only imagine what Maria Serena made of her still in bed in the middle of the morning. She took another sip of coffee. *Let them talk,* she thought defiantly. *Just think how jealous they'll all be when I tell them I've had real coffee.* Frank picked up the axe again, and she watched him for a moment before taking her coffee to the garden.

Among her herbs and vegetables she was happiest, or at least happier. Most were set out in neat rows, though some of the more rambunctious ones like mint were confined to pots. Around the garden was a low whitewashed fence hung with moonflowers and wild roses, its gate guarded by a potted bay tree she'd brought from Venice. And although she knew every plant name by heart, each was marked with a stake on which she had written its Latin name, just as she'd done in her parents' garden in Toronto, where a Saturday morning could be spent wandering the stone paths with her father.

And this one, Grace? he'd asked one such morning. He was wearing his tweed jacket with its leather patches on the elbows, redolent with the cherry-scented pipe tobacco he liked so much. It being Saturday, her mother hadn't bothered chasing him down with a comb, and his hair was sticking out in all directions. His shirt buttons were done up wrong, and toast crumbs were still lodged in his beard.

Bellis perennis. *Also known as the English daisy, or common daisy. Introduced from Europe. Good for injuries and bruises, especially those caused by trauma to the deeper tissues from an accident or surgery. In homeopathy, it has been found to be superior to Arnica in some cases. In medieval times, it was used externally on fresh wounds.*

Excellent, Grace. You are truly a botanist's daughter. Her father was the world's leading expert on the spruce budworm and had written a scholarly tome on the subject, *The Eastern Spruce Budworm: Population Oscillations and Effectuations on the Canadian Forestry Industry:*

A Paleoecological Study by Dr. Edwin Forrest, Ph.D. It was a title she and her brother, Westley, had loved to repeat as children, laughing as they tripped over the big words. Their father could wax on about spruce budworms for hours, making many a listener nod off. But never Grace, who shared both her father's passion for plants and her mother's zeal for politics. Her mother, a suffragette in her youth, had spent many hours volunteering in soup kitchens during the Depression.

But you've forgotten one thing, her father had added, plucking a bloom and placing it in the buttonhole of his jacket. *They make wonderful lapel decorations.* He laughed as if this were the funniest joke in the world, his whole body shaking until the daisy was in danger of being ejected from its buttonhole. Then he'd picked another one for her and tucked it in her hair. She found one now in her garden and placed it under one of the bobby pins in memory of that morning.

It had never taken much to make her father laugh. She remembered his laughter threatening the existence of her mother's crystal wineglasses as he howled over some silly joke Westley had made at a dinner party. Their guest of honor that evening was Dr. Norman Bethune, who was a friend of her father's from their time at the University of Toronto and who was on tour raising funds for the republican cause in Spain. He shook his head in amusement at her father and, leaning over, said to her in that sardonic tone of his, *If laughter is the best medicine, your father will live forever.*

But her father didn't live forever, and neither did her mother. Only three weeks later, four days after her seventeenth birthday, a streetcar derailed and overturned, crushing seven pedestrians, her parents among them.

Dr. Bethune attended the double funeral held at the nearby United church the family had always attended, though had anyone ever asked, at most they would have called themselves agnostic. Afterward, he sat with Grace and Westley at the same dining room table, the crystal wineglasses stowed away in the cabinets, the contents of the safe-deposit box and a shoe box in front of them. The shoe box largely contained bills with FINAL NOTICE stamped on them in red. They added the funeral bill to that pile. The safe-deposit box held useless stock certificates and insurance policies long cashed out. There were bankbooks in which the balance read zero and notices from the bank refusing further credit and threatening foreclosure. They also discovered the property taxes were in arrears and the house mortgaged beyond its value. Given the stack of notices from the grocer on Queen Street, it was a wonder they weren't eating at the soup kitchens where their mother had volunteered.

Reading through a packet of letters, they discovered it was Aunt Beth who had been keeping them fed and housed over the last several years, until even she refused to help. *I am not going to be your personal banker anymore, Edwin,* she wrote. *I have helped you out quite enough. You need to manage your finances better and stop giving money away to your wife's worthless causes. There is no reason why Westley can't work while he's at medical school. As for Grace, what man is going to marry a woman botanist? Find her a firm to work in where she can meet a man able to provide for her. It's time you became practical, Edwin, and removed your head from the trees! I swear those worms you like so much have bored themselves into your brain and made it soft.* Reading this aloud, they could guess their mother's reaction, her laughter winning out over fears for their future: *Don't worry, Edwin. Your sister always was a bit of a pill. We're lucky she helped out this long.*

In the end, she and Westley were forced to take Aunt Beth's advice, although it certainly was not the kind of work Aunt Beth had in mind. Even if one could get a job in those hard times, Grace wasn't about to start serving pie at the Woolworth's lunch counter, nor would Westley sell nuts and bolts at some hardware store. That wasn't the kind of future their parents had intended for them. Instead, being young, idealistic, and brokenhearted, they decided, much to

Aunt Beth's horror, to become medics for the republican side in Spain. So a few days later, they rode the streetcar to the Communist Party recruitment office near the corner of Queen and Spadina, a letter of recommendation from Dr. Bethune in Westley's pocket.

Scheduled to leave in two weeks' time, they returned home and were packing the last of the boxes just as the snow began to fall. They stood side by side at the darkened window in the empty dining room and looked out onto the garden. She loved the garden, but it was the greenhouse at its foot she would miss the most. Winters of her childhood were associated not with the Canadian cold but with the amber glow of the greenhouse. No matter how frigid the day, it was warm and humid inside, and condensation collected on the glass roof, dripping down like a tropical rain shower. There were beds of cacti, plants that came from jungles around the globe, and, her favorites, the gem-colored orchids her father had taught her to clone.

In winter, she and Westley had played in the greenhouse's circle of light, surrounding it with a protective ring of snow angels, their wings touching like a chain of paper dolls. For as long as she could remember, it was a ritual they had always performed with the first snow. They would lie next to each other, their arms waving up and down at their sides, their legs moving in and out.

And on their tongues they caught the snowflakes that spun toward them. To her, they were sweet and tasted of sugar cookies, although Westley said they were only water and couldn't taste of anything. When they were finished, their parents would put on their coats and come outside to admire the angels. Every year the angels grew a little taller, until she and Westley were too old to play such games, although she still secretly longed to.

But those days were gone and now the greenhouse was in darkness, all the plants having been donated to the university conservatory on College Street. She had watched the workers carry out every plant, every flower, feeling with each item's removal a finality not even her parents' funeral had invoked, the greenhouse's new emptiness seeming to mirror all the emptiness inside her.

For old time's sake? Westley asked. They put on their boots and coats and went outside. The snowflakes were wet and came down in clumps the size of cotton balls. Already a layer of white covered the stone paths, but over the years their feet had memorized the route to the greenhouse. They looked at each other, feeling a little self-conscious as they sat on the ground. Slowly, they lay back in the snow and moved their arms and legs. In, out. Up, down. *I wonder when they planned on telling us,* Westley said a little bitterly. The snowflakes that melted on her tongue no longer tasted of sugar cookies, though she could occasionally taste the salt of her tears.

They stood up and looked down at what they had created. The snow was so shallow they'd exposed the dirt with their movements. More mud angels than snow angels. *They'll soon fill in,* Westley said, brushing the dirty snow from the back of her red wool coat. They stayed there so long the outlines of the angels almost disappeared, and they themselves were shrouded in white. *When we come back from Spain,* he said finally, *we'll get you another greenhouse, I swear to you.*

Thanks, Westley. She had looked up at her big brother and known then she was stronger than he was, that despite his brave words he was making a promise she was fairly certain he wouldn't be able to keep.

"Are you all right?" Frank's voice brought her back to the present, and she looked up, blinking away tears. She'd been so lost in her memories she hadn't heard him.

"I'm sorry. I was going to make you an egg. I'll do that right away." Frank put a hand on her arm and helped her up. It had been a long time since someone had put out a supporting hand to her, and it confused her. She went to take another sip of coffee, but the cup was empty.

"There's no hurry," he said. "Signor Nevicato has gone for a nap, and I wanted to know if I could fix that broken shutter for you before it falls off. I could use a break from splitting wood."

"That's very kind of you," she said. "Now I'll get you that egg."

Still thinking about his hand on her arm, she left him and went to the well. She filled the chickens' water bowl and tossed them a handful of grain from the bag the miller had given her in exchange for the delivery of his wife's eleventh child. The chickens themselves had come from a grateful Zampollo cousin who lived at the very top of the mountain. Graziella had been unable to save the baby—no one could have or should have, it was so tiny and misshapen—but she had saved the mother, finally stemming the bleeding that threatened never to stop. Graziella suspected the chickens had been stolen, so poor were the cousins, but she didn't care, as she and Giovanni had eaten the last of their old hens in that final terrible winter, and she'd longed for fresh eggs.

This morning, the hens had produced five, a record output that slightly cheered her. She would make two each for Giovanni and Frank and one for herself. They could have the milk that Maria Serena had brought and the rest of the bread, and Giovanni would have the liver from last night's chicken too.

When she emerged from the henhouse, she saw Nino accepting a cigarette from Frank. She liked Nino. Unlike the Marias and in spite of his almost debilitating shyness, he had done his best to make her feel welcome and helped out as much as he could, given he could barely keep up with his own work. A large family to feed without the help of his two eldest sons—Dario killed during the Russian Campaign and Tazio now in Marghera. Tazio was trying to earn some extra money in what was left of the city before marrying Rosanna, the blacksmith's daughter from Il Paesino who had worked as a *staffette* during the war, delivering messages for the Resistance that had been stitched into the hem of her dress.

Graziella watched from a distance as the men stood up the motorcycle and Frank demonstrated it for Nino, making *vroom, vroom* noises like a child playing with a toy. Nino tried it next, looking quite happy, smoking his cigarette. Even the worry lines that had become part of his gentle face seemed to have relaxed a little. He got off when he saw her coming, and the awkwardness returned.

"I'm on my way to Il Paesino," he explained, glancing at the daisy in her hair before quickly looking away again as if he'd seen something he shouldn't have. The motorcycle was a safer place to look, and she could tell he would love to know more about it but was too shy to ask. "Maria Serena wanted me to get some motherwort from you. She came this morning but Papà said you were still asleep." Twisting his cap in his hands, he spoke slowly, as if even his own language was difficult for him. "Is there anything I can do for you while I'm in the village?"

She told him she couldn't think of anything and went to the house for the herb. She also added a vial of the *Calendula* cream Maria Serena hoped would fade the birthmark she always blamed on her mother. *Everybody knows,* she told anyone who'd listen, *you have to eat strawberries or your baby will get birthmarks!* Graziella's cream had little effect as really there was nothing that could be done, but Maria Serena applied it faithfully, hoping it would fade before Tazio's wedding. Back outside, Graziella handed the parcels to Nino and asked him to thank Maria Serena for the milk.

Later, as she was cooking the eggs over the fire, listening to Frank whistle slightly off-key as he hammered the shutter back into place, she realized she should've asked Nino if he knew anyone who could fix the motorcycle. She hadn't though, and a small half-formed thought crossed her mind that her forgetfulness might just have something to do with Frank putting out his hand to her in the garden.

3

The next morning the children arrived. Graziella knew them all, of course, offspring of the different Marias. Salvatore, Mario, Gaspare, and little Emilia. She came out of the house to find them gathered on the far side of the path, four little faces watching Frank from behind the cover of an ancient olive tree.

"Some of my nieces and nephews," she explained to Frank, who was sitting on one of the oak rounds looking back at them. "They aren't used to strangers. And some of the strangers who have been around here the last few years haven't been all that friendly."

Frank was dressed in a white T-shirt, his green army pants tucked inside his unlaced boots. Giovanni was already ensconced in his chair, his blanket draped over his knees. A fire burned in the pit between them, but she was disappointed not to smell coffee.

Frank smiled and wished her a good morning. "I was waiting for you before I made the coffee. I hope you don't mind me getting your father-in-law up. I didn't want him to start yelling like yesterday. Terrible racket for you to wake up to."

Thinking how grateful she was to be relieved of

this duty for the second morning in a row, let alone for the coffee, she barely had time to thank him before Giovanni announced it was going to storm. "I can feel it in my legs," he said loudly. "A big one's brewing."

"Are you sure, Papà?" she replied, looking out over the valley. Except for the fluffiest of white clouds hanging over the mountain she'd nick-named Mount Panettone for its Italian Christmas cake shape, the sky was a uniform sea of blue. It was one of those clear mornings when one could see the Alps around Lake Garda. No haze, no humidity. It was perfect. "I think your legs could be wrong today."

"They're never wrong. Tell Ugo to close up the barn tight or we'll lose the roof."

"Ugo isn't here, Papà," she said quietly, glancing over at Frank. "Do you mean Frank? The American?"

All the lines on Giovanni's sun-beaten face knitted together as he thought about this for a moment. "Yes, the American. You're right," he finally agreed, although Graziella could tell he was still confused. *My God, Ugo, hurry back before his mind goes completely.*

"I'll tell him, Papà," she said patiently, straightening the blanket back over his knees. "After breakfast."

Frank had put the coffee on and was now trying to coax the children over. He held something in his fingers, all the while making encouraging little noises as if he were trying to entice nervous sparrows to come and eat out of his hand. "See," he said, popping what was in his hand into his mouth and chewing. "It's gum. Yummy, yummy." He rubbed his stomach before taking another piece out of his pocket and holding it out. Coffee, cigarettes, sugar, gum. What else, she wondered, did he have in that pack of his?

"It's okay," she called out to the children in Venetian. "This is Frank. He's from America and speaks English. It's a different language, but I can speak it too." It occurred to her then she should start teaching the children English. It couldn't hurt. Maybe she could talk to Father Paolo, who ran a small school out of the church.

"He has some gum for you," she said when they still didn't move. "It's very sweet, like candy." In these hills candy was almost as rare as dragons, but clearly they understood and edged their way out from behind the tree.

It was Emilia who broke free of the group first and dashed toward Frank, a doll held firmly under her arm. She snatched the gum and stuffed it in her mouth before retreating behind Graziella. "Don't swallow," Graziella instructed her. "Just chew." Emilia obeyed, peering out at Frank.

"You're a funny little thing," he said with a light laugh, and the little girl's eyes grew wider at the unintelligible sounds. "I have a little sister. She was only a little bigger than you when I last saw her. Her name's Clara. What's yours?"

Graziella translated, and Emilia whispered her name into Graziella's dress. Of all her nieces and nephews, Emilia had always been Graziella's favorite, in part because she was the first baby Graziella had ever delivered. She'd been staying with Graziella the night the Germans had hanged her father, Lorenzo, and burned down the house with her mother and siblings inside. Poor little Emilia bounced among all her aunts' houses now, dressed in hand-me-down clothes too big for her skinny little frame. With a halo of golden curls, she was the only blonde in the entire Zampollo-Nevicato clan, an anomaly attributed to an Austrian grandfather, though Graziella knew differently. *Keep an eye on that girl,* Maria Serena had cautioned Maria Lisabetta, *or the gypsies will take her. You know how much they like blond babies.* Emilia never went anywhere without her ragged cloth doll with button eyes. For some reason, rather than playing with Maria Valentina's little girls, she preferred this trio of boys, and they seemed to tolerate her, including her in their games and watching out for her even though, at the ages of seven and eight, they still considered her a baby at four.

The boys, no doubt a little embarrassed that a girl half their age was the brave one, now swaggered over with an exaggerated air of nonchalance.

"By golly," Frank said to Mario as he handed him the gum, "with your hair sticking up like that, you could be Alfalfa." Mario's cowlick exasperated his mother, Maria Valentina, to no end, and there was nothing that could make him run faster than seeing her spit into her hand, ready to slick it down.

Graziella laughed. "You're right. They could be *Our Gang*. They get into enough mischief."

Salvatore, Mario, and Gaspare were a tight lot, and when they weren't sneaking stolen cigarettes behind the barn, their collective cunning was employed in avoiding all work, the backs of their mothers' hands, and any education Father Paolo tried to instill in them. They were followed everywhere by Gaspare's old dog, Lupo, and while his name might have meant wolf, he was in reality a mangy mutt with a limp whose cowering disposition was anything but wolflike. But to point that out to Gaspare was to invite a string of protests followed by elaborate tales of how the dog had taken down entire German regiments.

Graziella knew her own childless state was another source of derision among her sisters-in-law. After all, it was a woman's place to provide her husband with children. Maria Serena had twelve, Salvatore being the youngest. Mario's mother, Maria Valentina, had six and was pregnant again, and Maria Benedetta at least tried, even if all but Gaspare had resulted in miscarriage or stillbirth. Whether they thought Graziella was incapable of becoming pregnant or whether she deliberately prevented it with some mysterious herbal brew, she didn't know, but enough snide comments had been made that she knew they listed it among her many shortcomings.

Of course, she didn't tell them the real reason. They wouldn't have believed it anyway. To them, Ugo was infallible, except perhaps in his choice of wife, with no other defects, physical or otherwise. But she had been in Spain at the field hospital when it had happened and helped Westley remove the shrapnel from Ugo's groin and thigh, packing the wounds with aloe leaves gathered from the hillsides, their antiseptic properties drawing out the poison. Even though Ugo had told them he was preparing to be a monk at the monastery of Montserrat, it was still difficult for Westley to break the bad news to him. *You're very lucky to be alive,* he'd said gently. *And it's a good thing you've already chosen a vocation that doesn't include children, for I'm sure this will never be possible.* Ugo thanked him and said it wasn't important.

It hadn't been important for her either when a few months later in Marseilles he had proposed. *I do not know what kind of life I am offering you—a childless one for sure,* he'd said. She replied that it didn't matter. And she'd meant it then, believing Ugo was the only person she would ever need. But would it make it easier now if their children were here to help fill his absence?

"I could play baseball with the kids," Frank said as the children ran off. "I have a baseball in my knapsack. I just need something for a bat. Do you mind if I look through the barn again? Or maybe I should just wait for your husband to come back. You said he'd be home today, right?"

He looked at her, waiting for an answer, and she found she couldn't keep this deception up any longer. She was pretty sure he saw through it anyway, the way he kept pressing her. "I don't think my husband's coming home today," she whispered. "I don't know where he is. They don't say it, but I know they think he's dead."

Frank stared at her, his eyes as wide as the children's had been a few minutes earlier. "I'm sorry," he said. "Though I was starting to think that might be the case." The coffee boiled over the edge of the pot, but he didn't seem to notice. "So he never came back after the war? You haven't heard from him at all?"

"No, but he's not dead," she insisted, no longer whispering. "He's just not home yet." She ran back into the house before he could say anything else.

Once inside, she didn't know what to do, and so she sat down at the table and placed her head in her arms, her forehead against the cool wood.

She'd been planning to tell him but not like that. *And Ugo isn't dead, can't be dead. . . .*

She heard footsteps. A cup was placed close to her, and she could smell the fragrant coffee. "Drink it while it's hot," he said softly. "It'll make you feel better."

She lifted her head and thanked him. "I'm sorry I got so upset."

"I'm the one who's sorry," he said, pulling up a chair and sitting beside her. "I shouldn't have pushed you for an answer."

She took a deep breath, finding now that the truth was out she wanted to tell him everything. "Ugo was a leader of the Resistance," she said, starting at the beginning. "His code name was *Il Monaco*—The Monk, because that's what he was going to be before he met me. But even though he was in Venice, he used to come back here to the Hills every few months, to see me and help out on the farm. But I haven't seen him since January. I haven't even gotten a letter since late March, and I used to get one almost every week." She stopped for a moment to regain her composure. Frank pushed the coffee cup toward her, and she put her hands around it, seeking comfort in its warmth. "Our nephew Tazio used to work with him in Venice, but even he hasn't seen him since March. Tazio is going to Venice in a few days to try and find out more, but for now all we know is that Ugo led a raid on a Nazi storehouse in early April. The

Germans were stockpiling guns and ammunition, and the Resistance was so badly armed. The Allies were helping out, though Ugo said it was never enough. But something went wrong. Four men were captured and tortured to death because of that raid. Their bodies were dumped in the street for their families to find, and no one has seen Ugo since. . . ." Her voice broke over the last words, and she had to stop. She took a sip of coffee, her hands unsteady on the cup. It wasn't just Ugo. She'd known all the men who'd died, friends of theirs from Venice. Baldassare, a man who loved a joke, was once caught dumping a live canal rat from a trap into a police motorboat, a foolish stunt that had earned him an official dose of castor oil, one of the Fascists' favorite forms of punishment. Vincenzo and Biagio were brothers studying music at the conservatory, and Donato was a Jew whose family had fled to Switzerland.

She set the cup down on the table. "I keep thinking Ugo must've been wounded, or maybe he was captured and sent to a camp, or maybe he even went into hiding. But it's been so long now. The war's over, everybody else is home. . . . And he used to write all the time. He knew so many of the rail workers, and they'd somehow get letters to me. And if he'd been shipped to a camp in Germany or something . . . he'd be free by now. . . . He'd be back or at least would've sent word. . . . It's like he's vanished." She stopped, knowing she was repeating herself, knowing too how damning this sounded. "But I just don't believe it," she said. "He's too smart to get into such a mess, right?" And she looked at Frank, desperately wanting him to confirm this.

But he didn't. Instead, his response was to place his hand over hers on the table and hold it tightly, his fingers pressed into her palm. It was not a reassuring grip. It was far too hard for that. It was a grip that told her he thought the worst.

"It's no use, is it?" she asked finally. "He has to be . . ." The unspoken word *dead* hung on the air between them before she continued. "He has to be, because I just don't think he'd leave me here like this."

"I don't know how he could either," Frank said harshly. Startled by the sudden vehemence in his voice, she involuntarily pulled her hand out from his. "I'm sorry, Grace," he said apologetically, looking at his now empty hand as if wondering what had just happened. "I didn't mean it like that. It's just I know I couldn't do that to you. So I'm afraid you must be right." He reached out as if he might touch her again, but his hand fell short. "I'm so sorry," he repeated, his chair scraping over the stone tiles as he pushed it back. "I better get to work."

Father Paolo was telling one of his stories. It was the priest's day to eat with Maria Benedetta and

Roberto, but he had stopped by before dinner to see if Giovanni could be persuaded to play a round of chess. The board sat on the table between them, and already Giovanni had captured three of the priest's pawns and one bishop. Father Paolo's visit this evening was a surprise, and Graziella couldn't help but think his timing and choice of story had something to do with Frank's presence, as if perhaps he had come by to drop a gentle hint that she still had a husband named Ugo. She poured Father Paolo more wine as Giovanni knocked away another pawn with a knight in an illegal move the priest let slide.

"You remember, Giovanni, when the choirmaster of Montserrat came," Father Paolo said as Graziella went back to stripping leaves from a bundle of dried mint. "You remember how we couldn't believe the news of Ugo's singing had reached all the way to a monastery in Spain. It was a blessing. But such a mixed one. We knew if he loved Ugo's singing, then he would take Ugo back with him. Only ten years old and already leaving us. And yet we also knew how great an honor had been bestowed on us, for Ugo would be singing with the magnificent choir of Montserrat." Father Paolo shook his head wistfully.

"It was the Archbishop of Treviso," Giovanni piped in loudly. "He came and heard Ugo sing and wrote the choirmaster. They were friends. And Ugo was eight, not ten. And it's still your move, Paolo."

"Yes, you're right. Very good, Giovanni," Father Paolo said, praising this bit of recollection before pausing to contemplate his next move. A move, Graziella knew, calculated to end in his own eventual defeat.

"I still have the letter the choirmaster sent me, asking permission to hear Ugo sing," Father Paolo said as he finally pushed his rook up several squares. "It was dated June 10. June 10, 1926. I remember every word of it. It could be an important historical document one day. And yes, he'd learned of Ugo's singing from the Archbishop of Treviso. An enormous honor in itself. An archbishop! And all the way from Treviso! He'd written right away to Montserrat that as God had chosen a humble stable for his beloved son's birth, God had also chosen the humblest of churches for the most glorious of voices.

"Anyway, it was the Sunday after the Assumption when the choirmaster arrived. He stayed at my house, and Annunziata was terrified he wouldn't like her cooking. Maria Serena took care that the church was properly cleaned and set out only the very nicest flowers. And Maria Benedetta made Ugo a new white shirt. Heavens, how she fretted it wasn't going to fit right! Everyone was nervous. Everyone, that is, but Ugo, who wouldn't have been nervous if he'd been singing for the Baby Jesus himself.

"I'll never forget that day. He stood at the front

of the church in his new shirt, his hands folded in prayer, his eyes on the Virgin, so small and yet his voice soared to the heavens. It was a song no one had ever heard before—a song so beautiful God himself must have whispered it in his ear. Poor Maria Teresa had to be escorted from the church for fear her weeping would distract the choir-master, and every one of us was guilty of the sin of pride that day." Father Paolo's eyes glistened with the memory, and Giovanni's hand stopped in midair over the chessboard as if he too heard those notes from so long ago.

"Do you remember how your own father claimed his old cow gave milk again like a champion?" Father Paolo continued. "It had wandered through the woods and was grazing behind the church when Ugo started his song. It's a good thing Ugo went with the choirmaster the very next day or the poor child would've been kept busy performing miracles for the entire parish with his singing. Curing bunions and getting hens to lay eggs again." Father Paolo laughed here, the point at which he always laughed, and Giovanni used this opening to declare checkmate. The priest smiled his most innocent smile, as he always did when Giovanni won. "Yes, Giovanni. Looks like you got me again. Another game? But if you were a good Christian, you'd let me win for a change."

The family rarely saw Ugo once he left for

Montserrat, although he wrote to them faithfully, letters read and reread until every word was committed to memory. But between leaving for Montserrat as a boy and coming home from Spain with Graziella as his wife, he'd only made the long journey home three times to spend summer with his family. Visits in which his sisters constantly fussed over him, not letting him out of their sight while he worked beside Giovanni. News of these homecomings raced through the Hills, and on Sundays people traveled from miles around to hear him sing, filling the tiny Church of Santa Maria to the bursting point. They laid gifts of bread and wine at Ugo's feet, and she knew more than one miracle had been attributed to his singing.

The first time Graziella heard Ugo sing was that Christmas Eve just after Westley had died. In the weeks leading up to his death, Westley had declared utter defeat. He'd aged over the months, every week a year older, his handsome face drawn, all the easy jokes and laughter vanished as exhaustion and discouragement set in. Even his hair had thinned, and she knew then she saw death in his eyes. She remembered that day after their parents died, when she realized she was stronger than he was. *What's the use, Grace? There's no winning this war. Even if the Fascists are defeated, the West will intervene. British warships are anchored off the coast just to make sure the republicans don't win. So I save them now, and they die later. What's the point?*

You do it because it is the right thing, Ugo said. *And if no one ever fights back, then we are lost for sure.* Ugo had already told them that when the civil war had broken out, he'd felt it his duty to fight with the republicans, though he still planned to return to the monastery as soon as he could. He didn't know if it had survived the war, but he would rebuild it with his bare hands if he had to before finally taking his orders.

Over the next few weeks, Ugo gained strength as Westley lost it. She worked alongside Westley as he looked after the young men who came to him on stretchers, removed bullets, set broken bones, dug graves. He barely slept or ate. And the whole time he watched her and Ugo grow closer.

Would the scalpel have slipped had Ugo not been there? Did he see in Ugo someone who could save her? Was it just fatigue that made him careless, or had he cut himself on purpose? All she knew for sure was that after he'd cut his hand, the aloe wouldn't withdraw the poisonous infection. He told her to stay with Ugo, that he only wanted to sleep for a very long time.

The front moved on, but she and Ugo stayed behind to bury Westley on Christmas Eve in the makeshift cemetery in the field behind the hospital. After, they walked into the dusk, snow falling from a dove-gray sky, the frozen mud blanketed with white, and Ugo told her a story of the Great War, when the Germans and Allies had met in no-man's-land on Christmas Eve and sung "Silent Night" in their own languages. For one moment remembering they were all brothers.

But I miss my own brother. I miss Westley was what she said, and Ugo pulled her close. *You and Westley saved my life,* he said. *Barcelona is falling to the Fascists, and you cannot stay here. I will take you to France and see that you find a boat home.* He smelled of rubbing alcohol and hay, and she cried for a very long time while he whispered to her in a mixture of Venetian and English.

They returned to the hospital as darkness fell, built a fire with more of the shed they'd been dismantling for fuel, and cooked the last of the onions and potatoes from the cellar. A Christmas feast.

Later, when they held each other, still dressed under the blankets, she thought it strange how the first man to ever hold her was about to become a monk and would never hold another woman again. But that was when he sang to her. "Silent Night." So softly, his lips almost brushing her cheek, his breath warm against her skin—so close to being a kiss.

By the time the priest was ready to leave, an almost eerie stillness had settled over the hills, and the light was a watery pink. Graziella and

Father Paolo watched as a flock of swallows took flight from the branches of the giant chestnut, forming their own little dark cloud as they swooped over the barn. "Giovanni was right, it's going to be a big one," she said. "You could be spending the night at Roberto and Maria Benedetta's."

"Could be, dear," the priest replied. "I can't say I've ever seen the light such a strange color. Anyway, I'm sorry I missed the soldier." She didn't tell him she hadn't seen Frank since the morning, and she wondered if Frank was avoiding her, if she'd made a mistake by confiding in him. He'd acted so strangely. He'd even scared her a little—he'd been nothing but friendly until then.

After saying good-bye to Father Paolo, she looked to the barn. Was Frank up there now? About to go back inside, she was startled by the sight of Enza silently watching from the cover of the chestnut tree. Dressed only in a long white nightgown, with her dark hair hanging loose over her shoulders and that chronic look of shock and bewilderment, she made Graziella think of a frightened ghost.

"Do you want something?" Graziella called, knowing she wouldn't answer. "You should go home now. A storm's brewing." She took a few steps in Enza's direction, but the girl turned and ran down the path.

4

From the first cracks of thunder, Giovanni was inconsolable. He shouted to Graziella from his bed as he struggled with the covers, throwing them off his gnarled legs. "I told you Pippo would be back! Where's my cane? Where's Ugo?"

"It's okay, Papà. It's not Pippo. It's just a storm. Remember this morning? You said a storm was coming. You said you felt it in your legs." She put the lamp down on the dresser, picked up the quilt that had fallen on the floor, and tried to put it back over him.

"Get that off me, you stupid woman!" He was sitting up now, and his eyes, wide with terror, darted around the room as if lurking Germans might jump out of the shadows at any moment.

There was another loud clap of thunder, and Giovanni cowered against the wall, clutching the quilt he'd so recently rejected, his thin frame shaking violently. *Mother of God,* she wanted to shout, *you weren't this afraid when the Germans really were here!* She'd never seen him in such a state.

She took a deep breath and tried to reason with him. "Look, Papà. I'll show you. It's nothing but wind and rain and thunder." She went to the window, and the wind ripped the shutter from her hand and slammed it against the outside wall, shaking the crucifix over Giovanni's bed and blowing out the lamp. Rain whipped into the room, and a flash of lightning illuminated the wall and Giovanni's terrified face. "See. A storm, Papà. It's just a storm." She strained to close the shutters just as a loud knock came on the back door.

It was all Graziella could do not to scream herself. She left Giovanni, felt her way into the kitchen where another lamp cast a faint glow on the table, and went to the door. She opened it, almost expecting to see one of Giovanni's imaginary Nazis standing there.

But it was Frank, and she stood aside for him.

"My God, Grace, are you all right? I could hear screaming." He'd only come from the barn, but his clothes were soaked, his blond hair plastered to his head.

"It's Giovanni," she said as the thunder cracked again, detonating another round of screams and calls for Ugo. "I've never seen him this bad."

Frank peeled off his wet army jacket, flung it on a chair, and grabbed the lamp on his way to the bedroom. Graziella, only too glad to let him take the lead, followed him as far as the bedroom door.

"My God," Giovanni said, his voice flooding with relief as Frank set the lamp on the bedside table. "It's about time you came home, Ugo."

Frank turned and looked at Graziella uncomprehendingly. "He thinks you're Ugo," she said. Giovanni's grizzled face was now set in an almost beatific smile, all fear and panic gone. She tried to set him right. "No, Papà, this is Frank, the American soldier who's staying with us. Remember?"

"Don't tell me I don't know my own son," Giovanni snapped, the storm seemingly forgotten. He beckoned Frank to come nearer.

"What should I do?" Frank whispered to Graziella.

But before she could answer, Giovanni called for him again, and Frank went to sit beside him on the bed. *"Me fio, me fio,"* Giovanni repeated over and over, crying softly as Frank held him. Frank looked again at Graziella, his discomfort evident in the flickering lamplight.

"He's calling you his son," Graziella said, still standing in the doorway, close to tears. "I'm so sorry you have to see us like this. . . ."

"It's okay," he said uncertainly, his voice just audible over the wind and rain. "He's going senile, isn't he?"

She nodded as another crash of thunder rattled the house. Giovanni buried his face in Frank's shirt, and Frank held him awkwardly, patting him on the back. "He has some kind of dementia," she said. "He had a massive stroke a few years ago and smaller ones since."

"My grandfather was kind of like this right

before he died. He was always asking where my grandmother was, even though she'd been dead for years. At first we'd try to explain, but he'd only get upset. In the end, we decided to tell him she'd gone to the store for ice cream. He was happy then, but I felt bad lying to him like that. I hope you don't mind me pretending. . . ." His voice trailed off, as though he couldn't quite bring himself to say *pretending to be your husband.*

"It's okay," she said. "It's just . . ." And while she knew the end of his sentence, she couldn't complete her own. It was just *strange*?

The deception, however, calmed Giovanni, and she was grateful to Frank for that. And while the storm still raged, Giovanni laid back quietly now and allowed Frank to cover him with the quilt. His eyes never strayed from Frank as Frank dragged a chair over to the bed. "I'll stay with him until he falls asleep," Frank said, and Graziella, taking the burned-out lamp, left the two of them there, Giovanni gripping Frank's hands.

Back in the kitchen, she relit the lamp and leaned against the big copper sink for support, the stone floor cold beneath her bare feet. Above her, bundles of drying herbs swayed in the drafts, the lamp casting shadows like scurrying spiders across the rafters, while from the next room emanated the murmur of Frank's voice. She listened more closely and realized he was praying.

Now I lay me down to sleep . . . the next line lost in the thunder . . . *If I should die before I wake* . . . Poor Giovanni. The man he used to be would've died of shame to know he'd one day be afraid of a storm.

Graziella would never forget the time Giovanni had answered the door and found himself staring down the barrel of a pistol. *No, we don't have any foreigners in this house,* he'd said, while she, his Canadian daughter-in-law, an enemy alien, had stood wordlessly behind him.

There were three of them. Two Nazi officers and one Italian Fascist wearing a telltale black sweater. The Germans stood by their motorcycles as the Italian, who must've come from somewhere in the Veneto, questioned Giovanni in Venetian. Why hadn't they heard them coming? She imagined them turning off the engines at the church, coasting silently down the hill toward them.

What about her? the Italian asked. He tried to shove Giovanni to one side, but her father-in-law held his ground.

Shame on you, Giovanni said, *threatening an old man and a sick woman.* Thank God Maria Lisabetta's husband, Lorenzo, had just gone home. His position as a deserter was as precarious as her own, and as they knew even then, Lorenzo couldn't be trusted to act with caution, always bristling with bravado.

Get the wine from the cupboard, Giovanni

ordered. She obeyed silently, knowing if she spoke her accent would betray her.

This is the last of them, Giovanni said as he took the bottles from her and handed them to the Italian. It was another bold lie as their cellar was stocked from the fall harvest in anticipation of the upcoming winter. She stood behind Giovanni, keeping to the shadows, praying they wouldn't discover the cellar, trying to keep her eyes from straying to the trapdoor that was covered by a worn rug. Would they just take the wine, or would they kill them for trying to conceal it? Fortunately, these were still early days in the occupation, before everyone, including the Germans, were really hungry.

But the Italian accepted Giovanni's story, signaling with his gun for Giovanni to set the bottles on the step. *What's wrong with her?* he asked, waving the gun in her direction. Giovanni turned to her as if he wasn't sure who the man was referring to. He managed to give her the smallest wink of encouragement before looking back at the invader, lowering his voice so only the Italian could hear.

Graziella watched his face. He was very young. She tried to imagine who he was, tried to imagine he had a family, that behind the angry eyes was a person capable of pity. He looked from Giovanni to her again, and she detected something different—not pity though, more like disdain. She forced herself to meet his gaze, wondering what expression she should try to adopt, when he looked away quickly, turning to his companions still standing by the motorcycles, smoking cigarettes with an air of utter boredom.

The Italian looked back. *Flour? Sugar? Coffee?* He seemed almost a little desperate now, as if he needed to show the Germans more than a couple of bottles of wine for their efforts.

You expect us to have these things? Poor farmers like us? You want to take our rations too? Giovanni was defiant again, and the Italian seemed to be weighing his options before picking up the bottles and returning to the Germans.

Nothing here but an old man, he said. The Germans threw down their cigarettes and ground them under their heels. They were older than the Italian, with twin bushy mustaches over mouths set into bitter lines. They responded in heavily accented Italian, and Graziella only caught the word *woman.*

Too sick and ugly for you, the Italian said with another scornful glance in her direction. He put the wine into one of the saddlebags and climbed onto his motorcycle. *Let's go before it rains.* They exchanged more conversation she couldn't quite understand, but it seemed to have the desired effect as the Germans prepared to leave as well.

What did you say to them? she asked Giovanni as they watched them skid down the hill toward the village.

His eyes were still on the wakes of dust churned up by their wheels. *That some of his buddies had already given you a disease,* he said finally.

She felt a moment of hysteria as she thanked him, almost laughing even as she envisioned what could have happened.

It could've gone either way, he replied, closing the door. *Maybe they just wanted to get back to their camp before it rained.* Giovanni's hand was shaking, and he looked at it, as if fascinated by its quivering. He went to the cellar and brought up more wine, pouring them both generous cups before closing the shutters and lighting the lamp. She went outside to check for dangerous leaks of light, scanning the sky anxiously as she listened for Pippo's familiar buzz. When she came back inside, he made sure to bolt the door.

But that night Pippo didn't come, the sky above them quiet but for the gentle rain that came with the darkness, and she reread aloud some of Ugo's old letters, leaving out the passages written in English, meant only for her. *It snowed here last night. None of the men were very happy about it. They saw it as a sign of a long cold winter ahead. But not me. I watched it for hours, thinking of that other night it snowed in Venice, when you were here. Such a beautiful and rare event for our beloved city. I remember it brought tears to our eyes as it floated down, settling on the red tiles of the church, on the branches of the plane trees, on the bridge that crosses the canal. You showed me how to make snow angels. The moon was silvery behind a wisp of cloud, and the snowflakes were like feathers as they drifted down. You said the snowflakes tasted of sugar cookies. And they did.*

She put away the letters while Giovanni told her a story. Of how, as a boy, Ugo would climb from the abbey of Montserrat, following the trails as high as they went among the strange gray rock formations that reminded him of elephants. And there, far above the clouds, with the desolate lonely hills of Catalonia stretching to the horizon all around him, he would sing.

The sound of his voice, it was said, carried down past the monastery and beyond to the valleys and villages. Everyone stopped to listen. There were those who didn't believe it was a young boy, saying it could only be the voice of an angel. How Giovanni came to know this story, he couldn't say, but Graziella had no doubt it was true.

The next morning Giovanni called to her, unable to get up, his right side frozen from the first of his strokes.

When Frank finally emerged from Giovanni's room, Graziella had lit a fire, as much to ward off the chill of her memories as the damp of the night. They were silent for a few moments, standing side by side, watching the flames grow, while outside the rain lashed at the shutters and the wind whistled through the eaves.

"Poor old man," Frank said at last. "I feel sorry for him."

"Me too," she said, throwing another log on the fire. "It's strange because sometimes he stays quite clear. But it seems to be accelerating. I think it's the stress of waiting for Ugo to come home. Tonight was the worst I've ever seen him. Before the stroke, he ran this farm almost single-handedly. He was a proud, proud man because he worked his own land. The very first day I met him, he bragged that between this farm and the farms owned by his daughters and their husbands, they owned more than the Zizzos—and they didn't have to be Fascists or starve a bunch of peasants to boot. Not that they were as prosperous as the Zizzos. Even in the best of times, they grew barely enough to support themselves. Maybe a bit more for market, but that was it."

A rumble of thunder echoed among the hills, and she paused, waiting for it to fade away before continuing. "I know he hates relying on me to do everything for him. I think he realizes his mind is going, and it frightens and angers him. I know that's why he lashes out at me. I understand, but I'm getting so tired of it. I just wish Ugo would come back. He wants that so badly."

Frank fleetingly touched her arm. "I think you

must be a very brave person," he said quietly. "I can't begin to think how hard these past few years have been for you. I know you're worried and . . ." He stopped as if searching for what to say. "I wish I could make it up to you."

She could only nod, knowing if he continued in this vein she was going to cry, feeling with his presence he was in some way already making it up to her. Just being here, talking with her. "I'm okay," she said, letting the words out on a long breath. Unsure of what to say next, she hoped he wouldn't take her silence as a cue to leave. How could she ask him to stay? It was still storming and she wanted him here in case Giovanni woke again. Wanted him here even if Giovanni didn't wake again.

But she needn't have worried. "Why don't you go to bed then?" he said. "I can stay down here in case Giovanni wakes up."

"Thanks, but I don't think I can sleep any more tonight. I feel bad, though, keeping you up like this," she said, unable to put much conviction behind her words. "You need sleep too."

"I'll be okay," he said. "I don't sleep too well at night anyway. It's like Lady Macbeth walking around her castle all night, going on about Macbeth murdering sleep. Now I get what she means."

Graziella laughed, the air between them suddenly more relaxed.

"What's so funny?" He pretended to sound hurt. "Never had a farm boy from Vermont quote Shakespeare to you before?"

She shook her head. "Never. But it's nice. I love reading, but I have so few books here and I've read them all so many times."

"Well, that'll be both the first and last time you hear Shakespeare out of me. I don't even know why I remember that much. It wasn't like I paid any attention in school. Spent all my time staring out the windows and daydreaming I was on great adventures. Hunting lions and crocodiles, defending the Alamo, playing cowboy. I was always the hero, of course. Still, I wish I could remember more. It's good to hear you laugh." He looked at her as if he'd made her do something wondrous, and she smiled a bit self-consciously before offering him some wine.

"No point going out into the storm if you're not going to sleep," she said. "And I know I won't."

"Yes, please. I could use a drink."

She poured two cups and handed him one before setting the bottle on the mantelpiece. "Well, at least we don't have King Duncan's blood on our hands," she said.

Frank was poking at a log in the fire, but he paused for a moment, as if seriously considering this. Then he leaned the poker against the fire-place. "No, not Duncan. I can swear I had nothing to do with that." He held up his cup. "To sleep," he said in a rather bad English accent. "May it knit up the raveled sleeve of care."

She laughed again. "You do remember more!"

"Okay, so I remembered that much, but that's absolutely it. I'm all out of culture now. I'll have to find other ways to make you laugh."

"You've done so much already. You don't have to make me laugh too." She was close to adding, *I don't know what I'll do when you leave,* but didn't, scared by her own desperation.

"It's the least I can do." He took a long drink and refilled his cup. "Besides, all this farmwork is good practice for when I get back home."

She was envious for a moment, this idea of home. Were Ugo here, Italy would be home. Sometimes here on the farm but mostly in Venice, in their little apartment that filled with morning light and the sound of church bells, their potted bay tree back in the courtyard next to the monkey puzzle tree where it belonged. There was a passage somewhere in Shakespeare about a bay tree. An omen of sorts, but she couldn't recall the passage or even the play.

"Then you'll stay on the farm when you get home?"

He gave a half nod. "I think so. And I never thought I'd say that. I hated the farm almost as much as school. I'd go squirrel hunting in the woods when I was supposed to be doing barn chores. I didn't have to sign up, you know. I was exempt from the draft, farming for the war effort and all that. But I wanted to fight. Shoot Nazis, win the war. I thought I could do it single-handedly. I wanted to be a hero." He laughed a little contritely. "I was pretty young then," he added, as though he were talking about four decades ago as opposed to four years.

"But then I got here," he continued, "and I just wanted to go home. Go back to school, milk cows again, eat my mother's roast beef dinners, play with my little sister. There were a lot of days I would've happily sold my soul to do just that."

"I know what you mean," she said. "I was only seventeen when my parents died. My older brother, Westley, and I signed up to be medics in the Spanish Civil War. We were so idealistic. I can remember how we scoffed at the idea of working at a department store. But it wasn't long before the idea of serving pie at the Woolworth's lunch counter seemed like heaven."

"But then you met Ugo."

She stared into the fire for a moment before turning back to him. "You think I'm crazy, don't you, for wanting to believe he's still alive?"

"No, not crazy, Grace." He spoke more slowly than usual, and she could see he was picking his words carefully, trying to tell her what she didn't want to hear as kindly as he could. "But I know Ugo—"

She put her hand out to stop him. "No, it's okay.

I know Ugo wouldn't want me to be unhappy, but it's like I was telling you this morning. Just when I believe I can accept it, I think maybe he's somewhere lying wounded or on his way from some camp in Germany or something and I start to hope again. . . . I still look up and expect to see him standing there. I hear footsteps on the path and think it's him. Every time I hear the whistle from the train, I think Ugo's on it. The day you appeared on your motorcycle, I stood there praying it was him."

"I'm sorry it was just me."

"No, no. It's not like that. Please, though, let's talk about something else."

"But I'm worried about you, Grace. The other night, when I saw you at the edge of the cliff, I was afraid. . . ." He looked away, and she knew the words he didn't speak were *you were going to step off.* "I stayed awake the rest of the night watching for you, to make sure."

She was taken aback by this show of compassion from someone she barely knew. Had he saved her life that night? "I don't know. . . . I had this dream . . . about Ugo. . . ." *I wish I could make it up to you,* Frank had said earlier. How tempting to close this space between them, to feel his arms around her and let herself forget. How could she, though, longing for Ugo as she did?

But at what point would she accept he wasn't coming back? Another week? A month? A year?

When would she start mourning? Or had she been mourning for months already, this stubborn belief he'd return really only denial? If only she knew what had happened to him.

Thunder shook the house again, the loud boom followed by a whimper from Giovanni's room. It took her by surprise; she'd almost forgotten he was there. Almost forgotten Giovanni was Frank's reason for being here at all. They listened for a moment, but he made no further sound.

She and Frank had been standing all this time, and now she offered him a chair. "We'd better sit. It could be a long night." She went to take the chair opposite him, but that arrangement seemed too intimate. She still couldn't quite look him in the eye, so instead she climbed on top of the chair and brought down a bundle of dried herbs, placing it on the table between them. Fresh herbs sat on the counter, and she brought them too, along with the lamp and a wooden mortar and pestle.

Frank took a dry leaf from the bundle and crushed it between his fingers, wrinkling his nose in distaste. "What is this stuff?"

"*Bocca di lupo.* Wolf's mouth. It's good for the digestive system, among other things. While this," she said, pointing to the fresh herbs, "is San Giovanni's herb. It has lots of uses." This was a safe subject, better than dwelling on Ugo. "Once upon a time, people hung it outside their doors to keep demons away, but I put it in olive oil and use it as an antiseptic. I used to give it to Ugo for his wounded comrades. I gave him other things too, like lavender to repel lice. Ugo used to say that not only did he have the only lice-free brigade, he also had the nicest-smelling one."

She showed Frank how to strip the dried leaves by running her thumb and index finger down the stem. He imitated her, and the leaves fell with a whisper into a wooden bowl. "How do you know all this?"

She contemplated the San Giovanni's herb for a moment before selecting a tip and dropping it into the mortar. "Plants are what I know," she said, crushing the leaves to work out the oils. "When I hold them in my hands, I can feel their healing properties. My father, who was a botanist, always told me it was a gift, but I never really took him seriously. I didn't plan on becoming an herbalist. I studied botany with my father with the idea of becoming an academic like him. But then my parents died, and there I was with my brother in Spain looking after the wounded with almost no medical supplies. I found myself searching the fields and woods for anything that might help. Then I came here, delivered little Emilia, and sealed my fate as a midwife too." She spooned the pulpy mass into a brown bottle and added fresh leaves to the mortar.

"I haven't been much help to Giovanni, though," she continued. "The hot springs over by

Alba Terme might help his arthritis, but we'd need a car to get him there. So all I can do is put salve on his legs and give him white willow bark. But there's his mind too, and that's something else altogether."

A crack of thunder rattled the entire house, and they both paused in their work, looking up at the herb-festooned ceiling as if they expected it to fall on them at any moment.

"That was the biggest one yet," Frank said. "I hope it doesn't—" He didn't finish his sentence before Giovanni cried out.

Graziella sighed and placed the pestle on the table, ready to get up, but Frank put out a hand. "No, let me do it," he said. "It worked last time." He poured a bit of wine into another cup. "I'll take this to him. We should've soaked some of your herbs in it."

"I've tried, but he just spits it out and accuses me of trying to poison him." They started to laugh until Giovanni's cries put a guilty end to their brief merriment.

"Me fio, me fio," Graziella heard Giovanni mumble again, and if Frank didn't know he was asking for his son, he still gave the answer Giovanni would have wanted if only he understood. "Shhh, it's okay, I'm here," Frank said, and it wasn't long before he returned, announcing that Giovanni was sleeping like a baby.

She thanked him again. What did it matter for

now if he let Giovanni believe he was Ugo? She just hoped Giovanni wouldn't remember any of this in the morning. She could just imagine the reactions of her sisters-in-law.

Frank took his place at the table again. "Are either of these good for sleeping? "

She topped up their cups. "Yes, they can be, but it's tricky. It depends on the person. The best I've found for sleeping is valerian. But it's a narcotic, so it could give you nightmares." She sat down but didn't pick up the pestle. Instead, she folded her arms on the table and looked at him. "Do you know why you can't sleep?" she asked, her eyes drawn to a dusty-colored moth flying kamikaze missions against the glass chimney of the lamp.

He picked up another piece of wolf's mouth, not stripping it this time as she had shown him but carefully picking off each individual leaf. "It's hard to know where to begin." He contemplated a leaf for a moment. "I guess it all started going really wrong near Cassino." He seemed nervous, his voice a little shaky.

She put a hand out, placing it over his momentarily, wondering if asking him to talk was more about satisfying her own curiosity than out of any desire to be helpful. "I'm sorry. You don't have to tell me. It's none of my business."

"No, it's okay," he said, his eyes following her retreating hand as if he already missed it there on his own. She thought about putting it back, maybe even holding it, but he began again, and she felt the opportunity had passed. "We were up in the mountains near Cassino not long before the Allies broke through the line and marched to Rome." He spoke softly, and she had to strain to hear his voice over the pounding rain. "All that lay between my regiment and the Germans was this little river. We'd spent a couple of days firing back and forth whenever we saw anything moving. It was spring, but it was still damned cold. Sorry, *really* cold. Anyway, we weren't accomplishing much as we waited for this brigade of Brits to catch up with us. Then the real push was to happen. Cross the river and drive the Germans back. Keep pushing them north."

More thunder rattled the house, and they listened for sounds from Giovanni's room, but only his snoring was audible.

Frank took a sip of wine before resuming, the herbs in front of him forgotten. "Nobody was looking forward to this. In the hills, we were pretty safe, but once we were in that river, we were just sitting ducks. That's why we did it at night. They had this plan. Send forty or so guys to sneak across the river and take the Germans out in their sleeping bags. It sounded like a stupid idea even then. They should have sent in planes.

"I wasn't long in that river before I knew I was right. My feet sunk in the mud, and the water came up to my chest. I could barely move. By the time we reached the middle, the water was up around our necks. It felt like ice. Somewhere close to me a soldier began to cry, saying he couldn't swim. Everyone was going *shhh! shhh!* and it all sounded louder than bombs dropping. We were holding our guns over our heads, and my arms were killing me.

"I knew we should've turned back. I had this awful feeling about it. I was about to tell the guy next to me I was going back when the first shell lit up the sky. I couldn't fire my gun from that position. Wouldn't have known where to shoot anyway. So I just let the gun drop into the water. . . . And there we were, shells falling all around us, struggling back to shore with our boots sticking in the mud. . . . Everybody screaming and crying. It was a total snafu. . . . Afterward I was taken prisoner. . . ."

He broke off, pushed back his chair, and went over to the fireplace, giving the logs a vicious stab with the poker and sending up a shower of sparks. An ember fell onto the floor, and he stomped it out before turning around and facing her again. "Forget it. Forget what I just said."

"Why?" she asked, confused. "What happened?"

He put down the poker. Slowly this time, as if suddenly overtaken by fatigue. "Nothing. It's nothing," he said, the anger touched with weariness now. "Just another war story. I should go now. Maybe I can get an hour's sleep before Giovanni wakes up. And I sure could use a cigarette."

"I can get up with him," she said a little desperately. In the hopes he would stay, she went to pour him another glass of wine, but the bottle was empty. The thunder had become a distant rumble, and light was appearing around the edge of the shutters. Everything seemed to signal an end to the night. Still, she wanted him to stay. There was something disturbing about this abrupt change in Frank, this dismissal of his own story and the angry edge to his voice. He'd been like this earlier in the day too. Something wasn't right. It worried her, and she didn't want him to leave like this, instead wishing a return to their earlier intimacy. "I don't know what I would've done if you hadn't been here." She had been afraid to say it earlier, but she said it now.

He shrugged. "No, you sleep as long as you like. I'll come back to help Giovanni. Don't worry— I'll hear him. It's the very least I can do for you." And as there seemed like nothing else she could say, no excuse to make him stay, she saw him to the door.

She'd intended to thank him again and go to bed but instead found herself following him into the cool, wet morning. Rain still dripped from the roof, and the ruts in the path were filled with water. They had heard the storm's violence, but she hadn't considered what damage it might be doing. On the hill, the vines looked beaten down, and her hollyhocks beside the door were flattened into the mud. While she hoped that was the worst of it, she was already imagining every last plum and apricot smashed onto the ground.

But Frank noticed none of this. Instead, he was watching the water as it rushed down the ditch alongside the road. "Son of a gun, look at that water go!" he exclaimed, all the fatigue and anger of only a few minutes ago gone. It was an extraordinary transformation. He showed no sign of having spent a sleepless night in her kitchen, comforting an old man and talking about the war. He took off at a run and was halfway to the road before he turned and ran back again.

"Come on," he said, taking her hands. "Come and see the water. It'll be fun." They were standing close, and she looked down at her hands in his.

"No, I should go to bed," she protested, although why she couldn't say. Only a few moments ago she'd wanted him to stay. She tried to take her hands away, but he pulled her toward him, backing along the path to the road. Before she knew it, she was running beside him, splashing through the puddles.

The water was rushing from the top of the mountain, overflowing the sides of the ditch, tumbling over the rocks, sweeping along leaves and twigs. They crouched down and dipped their hands in the water, watching it flow over and between their fingers.

"It's like home," he said, "in the spring, when the snow melts. My friends and I would make little boats out of bark and race them. I made them for my little sister too. My God, it seems like a million years ago."

He told her to wait then and ran down the path toward the woodshed, returning soon with a chunk of bark. He broke it in half, plucked a couple of grape leaves from the vines that grew beside the ditch, and outfitted the pieces of bark with sails.

"Pick one!" he said, holding them out to her. She chose the one in his right hand, but he told her to take the one in his left instead. "I have a feeling that's a winner." He jumped over the ditch onto the road and held out his hand to her again. She took it and landed just short of the edge, up to her ankles in cold water. She was laughing, hanging on tightly as she scrambled the rest of the way.

They placed their boats on the water, holding them back. "Ready?" Frank asked.

She felt an excitement that went beyond a toy boat race. "Yes," she said a little breathlessly, and the boats were off.

Frank and Graziella ran together down the hill, racing after them—*Go! Go! Go!*—and it was her boat that Frank was cheering on as the bark spun and flipped, leaping over rocks, grape-leaf sails long ago spurned and left to make their own course. She was cheering too and didn't worry for even a moment what the Marias would think if they saw her running with Frank down the hill like a child, her mud-streaked nightgown billowing out behind her.

They chased their boats to the bend in the road, and Frank declared hers the winner before they started back up the hill, a little winded. "Wasn't that fun?" he asked. He put his arm around her shoulders and gave her a light hug. She agreed, thinking how maybe she would just stay up now. Check the trees, garden, and vineyard. She would make sauce with the bruised fruit. Perhaps she could ask Frank for a little sugar to sweeten it. Frank would get Giovanni up and make them both coffee. . . .

Just then, a gray rabbit hopped onto the road, and they stood as still as they could, but the rabbit wasn't fooled and, after sniffing a couple of times in their direction, darted back into the woods.

"It's good luck to see a rabbit at dawn," Frank announced quite seriously. His eyes weren't playful anymore.

"Really?"

"I don't know, but it should be." He pushed away the wave of hair that had fallen over his forehead, then looked up at the sky. "It's going to be a beautiful day, and that's good luck. And your boat won, which is also good luck. So who knows?" They had stopped walking. He was so close now, and she felt herself drawn toward him. He was going to kiss her. . . .

"Who knows!" she burst out, panic exploding inside her. "Maybe Ugo will come home today!"

He took his arm from around her shoulder and backed away, running his hand through his hair again, almost angrily. She found herself apologizing, wishing she could take the moment back. She could be kissing him right now. "I'm sorry. It's just so hard for me to let go," she said. "I really loved him. And now I don't know what I'm going to do. Oh, Frank. I can't. He could still come home. Any day. Maybe he really was wounded or, or, I don't know. . . ." Perhaps she should step back into his arms and let him hold her. Then maybe she'd be okay.

But just as she thought she might actually do it, she heard Lupo barking and Gaspare calling out Frank's name. The moment was lost. She stepped away from Frank and managed a smile. "The children are back. You should show them how to make boats."

He nodded and started walking again. She touched him briefly on the arm. "You understand, don't you? We can still be friends?"

"Of course," he said, though his smile was strained, his voice tired again. "Get some sleep. You need it. I'll look after things."

Enza was with the children, no longer wearing her white nightgown but a flowered dress Graziella couldn't remember seeing before, and she realized how dirty she herself was with her muddied feet and clothes. Enza didn't run with the children but hung back by the door, holding a crock, presumably filled with milk, the second such crock in four days, unusually generous for Maria Serena. Over Lupo's yelps and the children's excited shrieks at the sight of Frank, Graziella could hear Giovanni calling for Ugo.

"Don't worry about him," Frank said, extricating himself from a tangle of skinny arms and legs, leaving the children to play in the water. "I'll get him up." He followed her past the still-lifeless motorcycle to the door where Enza waited. But when Graziella went to take the crock, Enza thrust it out to Frank instead. Frank accepted it, thanking her in Venetian, but Enza never even looked at him before running off in the direction of home.

"What's wrong with her?" Frank asked as he watched Enza disappear up the path. "She doesn't talk a lot, does she? And she always looks so scared, like a frightened little animal."

Graziella took the crock from him. "There was this German soldier. . . ." She didn't elaborate, but Frank clearly understood.

"Those filthy Germans," he muttered. "God, I'd kill the bastard."

"Believe me, someone thought of that."

"Poor girl. She's so sweet and pretty too. Maybe I can cheer her up a little."

"I don't know," she said as a wave of exhaustion overtook her.

Giovanni let out a fresh volley of cries for Ugo. She looked to Frank for help, but he was still watching the spot where Enza had disappeared into the woods. "I'll go get him," she said wearily, pushing open the door that seemed to have grown heavier.

Her words brought Frank back to the present, and he shook his head. "No, no, let me. It's okay. You go get some sleep."

She thanked him, left the crock next to the bowls of herbs, and slowly climbed the stairs to her room.

5

It overwhelmed her sometimes, making her stop in the middle of some mundane chore, as it did now, looking out from the doorway over the valley as the day dawned, the broom she was holding forgotten. How was it that she, Grace Forrest, should find herself here? Here, in these hills she'd never even known existed, waiting for her husband to return from war, caring for his increasingly failing father, dealing with his ungrateful sisters. It was like some Greek tragedy unfolding with her at the center.

And now there was Frank. He came around the corner of the barn carrying a large basket of apricots. It was market day in Cinto Euganeo, and Frank was going with her brothers-in-law to barter fruit for other things they needed. As Frank set his basket on the ground beside Giovanni, he saw her and waved.

She returned the wave and watched as he disappeared around the corner of the barn before turning back to her sweeping. *I should've let him kiss me,* she thought for at least the hundredth time that week. After the storm, he'd cleared the fallen branches from the yard, gathered the bruised fallen fruit for stewing, and split yet more wood.

Every night after dinner, he set up the chessboard on the kitchen table and played with Giovanni while Graziella washed the dishes. Like Father Paolo, Frank always let Giovanni win, going so far as to make Giovanni's moves without the old man even noticing. Giovanni had persisted in calling Frank Ugo, believing Frank to be his son even though he couldn't understand a word Frank said. *You think he had another stroke?* Frank had asked. Graziella didn't know, but any attempts to correct Giovanni caused him so much distress they quickly gave up, preferring just to keep him happy.

Fortunately, Giovanni was always asleep whenever her sisters-in-law came to visit. They appeared with jugs of milk for their father or with messages from their husbands, though their real motive in coming was to see Frank. They asked Graziella to translate their mundane conversations, about the weather, their children, and had he ever met their second cousin, Poldo, who'd moved to America after the Great War and owned a butcher shop in New York City? Graziella noticed Maria Serena had started covering her birthmark in Frank's presence, something Graziella had never seen her do before. While sometimes she was followed by her other children, Maria Serena never failed to bring along Enza, taking every smile Frank gave her daughter as an encouraging sign. Graziella looked for these signs too, remembering his words the morning after the storm. *She's so sweet and pretty too. Maybe I can cheer her up a little.*

I should've let him kiss me, she'd almost said aloud as she translated some meaningless anecdote of Maria Valentina's. But as insecure as she felt, she saw nothing that could be interpreted as romantic in Frank's behavior. For her part, Enza stood silently next to her mother with her usual blank expression on her otherwise beautiful face, hands hanging limply by her sides.

Graziella knew it was foolish to keep hanging on to hope. She needed to accept that she might never hear confirmation of Ugo's death. Too many unmarked graves of too many men, and any one of them could be Ugo's. Tazio would be back any day now, and in her heart she knew he wouldn't have any good news. Good news could only arrive in the form of Ugo himself, and that wasn't going to happen. But even if she could accept he wasn't coming back, she needed time to put his memory to rest and to properly mourn.

But she didn't have time. Frank's boat was leaving at the end of the month, and she had to make a decision now. The idea of staying here, of living the rest of her life as Ugo's widow, playing midwife and nurse to his family in exchange for a bit of meat, milk, honey, and some old shoes, was too lonely an existence to even consider. She loved the Hills, loved Venice, but without Ugo it was almost impossible to imagine a life here in Italy.

Putting her broom away and going to wring out Giovanni's nightclothes, which had been soaking in the sink, she pictured herself falling back into the same malaise, standing on the edge of the cliff some foggy night without Frank there to call her away.

Of course, she could write to Aunt Beth and ask her to make arrangements to get her back to Canada. But she could envision the reply even now: *I'll do it, Grace, but I hope you've learned your lesson. I fear you are as impractical as your father, and look what happened to him.* As if being killed by a derailed streetcar was somehow his fault!

She hated the idea of relying on the charity of Aunt Beth just as much as she hated relying on the charity of Ugo's family. And she already knew Aunt Beth would oppose her going to university. Aunt Beth had always scoffed at the idea that women could have careers like men and would immediately find Graziella some dullard for a husband. Graziella already knew he'd be bald and his ears would stick out, and every Wednesday night she'd be expected to attend Aunt Beth's Imperial Order of the Daughters of the Empire meetings. All this sounded unbearably lonely and depressing, and yet, when she considered the possibility of returning to America with Frank, she felt hope. Which, she decided, could only mean one thing—she was falling in love with him. She might feel strange and guilty about it and still miss Ugo terribly, but it was happening all the same.

She wished she had Maria Lisabetta to talk to. She could've told her about this. They had been that close. From the first time they'd met, Graziella had sensed Maria Lisabetta's unhappiness and a deep resentment toward her life here. She was an outsider in her own family and, while at first she'd been as angry as the rest at Ugo's choice of a wife, she soon saw in Graziella an ally and someone she could trust.

It was Silvio Zizzo I always wanted to marry, not Lorenzo, Maria Lisabetta had confided one day. But Giovanni expected all his daughters to marry into the Zampollo family to keep their hold on the mountain. Besides, Giovanni had never liked Silvio's father, let alone his politics. And, as he was fond of saying, *El fruto no'l casca mai lontan da l'àlbaro*—The fruit doesn't fall far from the tree.

Graziella had never met Silvio, knowing only he'd died with Dario in the Russian Campaign, when Italy had been on the side of the Germans. Sent there on horses, the Italians had been mown down by the Russians' machine guns. Hundreds dead in a burst of gunfire.

As Maria Lisabetta talked, Graziella had suddenly realized it wasn't the Austrian great-grandfather who'd given Emilia her blond curls. Silvio Zizzo had. *Any secrets for me?* Maria Lisabetta had asked at the end of her confession.

Graziella hadn't then, but she did now. She was in love with Frank. It was so lucky for her he'd missed his boat back, although more and more she was convinced he hadn't missed it by accident. He kept saying he wanted to go home more than anything. Given the chance, how could he have done something as stupid as missing his boat? She was sure he was carrying some terrible guilt. Was he afraid of going home and facing his family?

He had taken his story as far as the mountain river. That was bad enough. The only one to survive. She couldn't imagine his terror. To be helpless as his friends died around him. But as soon as he mentioned being taken prisoner, he couldn't go on. *Forget it. Forget what I just said.* What had been worse than that mountain stream? Had he been tortured in a prison somewhere?

She heard a bark and, leaving Giovanni's damp shirt next to the sink, went outside to see the *Our Gang* children, Lupo, and her sisters- and brothers-in-law all pouring into the yard. Frank greeted the sisters with kisses on both cheeks, as if he'd been doing so all his life, and shook the brothers' hands. Between Frank and the brothers, there was no awkwardness or language barrier. The men joked and Frank laughed. He would pass out cigarettes and tell them about his farm in

Vermont in a mixture of English, sign language, his rudimentary Italian, and the few dozen words he now knew in Venetian thanks to the children. Cow, grape, wine, house, barn, dog. *Vaca, ua, vin, casa, stala, can.* The men would nod as if they understood every word. He rarely asked Graziella for help translating, recruiting on his own the brothers and Nino's middle boys to assist him with the grapes until the rows closest to the road were neat and orderly. They had made a scarecrow too that the children had named *Sior Todesco,* or Mr. German. She had donated an old shirt of Giovanni's to the project, and Roberto had brought a German helmet left behind in the retreat. The helmet made her shudder, but as it seemed to have the same effect on the birds, she raised no objections.

"You watch them," Giovanni said, ignoring his daughters as they approached him with yet another milk offering. He shook his cane as Frank placed a basket of plums on the cart. "They're a bunch of crooks in Cinto. Sold my father a blind dog once. No better than gypsies. Called that dog Gyp, we did. You hear that, Ugo?"

Frank agreed automatically, and Graziella cringed, waiting for the God-knows-what reaction from her sisters-in-law. She could have explained it was better not to correct him, but she knew Maria Serena would never listen.

"No, Papà, that's not Ugo. That's Frank, the

American soldier," Maria Serena said, her free hand shielding her cheek. She spoke to her father in that special voice, the one reserved for the very young, the very old, and the potentially crazy.

It enraged Giovanni. "Don't you use that tone with me," he shouted. "You think I'm stupid!" He waved his cane at her, knocking the pitcher, spilling milk down the front of her blouse and skirt.

Maria Serena screamed, her hand leaving her cheek, exposing the deep purple mark as she tried to brush the milk from her blouse. "Now look what you've made me do!"

Frank stood helplessly to the side, catching enough to know now he was the source of the trouble. He apologized profusely to Maria Serena in Venetian. *"Me despiase! Me despiase!"* He put down the basket and pulled a handkerchief from his pocket, about to wipe the front of her blouse. But when confronted with the enormity of Maria Serena's bosom, he seemed to change his mind, holding the handkerchief out to her instead. She took it from him, dabbing at the milk stain before handing it back with exaggerated thanks.

Graziella put out her hands to take what was left of the milk, but Maria Serena held the pitcher against her wet blouse, saying bitterly there wasn't much point now. To make matters worse, Roberto and Clario thought the whole thing quite hilarious (Nino knew better than to laugh at his

116

wife). Maria Serena, sputtering that it wasn't funny to be attacked by her own father, grabbed Maria Valentina's hand and pulled her toward the path.

It wasn't until everyone had left and Graziella had taken Giovanni for a nap that she realized Maria Benedetta hadn't gone home yet. She stood like some strange apparition in the cool dimness of the kitchen, twisting her apron in her hands. "I'm sorry" was all Maria Benedetta could get out before collapsing into tears, and Graziella realized the woman was pregnant again. Maria Benedetta knew it too, but she was not willing to wait this time. "I start to hope . . . and Roberto hopes too . . . and then four or five months later. . . . I just don't have the strength anymore. . . ." She was unable to go on, and Graziella handed her a dish-towel. She went to busy herself by the sink, waiting for Maria Benedetta to collect herself. Maria Benedetta cried so quietly. Slouched over the kitchen table, her head buried in her arms, her shoulders only slightly shuddering. Graziella sus-pected she did this often, crying silently so as not to disturb Roberto sleeping beside her.

Maria Benedetta was only a year younger than Maria Serena but shared none of her sister's sto-icism or belligerent sense of survival. The war, the numerous failed pregnancies, the constant fretting about Gaspare's and Roberto's health—they all had left her drained. Her face was pinched and lined, limp strands of graying hair escaping from her severe bun, and her clothes hung from her almost skeletal frame, so thin it was a wonder she could get pregnant at all, especially at the age of thirty-nine.

"I know it's a sin," Maria Benedetta blurted out, and Graziella turned to face her. Maria Benedetta crossed herself so often it had taken on the characteristic of a nervous tic. "But I just can't go through with it. I keep hoping it'll be different this time. And Roberto does too. I didn't want to ask you, but I don't know what else to do. I tried talking to Maria Serena, but she just says I should thank God—only one mouth to feed." And she started to sob again but loudly now, pressing the dishtowel to her face, the words flooding out with the tears. Graziella sat down and let her speak. "It's easy for her to talk. Twelve children. But Roberto . . . It's not good for a man to have only one child. What do people think?"

Graziella wanted to ask her why she thought the extremely fertile Maria Serena hadn't been pregnant in the eight years since Salvatore's birth. It wasn't exactly a secret she'd told Nino *enough is enough*. She'd in fact even bragged about it. Graziella had suggested she try a Dutch cap instead, but Maria Serena had replied with utter indignation (not to mention a bit of amnesia and hypocrisy) that she was a good Catholic woman, thus condemning poor Nino to a middle age as celibate as Father Paolo's. But Graziella didn't tell Maria Benedetta this, saying only that it wasn't Maria Benedetta's fault that she couldn't have children and that nobody blamed her, although Graziella knew Maria Serena and Maria Valentina did.

"It's not God's plan for everyone," she said, trying to choose words Maria Benedetta could relate to. "Look at me. No children, and I'd like even one."

Maria Benedetta seemed surprised by this revelation, and Graziella had to conclude again she wasn't a bad sort. She just lacked any spine when it came to standing up to her sisters. This, Graziella could forgive, but Maria Benedetta, too self-absorbed to wonder if their cruelty hurt her, didn't apologize for them either, and that was something Graziella wasn't able to forgive.

"And Ugo? He would like a child?" Maria Benedetta asked.

"We couldn't have children," she admitted, "but yes, when I think about it, I think he would have." She stopped for a moment, waiting to see if Maria Benedetta noticed she'd used the past tense when referring to Ugo. But there was no reaction and so she went on. "You're lucky. You have Gaspare."

Maria Benedetta nodded. "I know, I know." She twisted the cloth in her hands as if to wring out the tears. "You can help?"

"Yes, I can help. I can give you something, but you have to be sure. Can you come back later this afternoon?" Maria Benedetta nodded again, screwing up her face to keep from crying. "And there's something you can use to stop it from happening again, but it's not easy to get. You'll have to wait."

"Maybe, maybe. But not now." *One sin at a time,* Graziella thought, knowing Maria Benedetta would go straight to the church to find Father Paolo and confess. She could imagine him stifling a sigh every time Maria Benedetta walked through the doors, surely one of his most demanding parishioners. Would she even come back for the herb? "You won't tell anyone about this?" Maria Benedetta whispered. "You'll keep it a secret?"

"Of course."

"Not even the American?"

"No, of course not."

"I wouldn't want him to think . . ." But she didn't finish the sentence, instead getting up from the table and folding the damp towel before handing it back to Graziella. She glanced up at the old wooden crucifix that hung over the door, crossing herself one last time. "Give my love to Papà when he wakes. I must get home before Roberto and Gaspare return. I hope they found thread. I have to make Tazio's suit for the wedding, and thread's been so hard to find." Yet when she left, she didn't take the path to her house but rather the road toward the church, as Graziella had suspected she would. She doubted very much Maria Benedetta would go through with this, but she would get the herb anyway.

Waiting until after lunch when Giovanni was resting again, she took her battered trowel and wicker basket from the woodshed and walked down the hill to where the *Aristolochia* grew so innocently along the side of the road, only its noxious odor like rotting flesh warning of something more sinister. The children would pick it for her in May when its upright stems were adorned with hooded yellow blooms. *Zia Graziella—for you. Wash your hands,* she would tell them.

She grasped the stems and stabbed her trowel into the hard ground, prying out the brown rhizome and shaking off the dirt. This was not an herb that grew in their Toronto garden. *Aristolochia clematitis.* New to her but already holding memories. She curled her fingers around the root, feeling its power spread through her body. *Extremely toxic, has a drastic effect on the intestines, promotes menstruation, powerful abortive, a calmant for the nerves but only as a last resort.* She set the root in her basket, then drew her sleeve across her forehead, where beads of sweat had gathered, whether from the herb or the heat she couldn't say.

She'd given this to Enza, Maria Serena having brought the girl to her. Two months without blood.

Is this what you want, Enza? Graziella had asked. The girl had looked at her, but her eyes were dead. She could've asked Enza anything, and the response would've been the same—the girl no longer seemed to care anymore what happened to her. Maria Serena had interjected. *What are you asking her for? Do you think she can look after a child? You expect me to look after some German soldier's bastard? She'll never get a husband!* And so Graziella had reluctantly given Enza the herb, while still feeling she was overstepping some line.

And then there was Maria Lisabetta. Graziella dug again, breaking off another piece of the root. Not just an abortive but also a calmant for the nerves. *Give me some for Lorenzo,* Maria Lisabetta had said only last autumn. *I'll slip it into his food. He doesn't need to know.*

No, Graziella had replied. *It's too strong. Too unpredictable. You could kill him.* Maria Lisabetta had looked at her then, and Graziella had shivered. *It can't be that bad,* Graziella added, picturing even as she uttered the words Lorenzo pacing the room, his rage boiling out of him, his thoughts back on Mount Sole, where, alongside other Italian deserters, he'd fought with the local Resistance group. *The Nazis knew we were in the barn, but just killing partisans wasn't enough for them. They rounded up the women and children and threw them into the barn with us, shooting*

122

through the walls, lighting it on fire with grenades and incendiary bombs. A hole opened up in the side and I grabbed the nearest kid and ran. Others came behind me, some of them already burning, towers of flames. The Nazis were gone. On to murder the next village. I ran and ran and when I stopped I realized the kid was no longer breathing.

How naïve she'd been to think Maria Lisabetta hadn't borne the brunt of his anger. Why hadn't she seen the desperation grow in her friend's eyes? Probably because by then they all had that look, she herself half crazed with fear and hunger and worry.

I tell him to sleep in the tunnel below the church, Maria Lisabetta said. *I tell him it'll be safer for him there, but really I'm thinking of myself and the children. But he won't. He just starts screaming at me. "Are you trying to bury me alive?" Last night, after dark, when Pippo flew over, he took his pistol and ran outside yelling, "You bastard! You bastard!" He waved his gun in the air. "Come down here and fight like a man!" He was insane. I had to drag him inside to keep him from shooting. I told him he was going to get us all killed. The children were crying, and he was shouting at them to shut up. Even when Pippo was gone, he thought he could still hear him. He sat at the table the whole rest of the night in the dark, rocking back and forth with his hands over his ears.*

Graziella hesitated.

If you won't give me the herb, at least tell me what it looks like and where to find it, Maria Lisabetta said.

But Graziella refused, fearing what Maria Lisabetta might do. So she promised to prepare the herb herself, but by that same night it was already too late, and she couldn't help but wonder if she'd made herself an accomplice in all six of their deaths.

No, you did the right thing, Ugo had said when he came home for the funeral. *There was no knowing what was going to happen or what Lorenzo would do.*

But I should've noticed how bad it had gotten for Maria Lisabetta. Maybe I should have just let her do it. . . .

And what then? Have Lorenzo's death on your hands? No, it was not your fault. There are only bad choices to make anymore. You can only try not to make the worst one.

But how can we know before it's too late?

Sometimes, you cannot. Anyway, they are with God now. That is all we can ask for.

After the funeral, Ugo had gone with his brothers-in-law to cut down the Judas tree in the field across the path from the burned-down house. It wasn't the tree's fault the Germans had chosen its branches to hang Lorenzo from, but the brothers all agreed they could never stand in its shade again. They decided to burn it right there, and the green wood had smoldered for days.

She was smoothing the dirt back into place around the remaining *Aristolochia* when she heard laughter. She picked up her basket and went to wait in the shade of an oak tree by the road. Frank, Nino, Clario, and Roberto were all helping Nino's old donkey pull the cart up the steep hill. Without their help, the cart would roll back down, dragging the donkey with it. It was such a decrepit old beast, but Nino was extremely fond of it, seeing it as a war hero of sorts. After the Germans had stolen it in one of their winter raids, Nino had thought he'd never see it again. But the donkey had somehow survived, making its way back to the farm after the retreat, emaciated, its back scarred and missing clumps of hair from where it had been beaten.

The *Our Gang* boys and Lupo ran alongside. Only Emilia was allowed to ride. She waved, calling out to Graziella, trying to tell her something. Then Frank saw Graziella and he waved too, his smile reaching her even from this distance.

When they caught up with her, Emilia was ready to explode with excitement as she showed her the tiniest kitten, as dirty as the cloth it was wrapped in. "We just found it," Frank said, "or rather Lupo did, in a ditch at the foot of the hill. All the others were dead, but we heard this little meow. Poor thing. It's already lost one of its lives."

"More than one, I think. Giovanni's going to think you got cheated like his father. Not a blind dog but a half-dead kitten." Graziella handed it back to Emilia. "Be very gentle with it," she said, switching to Venetian, "and we'll give it some milk as soon as we get home."

"Okay," Emilia said. "It's a girl, and her name's Daisy. That's the name of Frank's cat in America." Emilia said *cat in America* in English, and Graziella was convinced the child would be fluent in English in a matter of weeks.

Graziella walked beside Frank, their steps sometimes bringing them close enough together that their sleeves brushed against each other's. She caught Nino's eye across the cart and asked him if there had been word from Tazio yet. He shook his head before looking away quickly. He'd been acting oddly the last few days, and she was beginning to wonder if he might be a little jealous. Just a few days ago, he'd stood in her kitchen torturing his cap in his hands as he watched her scrub the floor. Finally, unable to stand his silence any longer, she'd asked him if there was something he wanted to tell her. He turned deep red and, straightening his cap, attempted to put it on his head but instead dropped it on the wet floor. *You know, I could've fixed that shutter for you,* he stammered before rushing out the door. She'd almost laughed at the time, thinking she was going to have to invent some sort of love potion before he and Maria Serena made complete fools of themselves. But here he was looking at her with that same pained expression, and feeling uncomfortable, she found herself stepping slightly away from Frank.

When they reached the house, the men were in no hurry to go home and gathered around the well, passing the dipper and enjoying a round of Frank's Lucky Strikes. Graziella settled Emilia and the kitten in the kitchen with a dish of milk before rejoining them, and Nino poured them all some grappa. "To Frank's health," he announced, sounding like his usual self. Perhaps she was making too much of his moodiness.

"The grappa's for Tazio's wedding," Frank explained. "Nino wouldn't let me buy it at first, but I said it was for helping with the grapes. And of course as a wedding gift. He only had eggs and a couple of baskets of fruit to trade with. I've never seen anything like it. They just barter things. Some of them looked like they were trying to trade away their dinner. I was the only one with money, and I just wanted to buy everything and give it all back to them." He frowned. "The war might be over, but it's going to be a long recovery. From what I've seen, you're doing better than most up here."

"Who had the grappa?" she asked the brothers.

"The Zizzos," replied Roberto. "We had a good

laugh over that. Selling their grappa. Even they were hiding wine from the Nazis."

"And I'm sure a lot more," she said, imagining them burying their good silver in the garden by moonlight. Everyone had their limits, even Nazi sympathizers. "But what I really want to know is how Frank figured out you wanted the grappa for Tazio's wedding. Unless you've all learned English, that's a lot of information to convey."

"Oh, it was easy," Roberto said. He clenched his cigarette between his teeth and, pretending to hold up the edges of an imaginary gown, pranced across the yard while Clario whistled Mendelssohn's "Wedding March."

"Okay, okay," Graziella said while the boys hooted with laughter. She couldn't imagine them doing this at the market—the looks they must have attracted! But then Roberto did have a reputation for being a joker, perhaps his way of coping with the ever-gloomy Maria Benedetta.

They were laughing so hard they didn't hear it at first. The distant rumble from somewhere to the north. It was Nino who noticed it first, and they soon found themselves echoing each other's *shush, shush* as they strained to identify the source of the strange sound. "Thunder?" Frank guessed. She looked up but the sky was clear. It became louder until from behind Mount Panettone burst an airplane, cresting over the peak so low its underbelly almost grazed the trees.

They couldn't help it—a collective stepping back, a moment of fear. It had not been so long since the appearance of such a plane could only mean trouble. Planes like this one, flying low in broad daylight, strafing the road with machine-gun fire. Only too recent memories.

"It's an American plane," Frank said. It flew over the valley and the village, so low its wings were almost level with where they stood in the yard. They could make out the insignia on the tail, the blur of the propellers, even the pilot inside, and still they all stood there, mesmerized.

The boys recovered first, and they ran right up to the edge of the cliff, waving, shouting, jumping up and down. As if in response, the pilot tilted the plane slightly and the wings seemed to wave hello.

Graziella scanned the faces of her brothers-in-law. They were smiling now at the children and the plane's friendly gesture, but she could see they too remembered another day when the plane that had risen from behind Mount Panettone had been British, with a German one close behind. They'd all been here in the yard, bringing in the cherry harvest, and they'd dropped their tools and instinctively shrunk toward the house, seeking shelter behind the thick stone walls.

But they couldn't seem to stay there and went outside again, making their way to the cliff where the boys were now. Despite the very real danger of stray gunfire, they weren't afraid anymore, perhaps because this battle seemed personal, between these two planes only, fighters in a ring made of green hills, their punches bursts of white flame. The planes had been bombers, and with their bellies loaded with shells, they had maneuvered awkwardly at first, until one then the other released their loads, loud whistles ending with explosions, only narrowly missing Il Paesino but leaving behind a burning barn and several large craters in the roads and fields. They were more agile then, swooping at each other like angry swallows, then *boom*! A giant ball of fire, bright even in the brilliant afternoon sunshine, as the German gunner found its mark. There had been a sharp intake of breath among them, a synchronized step back from the cliff, and then a joint sigh of relief when the parachute opened and the English pilot drifted on the breeze as his plane crashed into the valley, flames rising from among the trees.

They watched as the German plane limped away, disappearing from view around Mount Panettone, heading back north where the Germans had an airbase. They lost track of the parachuter over Il Paesino, guessing he had landed somewhere near the village, perhaps low on the hillside among the trees. They did not hear the single gunshot, only learned of it later from the village postmaster. The Germans had left him there to the birds and animals, so sometime in the night the villagers had wrapped him in his bloodstained parachute and buried him in an unmarked grave. Graziella thought of how somewhere in England a mother and maybe a wife or sweetheart would never learn of this man's death, only know he'd gone down with his plane behind enemy lines and was presumed dead. She felt a connection with these unknown women, this not knowing, this constant wondering.

The American plane was gone now, only the faintest rumble in the distance, its departure seemingly a signal for her brothers-in-law to leave too. As Nino nudged the old donkey back onto its feet, Clario handed Frank his pack, and Roberto resumed his earlier act, prancing down the road while Gaspare, Salvatore, and Mario held up the train of his imaginary wedding gown.

"Roberto is such a clown," Frank said as the laughter faded away.

"Just wait until Tazio's wedding when he gets a little more of that grappa inside him," Graziella said. "Maria Benedetta will die of mortification."

"Roberto's wife, right? I don't know how you keep them all straight," he said with a shake of his head.

"It's not that hard," she said. "Maria Benedetta is the really thin one. Maria Valentina is very pregnant. And Maria Serena has the big birthmark on her cheek. And it's not all that important anyway. Remember how we were talking about *Macbeth* during the storm? Just think of them as the three witches and call them all Maria."

"Yes, but you're the one with all the herbs and potions. I bet they lay awake at night thinking you're out under the full moon stirring a big cauldron full of spiderwebs and bat toes and whatever else witches stir into their brews and wondering if they're going to wake up as toads."

"That's probably the only reason they didn't turn me over to the Nazis." They laughed, and she thought how he even made the Marias tolerable. Maybe later she could tell him she'd rethought things and would he kiss her now please?

Frank had bought a fish wrapped in a copy of the Resistance newspaper, *Il Patriota*. "This old guy had them in a barrel," he said. "And there was another barrel with eels."

"I'm glad you got the fish," she said, smoothing out the paper to read later once it dried. It was in the pages of this paper a few years before that she'd learned of the death, in China, of her family's old friend Dr. Norman Bethune. A case of blood poisoning, just like her brother, Westley. "Eels make me shudder. They're so long and slimy-looking."

"I agree," he said with a smile. "I think our ancestors immigrated to North America not because of religious persecution or anything like that but because they didn't want to eat eel anymore."

She laughed again. "I'll grill it over the fire. It'll be a wonderful treat. I'm sure even Giovanni will be excited. He hasn't had much of an appetite this week."

"A real feast. But I'm going to cook it. I'm giving you the night off." He opened his pack. "Look what I found for you. It's in English too. I think it's from Canada."

"A present?" It was a battered book called *Glengarry School Days*. "You're right, it is Canadian. I'm sure my brother read this. It must've belonged to some Canadian soldier."

"Probably. I can't see how else it would get to a rural market in northern Italy. I was really excited when I found it because you mentioned how much you love to read. I know it's not Shakespeare but . . ."

"No, no, don't apologize. This is one of the nicest gifts I've ever received." She wanted to hug him but, afraid of his reaction, instead resumed rummaging through the parcels while he dealt with the fish. He'd bartered the fruit well: a tiny round of cheese, a couple of small sacks of dried beans and rice, another one of dark flour, a postage-stamp-sized packet of salt left over from someone's war rations, and a jar of chestnut honey.

It was the last item that excited her the most. "Oh, I can't believe you found honey!" she exclaimed, removing the wooden stopper from the jar. She dipped her finger inside and tasted the honey with a sigh. "Try it," she said, holding the jar out to Frank, and he too licked his finger with an identical sigh. "We can have some with pancakes tomorrow morning," she said, replacing the lid. "And with the rest I'll make an apricot bread pudding for Tazio's wedding."

She went on to tell him that Clario used to have beehives. "Six of them. But the Germans found a radio transmitter hidden in one near Arquà Petrarca, and they made a point of smashing every hive in the Hills to smithereens. It was winter, and the bees all died. Clario wants to rebuild them. But they're so much work, and supplies are so short. Perhaps this winter, and then we can have honey again next year."

"Honey next year?" he asked, and only as she put her hand back into his pack did she realize what she'd just said. That she'd still be here next year as opposed to far away.

She was trying to think how she could correct this, how she might say something that showed she'd changed her mind about that interrupted kiss when her hand touched something cool and metallic at the bottom of the pack. She pulled out a small silver-plated hand mirror, not unlike the one that had once sat on her mother's dressing table, part of a set that included a comb and brush. Only this one was more intricate, the handle twined with silver morning glories, while on the back was a bird, beak open in song against a backdrop of roses. She turned it over and caught the reflection of her smile in the unmarked glass. This was even a nicer present than the book. Was he keeping this as a surprise for her?

Frank looked up from gutting the fish and saw her holding the mirror. "Oh, that's for Enza. Do you think she'll like it?"

Turning it over and stroking the silver bird with her finger, she felt the joy of her discovery dissipate. "Of course. Any girl would like something so beautiful."

Just then, Giovanni called out weakly from his room. "*Ti xe ti,* Ugo?"

Frank understood the simple question. "Yes, it's me, Papà. I'll be there in a second." It didn't seem to matter to Giovanni that he couldn't understand what Frank said. His voice was reassurance enough. Graziella wondered when Frank had started calling Giovanni Papà. She hadn't even noticed—it seemed so natural.

"Don't worry about Giovanni," Frank said, setting down the knife and wiping his hands on a cloth. "I'll look after him. You go find a cool place to read your book. I'll call you when dinner's ready."

She looked at her reflection in the mirror again before slowly returning it to Frank's pack. Taking her book, she went to sit in the garden beside the potted bay tree. She flipped the book open but couldn't get past the first line. *The school was built of logs hewn on two sides. . . .* It was the mirror. It bothered her. And it wasn't hard to figure out why. She was jealous. She'd almost convinced herself that Frank wasn't interested in Enza, but clearly he was.

She had been sitting for a while, staring at the book, when she heard Frank talking with Giovanni. She got up and, from the cover of the sumacs at the corner of the chicken coop, watched while Frank helped Giovanni to his chair. Since Giovanni had started calling Frank Ugo, he'd stopped asking for his blanket, and she could only conclude he no longer needed the security it used to provide him.

Out of nowhere appeared the sparrows, flitting around the chair, waiting for Giovanni to drop crumbs. Giovanni waved his cane at them half-heartedly before ignoring them entirely. One landed briefly on his knee before flying up into the chestnut tree.

Frank held up the fish and Giovanni nodded in approval, surmising aloud that it couldn't be old Pasquale down in Cinto who'd sold it to him or he would've cheated him for sure, and it was a damn shame he hadn't bought eel instead. Graziella smiled, thinking how Frank would've laughed if he could've understood. But Frank laughed anyway, and Giovanni joined in.

Grabbing some kindling, Frank started a fire in

the pit. "On our farm, we have a trout pond fed by a spring," Frank said. "My grandfather built it, and when I was younger, it was my job to shoot the muskrats that built their tunnels in the banks. I did a good job, not just because I liked shooting muskrats, but because I kept getting this nightmare where I would come out in the morning and all the water would be drained out of the pond, all the poor fish flopping around on the dry bottom. Still have those nightmares sometimes, even after everything else that's happened."

Giovanni nodded as if he understood every word. "We have to build a trap for Pippo," he said in response. "I've been giving it some thought. Tonight, before he comes back. Take the nets from the fruit trees. Get . . . can't remember her name, one of my daughters, the one who sews a lot . . . but get her to sew them all together. We could hang it between the mountains and Pippo would be caught like a bird. Where are those nets?"

"Can't say I know what you're talking about," Frank said, "but it sounds swell to me. Looks like there's already a good bed of coals. You think it's ready for the fish?" He held up the fish again and pointed to the fire. "Got to remember to ask Grace what Pippo means. I've heard you say it before. The kids too. Funny word. Pippo, Pippo, Pippo."

Giovanni shook his head. "What you going on about Pippo for, Ugo? The war's over. The Americans have got Pippo for sure. Got him locked up in that big tower they have now. Tallest tower in the world. That should keep him. Sure hope you didn't get that fish from old Pasquale down in Cinto. He'd cheat you for sure. Probably no good. Should've got an eel."

Her desire to laugh at this conversation was cut short by the thought of how lonely life would be after Frank left the Hills, for both her and Giovanni.

"I never hear you sing anymore, Ugo," Giovanni said, suddenly wistful. "Sing for me."

"You know, I sure wish I knew what you were saying," Frank said as he placed the fish on the pan. "Must be terribly frustrating for you. I'd get Grace to translate, but I've given her the night off." If he'd glanced toward the garden, he would've seen her there lurking among the sumacs. She had to admit she was spying on him, waiting to see if he might give something away in his one-sided conversation with Giovanni.

"Canta, canta," Giovanni said, urging him on with one hand, and now Frank was echoing his words back to him. *"Sì, sì,"* Giovanni said, and in a wavering voice he sang a few notes of "Ave Maria."

"Ah, you want me to sing. Because Ugo sings. But I don't sing at all, and they say Ugo sings like an angel."

"Canta, canta." Giovanni was insistent.

"Okay," Frank said, and so he sang. "Amazing

Grace." The hymn that as a child she'd thought was written about her, only to have Westley tell her it wasn't. *Because you're not amazing,* he'd said with a laugh. She'd cried then, and her mother had assured her she was indeed amazing before admonishing Westley. *Don't tease your little sister like that.* She'd like to think Frank had made the connection to her name, but more than likely it was just the first song that came into his head.

He wasn't too far off when he told Giovanni he didn't sing at all. These weren't notes like Ugo's that invoked the gods and took their place among the stars, nor would he ever be mistaken for an angel. He sang quietly, self-consciously, as if he were afraid of being overheard. But there was a melancholy sweetness too, the notes like dandelion seeds drifting through the air on silken parachutes. And he more than convinced Giovanni. "I curse the day that archbishop came and heard you," Giovanni said, wiping the tears from his eyes. "You've been away too long."

"Damn it, don't cry," Frank said, getting up and flipping the fish on the pan where it sizzled. She came out of the sumacs then, ready to tell him how she felt. It was absurd to be afraid to speak her mind. Once, she'd been stopped by a Fascist patrol while delivering grenades hidden in her market basket to a partisan hiding at the miller's. *What've you got there?* one of the Fascists had asked with a smile. *Bombs,* she'd replied very

139

sweetly, keeping her words to a minimum, smiling her most flirtatious smile, her heart pounding as she gave them each a piece of bread from the top of the basket. They'd laughed, thinking it was a joke as she walked away as quickly as possible. It was a situation she could've paid for with her life, and yet she was more afraid of telling Frank she was falling in love with him. She had to take this risk though. Maybe if he knew she'd regretted not kissing him, he'd change his mind about Enza.

He smiled at her. "How long have you been standing there?"

"I heard you singing to Giovanni. It was lovely."

He dismissed her compliment with a wave. "Come eat some fish. And then if you don't mind, I want to go and give Enza the mirror." With his mention of Enza's name, all her resolve drained away again. She must've shown her disappointment because he was quick to apologize, though he got it all wrong. "Don't worry. I'll help you feed Giovanni and get him to bed first."

She remembered that morning after the storm when the water had rushed down the hill and he'd held her hand as they chased after the bark boats. Her boat had won, and for a moment she'd been uncomplicatedly happy. But then she'd asked him to be her friend and now he was going to see Enza. She looked at him cutting a piece of fish for Giovanni and thought once again, *I should've let him kiss me.*

$$\bullet \quad \bullet \quad \bullet$$

After Frank left, Graziella sat at the kitchen table and took out her book. But still she couldn't get past the first line. *The school was built of logs hewn on two sides. . . .* She kept imagining Enza's reaction to the mirror, Frank coaxing her out of her silence. She read the line again. *The school was built of logs hewn on two sides. . . .* With a sigh, she closed the book. She might as well go to bed, though she doubted she would sleep.

The *Aristolochia* still sat on the counter beside the sink where she'd left it. She picked up one of the hard brown roots, feeling a tingle like an electric current in her fingers. Maria Benedetta hadn't come back for it. Graziella hadn't seen her since she'd left the house in the direction of the church, and she imagined her cutting through the fields and vineyards to get home. Graziella thought her sister-in-law would continue to avoid her for a while, wracked with guilt over her request, only seeking her out when this pregnancy failed too. Graziella wondered why she'd even bothered to dig the root. She'd known Maria Benedetta wouldn't come back and, even if she had, Graziella would never have given it to her anyway, realizing Maria Benedetta would've spent the rest of her life wondering if this baby would've been the one to survive.

Graziella closed her fingers around the root, feeling its power spread from her hand up her arm.

Not just an abortive but as a last resort a calmant for the nerves. She felt it now, a seductive numbing of the senses, the promise of sleep. Deep sleep without dreams of Ugo, Frank, or Pippo. *Sleep that knits up the raveled sleeve of care.*

She quickly dropped the root back onto the counter, rubbing her palm hard against her dress as she took a pan down from its hook. She swept the roots into the pan and, holding it in front of her as far as she could, walked across the yard to the edge of the cliff. She looked down into the shadowy darkness, then flung the roots as far as she could.

6

The next afternoon as Graziella heated water for laundry over the fire pit, Clario and Maria Valentina delivered a letter from the monastery of Montserrat. They'd been to the postmaster's in Il Paesino and were now on their way to see Tazio, who'd finally arrived home sometime in the night. He hadn't been to see Graziella yet, and she took this as a sign that he had no news for her.

Maria Valentina kissed her father quickly on both cheeks before handing Graziella the letter. "To save you the trouble," she explained. She put her hand on her swollen stomach, as if to emphasize the amount of effort she'd gone to on her sister-in-law's behalf. Until Frank's arrival, Maria Valentina had rarely dropped by to see her father, let alone do anything to help Graziella. Graziella knew Maria Valentina believed Giovanni to be entirely Graziella's responsibility and saw no reason for anyone else to ease the burden of caring for him, often reminding her of her own six children, with another on the way.

Still, Graziella thanked her and took the battered envelope. Her name written in a spidery hand, it was covered with official-looking stamps, a record of its journey from Spain. She had written

143

the monastery at the end of May in the midst of a frantic period of letter writing, hoping that somewhere someone had word of Ugo—in this case, even entertaining the possibility he might have gone back to Montserrat, inventing a hundred implausible stories as to how that might have come to be. Now it just seemed ridiculous. Could she really have thought Ugo would have returned there, leaving her here without so much as a word? From all those letters, though, this was one of the few replies she'd received, and it was at least possible Ugo had written to them, leaving some clue to his final days.

"You'll tell us what's in the letter, I hope," Maria Valentina said. "The twins especially are anxious on his behalf."

The twins? Graziella was momentarily confused. Of course, the Zampollo twins. She pictured their sullen, accusing faces. They needed to get married and get over this silly idea she'd stolen Ugo from them. But they were an unimaginative pair, and as long as the Marias kept nourishing their resentment, that was unlikely to happen.

Graziella slipped the envelope into the pocket of her apron. *Let her wait,* she thought, but she fixed a smile on her face and answered as sweetly as possible. "Of course," she said. "If there's any news, you'll be the first to know." She never showed any of the Marias how much they bothered her. It was one of her few weapons against them, and she took a guilty satisfaction in knowing it irritated them to no end.

"You're looking fat," Giovanni said to his daughter.

"I'm having a baby, Papà," Maria Valentina said, rolling her eyes. Her white blouse, stretched to the breaking point over her belly, had wet spots on the underarms from the long climb up the hill, but she'd clearly dressed with care, no doubt in the hopes of seeing Frank again, her last attempt having been cut short the day before when Giovanni had knocked the pitcher of milk from Maria Serena's hands. She'd washed her hair too, and whereas she used to wear it in a long braid curled over her head, it was now styled into a shoulder-length bob.

"You cut your hair," Graziella said. "It looks nice."

It was Clario who answered, as if to spare his wife the difficulty of acknowledging a compliment from her sister-in-law. "Lidra cut it last night," he said, referring to the eldest of their five daughters. "Copied it from a magazine. I told Maria Valentina she better not come with me or your American soldier might carry her off." Clario winked at Graziella over his wife's shoulder before Maria Valentina could turn and give him a withering glance.

Clario seemed to take his wife's ill nature in

stride, even finding it rather amusing, as if he didn't take it seriously or had just enough good-will to compensate for her lack of it. Her ban on helping Graziella naturally extended to him, but he quite easily ignored it, showing up once a week with an offering of some sort—a skinned rabbit or a bit of wine or honey from the beehives he'd kept before the Germans destroyed them. *Don't mention it to my wife, should you see her. She'll accuse me of stealing food from our children's mouths,* he'd say, sealing this deal between them with a wink. Sometimes he'd bring his accordion, playing old songs for Giovanni that would inevitably lead to talk of Ugo.

In Clario, Graziella saw a man content with his lot and who had come through the war grateful his and his family's suffering had not been greater. *Things could be worse* was his motto, and he had repeated it over the past years as often as Maria Benedetta said her rosary. When the Germans stole his ox, he was grateful they left the cart. They took the harvest but didn't find the wine. When Maria Lisabetta and Lorenzo were killed, he was only too aware the Germans could have sought revenge on the entire family, that it could have been all their children burned alive inside their houses, with himself and the rest of his brothers swaying from the branches of the Judas tree.

And so when the war ended, Clario breathed a

sigh of relief and said a word of thanks. He made a plaque and hung it beside the front door: *Thanks be to the Blessed Virgin for sparing this house and this family.* Envisioning a winery on the ruins of his brother's house, he planned now to take over Lorenzo's land and was striking a deal with Tazio to turn it all to grapes. *Who knows,* he'd already told Frank, *maybe you'll be drinking our wine in America one day!* He already had the expertise to make it happen—his prosecco was said to the best in the Veneto, the only point of contention being whether his prosecco was as clear and sparkling as the mountain air or whether the mountain air was as clear and sparkling as his prosecco. He was ready for the modern world, saw it rising from the ashes of the old. And for this reason he was full of questions for Frank, whose family farm in Vermont with its tractors, electricity, and milking machines represented for Clario the height of modernity.

Just then Frank himself appeared from around the barn, eating a plum. *Your American soldier,* Clario had said. But it wasn't true. He wasn't her American soldier. He was Enza's American soldier. She was going to have to accept that. The night before, Graziella had lain awake, the still-unread book he'd given her on the pillow where Ugo had once rested his head, listening for the click of the barn door. But she had heard nothing except the chirp of crickets, and when she awoke this morning, it was pretty much like every other morning since he'd arrived: coffee ready and Giovanni sitting in his chair complaining about nothing in particular. The only thing different was that instead of chopping wood Frank had collected a small pile of boards and was building a bench by the cliff.

Frank tossed away the plum pit before kissing Maria Valentina on both cheeks and shaking Clario's hand. Frank's hair had grown in the two weeks since his arrival, and he combed it back with his fingers. Graziella imagined Maria Valentina offering to let her daughter Lidra cut it for him, but then Maria Valentina would never risk Maria Serena's wrath should she be seen as competing with her own matchmaking efforts.

Graziella interpreted as Frank asked after the health of Maria Valentina's five daughters and complimented her on what a fine boy Mario was. "He reminds me of myself when I was little," he said, "full of energy and mischief." Overcome with an uncharacteristic bout of bashfulness, Maria Valentina barely managed a weak *"Benissimo, sior"* and *"Grassie, sior,"* but still, she looked pleased and no doubt planned to pass along this praise of her only son to her sisters. She made no further mention of the letter, forgotten in the glow of Frank's compliments—he'd even mentioned her new hairstyle. Clario asked Frank for a hand with replacing a beam in his barn before inviting him to dinner, and Frank readily agreed to join him later that afternoon.

After saying good-bye, Frank went back to work on his bench while Graziella took her letter into the garden. She sat down next to her bay tree, surprised to find it looking sickly, its usually thick, shiny leaves limp and droopy. Only yesterday it had looked fine. How had it deteriorated so quickly? She put the letter back in her apron pocket and found her answer in the hard, dry soil.

With a pail, she scooped some water out of the rain barrel at the corner of the chicken house and poured it around the plant's base. No ordinary bay tree, it had come from their tiny courtyard in Venice. Neglected in a cracked terra-cotta pot, it had been little more than a stick, but she'd watered it with cold coffee and an emulsion of fish heads, trimmed off the dead branches, and praised every new bud that appeared.

What a strange sight she and Ugo must have made as they walked to the train station, she in her bright yellow dress, tears flowing down her face, clutching a cardboard suitcase, while Ugo carried his violin case in one hand and the potted bay tree in the other, his face set into a determined expression. On the platform, he first handed her the violin. *There will be no more music for me until the war is over,* he said sadly, and she promised to keep it safe for him. Then he passed her the little tree. *Take it. I will surely neglect it. It is important that you keep it alive.*

She made one last plea to let her stay. She could help, she would stay hidden, but at least they would be together. But he wouldn't relent, imploring her to please, please get on the train. *Do you think I would send you away if I did not think it absolutely necessary? Do you think I want this? But it is for the best, and we will be together again soon, I promise!* The whistle sounded, the conductor telling her impatiently the train was leaving—*Make up your mind, lady! Take care of the bay tree,* Ugo said, his final *I love you* lost in the grinding of wheels.

And he'd been right to be so insistent. The very next day, the English wife of a known anti-Fascist had been taken away, her whereabouts never discovered. An example, it was said. It was one thing to be the foreign wife of a Fascist party member, quite another if you were the foreign wife of an anti-Fascist.

Her tree was already looking somewhat relieved as she took out the letter. Breaking the seal, she removed the single folded sheet. She read it quickly, then again more slowly, but it was as she suspected. Not even a clue. The monastery's brothers hadn't received a letter from Ugo in more than a year, but they would pray for his safe return.

She stuffed the letter back in her apron pocket

and returned to the laundry, adding ash to the cauldron before stirring the dirty clothes into the hot water. After a few minutes, she lifted each item with a wooden spoon, rubbed it against the washboard, then put it through the wringer. A little pile of sodden though clean clothing and sheets formed on the oak round next to Giovanni's chair.

"What's Ugo doing?" Giovanni asked.

"He's building a bench. Maybe later you can sit on it."

"That would be nice, Maria," he said. "Maybe you could sit with me."

"Maria?" She looked up from her laundry, wondering at first which of his daughters he was referring to when it struck her. "Your wife, Maria?"

He stared at her for a moment. "Did I say Maria?" he asked sadly. "What's wrong with me? Maria's been gone more than twenty-five years. The midwife handed me my only son and told me my wife was dead." He groped around as if searching for the security of his old blanket. "She was a good wife," he said. "I wish you could've met her. She would've liked you."

"Oh Papà." Shaking her head sadly, she realized in some way that Giovanni was trying to tell her that he himself liked her. "I'm sure I would've liked her too. You must miss her." But Giovanni didn't answer, his mind already slipping away, his wife forgotten.

Just then Frank called for her. She left Giovanni

and came to admire his work—two planks for the seat, another for the back, legs like the letter X. Simple but solid, everything salvaged from a manger that hadn't seen hay in five years. She would've liked to sit with him all afternoon, but Frank had promised to help Clario and felt he should be going.

He took Giovanni inside for his nap before leaving while she went to hang the laundry. Sheets, towels, underclothes, pants, shirts, aprons, her brown-flowered dress. As she was hanging the last item, she looked up and saw a smiling face. Ugo!

But of course it wasn't Ugo—it was Tazio. "Zia Graziella. It's so good to see you!" Oblivious to the shock he'd just given her, Tazio picked her up, swinging her around in circles before setting her down again, and for a moment his face was a dizzy kaleidoscope of smiles and dark sparkling eyes.

"You know I hate when you call me *Aunt,*" she said, hugging him back, her voice a little shaky. "I'm only one year older than you, don't forget that. But I'll forgive you since it's so good to see you too." She'd forgotten how much they looked alike. Ugo and Tazio were uncle and nephew, but between the similarities in looks and closeness in age, they were often mistaken for brothers. Even their voices were similar, and although Tazio would say he couldn't carry a tune in a bucket, it wasn't entirely true. She'd heard him sing and, while his voice lacked whatever it was that made Ugo's so magical, it was still a fine voice.

As children, Ugo, Tazio, and Tazio's older brother, Dario, had been as inseparable as Salvatore, Mario, and Gaspare were now, and both Ugo and Tazio had grieved deeply when Dario was killed in Russia. During the year she and Ugo had lived in Venice, Tazio had been studying engineering at the university and was a frequent guest at their apartment. He'd reminded her of Westley, with his easy nature and quickness to laugh, and she'd come to love him like her own brother. He'd been with them too that day in 1940 in crowded Piazza San Marco, the day Mussolini had declared war on Britain, the day Ugo had decided she needed to leave Venice immediately.

"I'm surprised Maria Serena let you out of her sight," she said now.

"You know Mama. She's driving everyone crazy getting ready for this wedding. When I left, she was busy yelling at Zia Maria Benedetta about my suit. The poor woman made the pant legs too short, and Mama was asking her if she wanted me looking like some ignorant peasant farmer at my own wedding. 'You want all our neighbors laughing at him? A son of a Zampollo and a Nevicato and a hero of the Resistance!'" He captured his mother's gestures and the indignation in her voice perfectly, laughing indulgently at her

153

dramatics. "Anyway, I saw my chance to escape and took it."

Graziella laughed at this story but only half-heartedly, sensing Tazio was stalling, afraid to tell her what he was really there to say. In the silence that followed, she slipped her arm through his and led him to the newly finished bench. "There's no news, is there?"

He shook his head. "There is actually, but I'm afraid it's not the news you were hoping for. I've been trying to tell myself we've known for some time, even before I said I'd go to Venice, and that there's comfort in just knowing what happened, in not wondering anymore. . . ."

He broke off as a train whistle blew in the valley below. It was the whistle that brought what he was saying home to her. Never again would she wonder if this was the train that would be bringing Ugo home. There was no doubt anymore, no hope—Ugo was gone. She didn't cry, just held tightly to Tazio's arm, thinking how this was what she thought she wanted. Just to know. But now that it was happening, she wasn't so sure. She found herself wishing she could go back to living with her old illusions that Ugo was out there somewhere, still trying to return to her.

"Do you want to know what happened?" Tazio asked finally.

She nodded, afraid of what was coming. For there was dying and then there was how one died.

She thought about Maria Lisabetta and her children in the burning house, those final minutes of fear and agony. *Oh God, I hope you didn't let Ugo suffer.*

Tazio took a deep breath. "I almost gave up, you know. I'd been in Venice for several days and had spoken to everyone who knew Ugo, but it was always the same story—no one's seen him since the raid on the storehouse. And though his body's never been found, everyone's concluded he must've died with the other men."

"But the other men," she said, thinking already her fear was about to be confirmed. "They were tortured. . . ."

"No, it didn't happen like that," Tazio said, pulling his arm out of hers and putting it around her shoulders. "It's just what people thought. I was ready to believe it myself. But then just as I was about to give up and leave the city, I ran into Michele Corinaldi. I don't think you knew him, but we both left Venice at the same time in March, long before the raid on the storehouse. I joined the Resistance in Padua, while Michele headed to the mountains north of Venice to help the partisans there. He was wounded on the final day of fighting and had only just returned to Venice. Had I left a day earlier, I would've missed him. But he told me he saw Ugo up there."

"In the Dolomites?" Of all the scenarios she'd imagined, this wasn't one of them.

155

He nodded. "I know, it's strange, but he must've gone there right after the raid. Michele told me they didn't speak much. The fighting was so fierce, and there was little time for talking. Ugo didn't say anything to Michele about the raid—only that he had to leave the city. Michele was surprised no one else knew Ugo was up there. I don't know what happened, Graziella. I'm sure he would've written you if he could have."

"Oh Tazio," she said. "It doesn't matter. Just tell me he didn't suffer long."

"No, he didn't, and we can thank God for that. Michele said it was the last day of fighting, and Ugo was in the thick of it. He said Ugo was fearless and when he was shot, he loaded his gun again and passed it to Michele before collapsing. Michele said he didn't suffer, that he went peacefully." Tazio stopped, and there was a very long pause in which they didn't look at each other. She imagined Ugo's blood staining the spring snow as he struggled to do that one last thing, load his gun. He never gave up, not until his final breath. She wanted to ask Tazio if he'd said anything before he died, but surely Michele would've passed on any words if he'd heard them. She remembered her dream, the one she'd had the night Frank arrived. Ugo had sat on the side of their bed and said, *Do not forget how much I love you,* and then he'd kissed her. Those were his last words to her.

"So he's buried there?" she asked very quietly at

last, and Tazio nodded. On a clear day, one could see the Dolomites from Venice, jagged shadows on the northern horizon. She remembered how Ugo had pointed them out to her as they walked along the Fondamente Nuove. It had been a bright winter day, cold enough they could see their breath. She'd put her hand in the pocket of Ugo's overcoat and he had held it. There'd been no dark premonitions to spoil the mountains' beauty or their own happiness.

"Yes," Tazio said. "Michele told me he himself was injured shortly after Ugo fell. When the fighting subsided, he and the rest of the wounded were brought to a hospital, but he saw the monks from the local monastery take away the dead, Ugo among them."

They sat silently, watching without really seeing the clouds drift eastward, casting their giant shadows on the ground while a hawk circled over the valley.

"I'm just sorry I didn't know this sooner," he said at last. "That you had to wait so long."

"It's not your fault," she said. She looked at him then, this man who resembled Ugo so much and who loved him too. This was hard for him as well. It would be hard for everyone. "Would it be okay if we don't tell the family until after the wedding?"

"But that's a whole week away. It doesn't seem right."

"Please, Tazio. For me then. I know it's selfish, but I could really use some time to absorb it all before I have to deal with everyone else. You know how upset they'll all be."

Tazio looked unconvinced, but he agreed anyway. "I'll do it for you, if you really want me to. It's true—I don't know how I'm going to handle Mama. She's been holding out hope all this time too. She's not going to take it well. And if we tell everyone now, they'll want to postpone the wedding. Everyone is looking forward to it, and, well, I suppose Rosanna and I have our own reasons not to put it off. But you don't mind if I tell Rosanna, do you?"

Graziella shook her head. "Of course not. I just need some time."

Tazio took his arm from where it still rested around Graziella's shoulders. "Okay then, but speaking of Mama, I should go back now. If I miss dinner, I'll never hear the end of it." They both managed a slight smile.

"I'll walk you part of the way," she said, not wanting to be alone just yet. "Giovanni should be okay for a little longer."

Tazio had one last look out over the valley where the distant Alps were starting to take on the blush of evening. "This is a perfect place for a bench. I don't remember it being here."

"Frank made it," she said, feeling suddenly strange, not sure how everything she'd just learned changed things. She didn't bother to explain who Frank was. Maria Serena would have wasted no time doing that.

"The American soldier," he said. He took her arm as they crossed the yard and turned onto the path. "He's certainly caused quite a stir. Mama, Papà, Zio Roberto, Zio Clario, the kids—it's all they want to talk about." She didn't respond, and Tazio looked at her searchingly. "Perhaps this isn't the best time to ask you, after everything I've just told you, but are you and he . . . ?"

She looked up at him. "I've been so unhappy, Tazio. You have no idea. I had this dream the night Frank arrived. I thought Ugo was really home. It was so wonderful, but then I woke up and he wasn't there. I went outside, not even thinking. I walked down to the cliff, and the valley was full of fog. And then Frank appeared. He was worried I was going to step off."

"Were you?"

"I don't know, but I do know I wasn't thinking right."

"But since then?" Here the path entered the woods, the trees forming a great canopy of green, letting the evening light filter through, while a nightingale sang somewhere above them.

"I don't know about that either." She tried to explain how helpful and kind Frank had been to her, even how she thought maybe she was falling in love with him and how tangled up it was with accepting Ugo's death and thinking she couldn't stay here. She told Tazio too about the night of the storm, how Frank had tried to kiss her and how later she'd changed her mind, but it was too late.

"Why is it too late?" Tazio asked, and she told him about Frank giving Enza the mirror.

"Oh, the mirror," Tazio said dismissively. "Mama's acting like it's an engagement ring. You women read far too much into these things."

"But did you see it? It's so beautiful and made of real silver too."

"Look, I'm pretty sure Frank isn't reading that much into it. He just saw it at the market and thought of it as a pretty trinket a girl might like. I bet anything it was priced very cheaply."

"Nothing's cheap in the markets right now," she said, pulling out a bur that had caught on her dress.

"I know, for us. But for Frank? I'm sure it didn't cost him any more than what he would've paid for a chocolate bar in America. Look, I can't see Frank being interested in Enza, pretty as she is, and I'm even more certain Enza isn't interested in him."

"How do you know that?"

"Well, she wasn't all that impressed with the mirror, from what I could tell. It's Mama who keeps looking at herself in it. And you know how Mama is—I'm sure she's been pushing Enza on Frank without any consideration for what Enza feels. Enza's not looking any better since the last time I saw her, and I doubt very much she'll ever recover. The best thing we can do is send her to the convent with Zia Maria Teresa." He shook his head. "Poor Enza. I'm sure Frank just wanted to cheer her up. She certainly needs it."

"You think so?" she asked uncertainly.

"Look, he made you that bench. He chopped all that wood. He fixed your shutters. He bought you a book, something he knew you'd like. He helps take care of Nono," he said, referring to his grandfather, Giovanni, "no easy task. Yes, Papà told me all the things Frank's done for you. He even bought the grappa for my wedding, which in my opinion is just another way to impress you. No man would do all that if he wasn't at least a little in love with you."

She thought how only an hour ago this would've made her happy, but now it only added to the turmoil. "But even if that's true, it's still too late. I need to go to the Dolomites and find out where Ugo is buried. I have to put up a cross up for him. And have a funeral. By the time I do all that, Frank'll be gone. And right now, I don't even know if I care. I just want Ugo back."

"Graziella," Tazio said, stopping and turning to face her. "I can go and put up a cross for Ugo. It doesn't have to be you. Ugo would understand." He spoke gently, taking her hands in his. "I can only imagine how hard this is for you right now.

But Frank has clearly been good for you. You look so different than when I saw you in May. You were almost as bad as Enza then. So thin and sad-looking. But today when I saw you, I thought how much you'd changed—almost like the girl I remember in Venice." He smiled. "I'll never forget the first time I met you. I'd gone to the window to see who'd rung the bell. You were below in the square, wearing a yellow dress. Ugo whispered something in your ear, and you threw back your head and laughed. It was like the sun had fallen out of the sky and into the square. Our eyes met then and you waved. My God, was I jealous! If it had been anyone other than Ugo, I would have dueled to the death for you," he said with a laugh. "And now Frank will get you. Lucky Frank. I'm looking forward to meeting him. And don't you worry about my mother. I'll take care of her."

She managed a weak smile in spite of herself as they came to a stop in front of the ruin of Lorenzo and Maria Lisabetta's house. It was always a shock the way it appeared so suddenly around the bend in the path, one moment hidden in the copse of poplars, the next moment there, four stone walls with everything but the silence burned away. If the nightingale still sang, it couldn't be heard here, and even the breeze moved noiselessly through the treetops. Inside the empty doorway, grass and weeds grew knee-high among the charred remains of the floor, the small root cellar filled in with rocks by Clario, who feared the children might fall into the open hole. There was little danger of that though, as the children were scared of the place and always ran, not walked, when they passed by. She wondered if like her they sometimes saw a flash of flame, a terrified face behind a glassless window. She rubbed her eyes on her sleeve as if to blot out the images.

"Zio Clario and I are going to tear it down," Tazio said. "Rosanna and I don't want our house on the same spot. But we'll reuse the stone. We'll build a shrine first, here by the path, before anything else."

"I'm surprised you're starting this vineyard with Clario," she said. "You were a good engineer."

"How would you know that?" he said with a slight laugh. "All I ever did during the war was blow things up." He kicked at a tall thistle, breaking it off at the base. "This mountain's in my blood. I would wake up at night and dream about the grape harvest. A grape hook in my hand instead of a gun. My hands stained with grape juice instead of blood. Don't get me wrong—I'm as proud as the next partisan at what we accomplished. But I don't want to go back to eating boiled chestnuts that make my stomach hurt, shivering under blankets infested with bedbugs, wondering every day if I'm going to die. I just want the soil, the seasons, the sun, the rain. Rosanna as my wife. Children. Does that make any sense?"

"Yes," she said. For the first time since Tazio had broken the news to her, she felt close to crying. She looked at the burned-out house and the dark woods beyond. "I'm so tired, Tazio. Of everything."

He hugged her. "Then talk to Frank, Graziella. Don't throw away this chance. I have no doubt Ugo would've wanted you to be happy."

Giovanni was awake and muttering to himself when she arrived home, but he was content to let her feed him his dinner of scrambled eggs, satisfied with her explanation that Ugo was at Clario's fixing the barn. "Maybe Pippo would fit in Clario's barn," he said thoughtfully. "We could chop him into pieces and put the wings in the horse stalls. But do we have enough hay for that?" She nodded absently, picking at her own dinner, her thoughts on Clario's barn too, wondering when Frank would return, imagining Clario refilling Frank's glass with grappa into the small hours of the morning. She thought how this time yesterday she'd been hiding in the sumacs, ready to tell Frank how she felt, only to have thought she was too late. Now Tazio was telling her she hadn't missed her chance—and that she should take it. *Oh Ugo, forgive me.*

She went outside and took down the laundry, folding and putting it away before going out again to feed her chickens and draw water from the well for the morning's breakfast. But when she was finished, Frank still wasn't back, and she had no idea what she would say to him when he arrived.

She put Giovanni to bed and went out to sit on Frank's bench just as the first fireflies appeared. From her garden wafted the heady perfume of *Nicotiana*, and over the little garden fence the moonflowers, bright white moons themselves, opened for the night. It was perfectly clear, the stars splattering the sky from one horizon to the other.

When I was growing up, Ugo had once told her, *Maria Benedetta would say prayers with me. She would point to the stars and tell me one was Mama looking out at me from Heaven.* He had found that story comforting as a child, and she found herself naming a star for her mother, her father, Westley. Over the years, the number of stars had grown: Norman Bethune, Maria Lisabetta, Lorenzo, Dario, friends lost in the war. . . . So many. And now there would be one for Ugo.

She went over what Tazio had told her and kept coming back to that dream. Was it more than a dream in the end? At the time, she'd been so convinced that Ugo was truly there, had even felt his lips on hers. She had never been sure about an afterlife, had never shared Ugo's deeply held religious beliefs, but she knew now this was more than a dream. Ugo had been there, somehow, in her room, really there. And maybe it wasn't a coincidence he'd come to her on that particular night. Did he know Frank would be there for her at the edge of the cliff? Frank had stayed up the rest of the night watching for her, worrying about her. Had Ugo in some way sent Frank to look after her since he no longer could?

Her eyes still on the stars, she heard Frank whistling as he came along the path. Still not sure what she was going to say, she got up from the bench and called out his name. He came over to her, and she could just make out his features in the darkness.

"Hi there," he said, and she could hear the smile in his voice. "I wasn't expecting to see you. I figured you'd be asleep already."

"I was waiting up for you."

They stood facing each other, only a foot or so between them, and for all her uncertainty she knew more than anything else she wanted his arms around her.

"I'm glad you did," he said. "Putting up that beam took longer than we thought, and then both Mario and Clario wanted to play a round of baseball—Clario's made a really good bat, you know—and so we sat down to dinner really late. I have to admit I'm dog-tired from trying to figure out what they were talking about. . . ." He broke off, as if detecting something different in her. "Is everything okay?"

She paused, searching for the answer, not knowing how these emotions could exist side by side in her. This longing for Frank next to this grief for Ugo. But she couldn't express that yet, so she related everything Tazio had told her, stopping now and again to steady her voice.

When she was finished, Frank let out a low whistle. "Son of a gun. That's really something, isn't it?" Then he looked at her, seeming a bit stunned by his own words. "I'm sorry. I didn't mean it to come out that way. How are you? Are you okay?"

She nodded. She didn't know what kind of response she'd expected, but not *How are you? Are you okay?* As if she'd told him she'd stubbed her toe.

It seemed pointless to go on and she excused herself, saying she should check on Giovanni. Frank seemed to recover a bit but only to ask if Giovanni had caused her any trouble, and she said no. *Would it make a difference if I told you I loved you?* Because, in spite of everything she'd learned today, she still knew that part was true. But the moment seemed lost now, all wrong. And so she left him at the bench and went to the house, listening briefly at Giovanni's door before going up to her room.

Slowly, mechanically, she took off her clothes, put on her nightgown, and brushed her hair before plaiting it. Then she climbed into bed, listening to the chorus of crickets. This was not the way she had wanted it to go with Frank. What had happened out there?

Maybe she wasn't being fair to Frank. She'd just told him of her husband's death. Even though he already suspected it, it still must've been surprising. And surely he realized this changed things between them.

Yet what if Tazio was wrong? Frank might not be in love with Enza, but perhaps he was still content to stay friends with Graziella. That attempt to kiss her may only have been the result of the night they'd spent talking, the ferocity of the storm, the excitement of the water rushing down the hill.

But then she remembered his disappointment when she'd turned away from his kiss. She threw back the covers and went to the window. The moon had risen, and so she could make out the silhouette of the bench and Frank still standing beside it. In less than a month his boat was leaving, and she would never see him again. And she would once again be here alone, having lost not just Ugo but Frank too.

She couldn't let that happen. She had to risk it. She had to find her courage and tell him she was in love with him. And if he wasn't in love with her, then at least she'd know.

She heard the scrape of a match, and his face was lit for a moment as he brought the flame to a cigarette. But he didn't light it, just held the match as he looked up toward the open window. And then she knew she no longer had to say anything at all. For in the flare of the match, she saw the same longing on his face. And before the match went out, he had thrown down the cigarette and was running toward the house.

7

"One hundred and seven people plus one dog and one doll," Maria Teresa said, peering out at Graziella from under her black wimple through thick wire-rimmed glasses. Graziella, wearing her yellow dress, watched the people spilling out of their little Church of Santa Maria and onto the steps as the bells pealed. She would have guessed almost twice that many but had no doubt Maria Teresa's count was accurate. Ever since her arrival two days earlier from the convent in Padua, Maria Teresa had been cataloguing the contents of the house, from the number of dishes in the cupboards to the plums sitting in the bowl on the table to the stone tiles covering the kitchen floor.

The photographer was a distant cousin from Este who had made false identity papers during the war for the refugees Father Paolo had harbored in the church tunnel. Already looking sweaty and harassed, he was trying to organize the wedding guests for the group photo. Tazio and Rosanna on the lowest step, immediate family to their left and right, children on the ground in front, the rest of the guests behind them. His camera was ready, carefully arranged so as to include the bell tower. "I've never seen a more unruly lot," he mumbled crossly in Graziella's and Maria Teresa's hearing.

Maria Teresa did her best to help. "Yes, yes, a difficult problem indeed. One hundred and seven divided by 10 would mean 10.7 guests per step. But if we count Maria Valentina as two, that would give us 10.8 guests per step. If we add in the doll and the dog and subtract the children . . ." The photographer looked heavenward as if wishing the bell tower would come crashing down on them all.

Tazio and Rosanna, seemingly oblivious to the photographer's wishes and the chaos around them, stood on the top step talking and smiling. Rosanna looked lovely in her mother's old wedding dress of ivory silk, and Graziella wondered fleetingly if the glow she exuded meant she was newly pregnant or if it could all be attributed to the excitement of the day. Tazio was handsome in the suit Maria Benedetta had made him, the too-short legs that had caused Maria Serena so much grief now the perfect length with the addition of extra-deep cuffs.

That morning, Maria Serena's and Maria Valentina's girls had decorated Nino's cart with flowers and cushions, and Tazio, together with his father and various other family members, had met Rosanna at her parents' house down in Il Paesino. The donkey slowly pulled the couple through the streets while the villagers cheered them on. Then, with the help of the brothers, it made its painful way up the hill past Frank's motorcycle, still leaning against the house. Graziella walked with Rosanna's family. Usually so good-natured, they'd grumbled all the while that if they'd had the ceremony in the church in Il Paesino they would've been spared the grueling climb in their Sunday clothes, but Maria Serena had insisted it be held in *their* church with Father Paolo presiding, and so it was. Graziella watched now as Rosanna's family pressed themselves along the church walls as if ready to retreat inside and declare sanctuary from the groom's relatives.

Lupo gave a loud yelp and strained at the rope that held him. Roberto had locked him in the barn for the day, but Graziella suspected Gaspare had left open an escape route, and the dog had burst into the service at the point of *If anyone has any objections.* . . . There had been laughter from everyone but a steaming Maria Serena and a mortified Maria Benedetta, who'd made Gaspare take the dog outside and tie him to a tree, where he'd been barking ever since.

Maria Serena seemed to have her own ideas as to how the photograph subjects should be organized. With one hand pressed over the mark on her cheek, she tried to shoehorn Enza into position next to Frank, who stood on the bottom step, holding Emilia, surrounded by little boys all jostling for the honor of standing beside him. This competition wasn't limited to *Our Gang*, for now there were even more boys, at least another half a dozen cousins all wanting their picture with the American soldier in his uniform. Enza, in a new dress of ugly green organza that did nothing to dampen her beauty, was thrust to the side. She sat beside Lupo and plucked listlessly at the grass, seeming not to notice his constant barking.

Loudly adamant that he was not leaving his son's side, Giovanni had also planted himself next to Frank. Nino pleaded with his father-in-law to take his proper place beside the bride and groom. "Just for the photograph, Papà," Graziella heard him say desperately. "We don't want Maria Serena to get upset with us." He wrung his hands, no doubt wishing he had his cap with him, but today his hair was carefully combed and slicked back, making him look oddly stiff and formal. Giovanni, usually so tolerant of Nino, responded by giving him a quick crack across the knees with his cane.

Maria Serena's middle girls, aged thirteen and fourteen, were also vying to stand beside Frank. As they'd been sent to board in Monselice, where Nino had found them work as maids, this was their first sighting of the American soldier, and *dreamy* was the adjective Graziella had heard whispered back and forth as she sat in front of them during the ceremony. They had giggled all the way through Father Paolo's somber sermon on

173

fidelity, obedience, and the sanctity of marriage, and when Frank had turned around at one point from where he sat next to Giovanni in the front row, they had let out sighs that lasted the duration of the Lord's Prayer.

The commotion around Frank grew. Mario, crowded out by his sisters, gave one of them a push. After nearly falling backward, she in turn called him a *canaja*—a brat—and swatted him across the head. Nobody seemed to know how Salvatore had gotten a bloody nose, but Maria Serena clearly thought it was Gaspare's fault and told Maria Benedetta surely she could keep *one* child under control, an admonishment that caused Maria Benedetta to burst into tears and Roberto to reproach his sister-in-law with a now-look-what-you've-done glare. The altercation brought Maria Valentina storming over, using her enormous belly like a ship's prow to ply the human waters. Mario protested loudly that he had nothing to do with it, but she boxed him on the ears for good measure anyway.

When Lupo broke free and charged through the guests, the photographer clearly had enough. He stamped his foot and roared at the crowd, *"Basta! Basta!"* There was a moment of silence as a sea of stunned faces turned toward the camera. Only Salvatore made any sound, whimpering as he held his father's handkerchief over his bleeding nose.

Just then, Frank looked over at Graziella, and

they smiled at each other. She barely heard the photographer's shouts for silence and was still smiling at Frank when there was a loud click and a great flash, the moment frozen for posterity. Maria Teresa was the first to recover, her gaze following Graziella's, her voice carrying over the crowd. "That American soldier of yours sure is a handsome young man."

Graziella's cheeks burned as 106 pairs of eyes turned on Frank. Roberto reached over the heads of the children and gave him a great slap on the shoulder. *"Merican! Che belo!"* he exclaimed as everyone laughed.

Frank glanced at Graziella with an I-don't-know-what's-going-on look as Graziella, trying not to laugh herself, took Maria Teresa by the arm and led the way past the priest's house to where the feast had been set up in a small field. Three wild boars caught earlier that week by Nino's middle boys roasted on spits over fires attended to by Father Paolo's housekeeper, Annunziata, and the smell of roasting meat filled the air. Two long rows of tables built of sawhorses, planks, and old doors were connected by a shorter head table. Maria Teresa, glancing at the tables, announced to Annunziata they were short seven plates and four cups. Annunziata glared at Maria Teresa with her good eye, and Graziella, attempting to diffuse the situation and seeing an opportunity to spend a few quiet moments alone, volunteered to get more dishes from the house. Frank was still in the middle of the crowd that was slowly moving toward the tables, and although no one was paying any attention to her, she tried not to look too long in his direction as she passed.

While they'd tried to guard their secret from everyone except Tazio, who had given her his blessing, it was clear Roberto and Clario were neither averse to the arrangement nor above making slightly lewd comments outside the range of their wives' hearing. Even Nino seemed fine with it, and Graziella concluded she'd been wrong to think he'd ever been jealous.

As the relatives arrived for the wedding, a steady stream of them had stopped by the farm on the pretext of procuring herbs from Graziella for their various ailments: boils, bursitis, constipation, piles, shingles. . . . And while Graziella was grateful for this brisk business (she'd even been given a little white sugar and a pair of a stockings), she knew they'd really come to meet the American soldier they'd heard so much about.

Maria Serena had seized upon the opportunity to give them a constant chaperone in the form of Maria Teresa, a move that meant Frank was spending his nights in the barn again. And Maria Serena couldn't have picked a better one, as Maria Teresa rarely left Graziella's side, providing her with a day-by-day account of her life in the convent from the time she'd arrived there as a girl of fifteen. *On June 17, 1931, the bishop arrived, and it was my pleasure to prepare the noon meal. Three hundred sixty-two slices of black bread, 181 slices of tomato, 181 slices of provolone, 97 bottles of wine. I made the sandwiches in record time, one hour and six minutes, and the bishop praised me for my service. . . .*

Just that morning Graziella had laughed when she found herself counting the birds eating the crumbs Giovanni dropped during breakfast. *It's happening to me,* she told Frank. Frank had suggested they give Maria Teresa a task like counting the jujube fruits ripening on the trees or the number of grapes on the vines, but they didn't. Really, even with this strange mannerism, Maria Teresa was the most likable sister of the entire lot, and so they humored her, snatching brief moments alone while Maria Teresa and Giovanni snored away the hot afternoons.

Along with Maria Teresa, Maria Serena had sent Emilia, as the other Marias' houses were steadily filling with relatives. *They can share a bed,* Maria Serena had said, but Emilia found her aunt a little too disconcerting and so had retreated to Graziella's room with her kitten and doll in tow. At night, Frank sat with her as she climbed into bed, telling stories about Vermont, always starting with *Once upon a time. . . .* She understood a little, and his voice was gentle and soothing. Graziella sat with them, hoping these stories were meant for her too. Stories of a life that might soon be hers. When Emilia had fallen asleep, Graziella slipped out to the barn with Frank, only crawling back into her own bed in the small hours of the morning.

The house was quiet and cool when she arrived now, and she succumbed to the desire to sit and rest for a few minutes. The plates would not be needed for another half hour, and she would not be missed in the interim. On the table was the book Frank had given her, a ribbon marking her place. Daisy jumped into her lap, and Graziella told the kitten she was missing quite the wedding.

Her own had been nothing like this. She and Ugo had married in Marseilles, a brief civil ceremony with no guests, the subsequent license changing her name from Grace Forrest to Graziella Nevicato. It also listed her religion as Catholic, something she didn't object to, seeing it as a way to expedite the ceremony. As she told Ugo, she didn't think they would agree to list her religion as agnostic anyway. And while she found Ugo's mix of revolutionary politics and deep religious belief strange, he did not seem at all concerned by her ambivalent faith. Indeed, after all they'd been through together, it seemed of little importance.

She never could have made that trip over the Pyrenees by herself. With death dogging their every step, the hunger alone would have killed her. But Ugo seemed to thrive on cold air and danger, insisting she have what little food and wine they came across. Did he eat or drink anything besides snow in those days? And although she sometimes saw pain in his eyes, he never complained. At night she would fall asleep to the murmur of his voice and wake up with his arms around her. *I have never questioned my commitment to taking orders at the monastery, but I am getting very used to sleeping with my arms around you,* he said. These words didn't take her by surprise—she'd known from that Christmas Eve in the snow they were already in love.

So when they reached Marseilles, it wasn't for her to catch a boat home. It was to be married. Only after the ceremony did they learn from a Nova Scotian boat captain that the Canadian government was threatening to arrest any Canadians who'd fought in Spain against Franco's Fascists. That news, though shocking, seemed just another sign they were meant to be married, as if everything in the universe was working toward them being together.

How would things be different now if Ugo had been home the day Frank arrived? She could imagine Ugo liking Frank. She pictured them together discussing the state of Frank's motorcycle—Ugo would've known what to do even if he couldn't actually make the repairs himself.

Maybe they would have walked over to the Zizzo farm together. Then Ugo would've asked him to stay for dinner, and they would've all eaten together—Ugo, Frank, Giovanni, Father Paolo, and herself. Ugo might even have asked him to stay for a few days, or as long as he liked, maybe even until his boat left. Ugo, who was interested in everything, would have asked about his politics, how he came to fight in the war, his farm in Vermont, what he would do on his return.

And herself? She already knew she would've liked Frank, of course, but would she have fallen in love with him if Ugo had been at her side? Would she have noticed just how blue his eyes were, how warm his smile? And if he'd touched her arm in passing, would she have wanted him to touch her again? It was strange now to think of not falling in love with Frank—that she would've simply liked him and he would've gone on his way, never to be seen again, only remembered as that nice American soldier whose motorcycle had broken down the summer after the war. It seemed so unlikely now, and as she once couldn't imagine life without Ugo, she now couldn't imagine it without Frank.

Still, she wished she could talk to Frank about Ugo. It was the one small thing she would change. It seemed necessary. About the trip from Spain, the year in Venice, his visits home throughout the war. But she found the subject made Frank uncomfortable, and she suspected he might be a little jealous, as if he worried he couldn't compete with Ugo's memory. Maybe it would have been easier if there had been someone important in Frank's past, but there hadn't been. He'd once kissed a girl named Wendy behind the church after a prayer meeting, but that was it. *I bet you broke her heart,* she said. *More like she broke mine, then went on to marry a French Canadian with a big mustache,* he replied. *But I probably deserved it. I was too busy avoiding chores and dreaming up adventures to really bother with girls. And these past couple of years?* she asked. He shook his head. *No one special, that's for sure.* She wondered if *no one special* meant the prostitutes who solicited soldiers or maybe some local southern Italian girl, but he took her into his arms then, and she decided it was unimportant. *I think I was waiting for a beautiful damsel in distress. And luckily my motorcycle broke down at her door.* He kissed her. *And you, besides Ugo?* She'd shaken her head. *Remember, I was only seventeen when I left for Spain, though I might have had a small crush on Dr. Bethune.*

Back at the wedding, she handed over the dishes to Annunziata, who told her crossly she'd taken long enough. The huge feast seemed all the more magnificent after so recent a famine, and if there were a lack of delicacies due to the shortage of

181

white flour and sugar, nobody seemed to notice. Quantity made up for everything. Roberto and Clario had recruited help to take down the boars, and great platters of meat now lined the tables that almost sagged under the weight of food: salads, new potatoes, beets, rounds of unripened cheese, peaches, her own apricot bread pudding, olive oil for the dozens of loaves of bread, and quantities of wine so vast as to suggest it wasn't only the Zizzos who'd buried their alcohol to keep it from falling into enemy hands. Clario was pouring prosecco as if it were water, and the guests drank with delighted abandon.

Chairs had been brought out from every nearby household, and some of the men had moved benches from the church. Maria Serena, busy directing people on where to sit, was having about as much success as the photographer had had earlier. All the little boys clamored to sit beside Frank, while Giovanni tried to keep them at bay with his cane. After many threats from Maria Serena, the 107 guests plus one doll were at last seated, with Tazio and Rosanna at the head table. Giovanni was to sit with them but refused to do so without Frank. So Frank sat there too, the only person other than Father Paolo who was not a parent or grandparent of the bride and groom.

Graziella was seated at the very far end with Maria Teresa on one side and the tedious Zampollo twins on the other. Maria Serena's middle girls sat across from her, and next to them was their sister Enza, as silent as ever, clearly wishing she were somewhere else. *At least we have that in common,* Graziella thought. It was hard not to conclude that Maria Serena wanted Graziella's meal to be as trying as possible. Her middle girls talked nonstop about Frank, constantly stealing glances down the table. They solicited the opinions of the Zampollo twins, who admitted that except for the crooked nose he was very handsome. The girls told them quite indignantly that it only added to his appearance and besides, with those dreamy blue eyes his nose could be the size of a zucchini and it wouldn't matter. Maria Teresa thought this hilarious and said she didn't think Frank would be nearly as handsome with a zucchini for a nose, so it was a good thing it was just crooked. One of the girls then told Graziella she was jealous Frank got to stay in her barn, "but I guess you speak English. Still, it isn't fair, since you're already married."

Through all this, Enza just sat looking at her plate, picking at her food. Graziella watched her, wondering how she'd ever been worried about her and Frank. Seeing her with everyone today, it was obvious that of all the family Enza was the least affected by Frank's presence. Frank had been surprised to learn of Graziella's jealousy, protesting that he was only trying to cheer Enza up. *And that mirror almost did the trick,* he'd said.

She was so close to smiling, but when Maria Serena made a big fuss over it, she ran away. I think it's going to take her a very long time to get over what happened—if she ever gets over it. And I don't think her mother is much help-she's so desperate to land her a husband. Across the table from her now, Enza put down her fork and turned around on the bench to stare out over the field. Graziella felt a new rush of pity for her. She was relieved she'd been wrong about her and Frank, but she still wished Enza happiness or at least an end to this silent hell in which she lived.

The meal seemed to go on forever. As much as she was happy to share this day with Rosanna and Tazio, she really just wanted to be alone with Frank. And she was tired too. Neither of them had slept much these past few days, their only time alone at night and during siesta.

Around her, the conversation flowed as freely as the wine, giving a sense that this was a day to forget about the war behind them and the long road to recovery ahead. A day in which to live as they wished they could every day—eating rich food, raising many toasts, sitting in the warm Italian sun, all bad memories banished.

Graziella knew only one thing hung over the day—Ugo. Ugo, who wasn't here with them. All those years he'd been away he was always a presence at these family gatherings, his name always invoked, his stories and music always remembered. But today his name was only whispered. Graziella recognized the signs of a conversation about him—the low, hushed tones, the shaking of heads. Everyone was especially kind to Giovanni, never correcting him when he called Frank Ugo. After dinner, as the men drifted toward the shade, they clapped Frank on the shoulder and told him he was a good man for helping out with Giovanni. *Ugo,* they said, *would've been happy.*

The grappa came out, and Frank offered Lucky Strikes to the men and broke off pieces of Hershey's bars for the children. One of Maria Serena's girls took a cigarette too and lit it, much to her mother's horror. "Stop that! You look like a floozy."

But the men laughed it off. "Don't be so old-fashioned. Lots of girls in America smoke. In Italy too." Maria Serena let it go, if reluctantly.

Graziella took advantage of the laughter to ask Maria Benedetta how she was feeling. "I'm sure I'll miscarry any day now," Maria Benedetta said, pushing away the hand Graziella tried to place over her stomach. She made Graziella swear again not to tell anyone about anything before crossing herself and going back to stacking dirty plates, and Graziella wondered if Maria Benedetta's gloomy outlook might give this baby the tenacity it needed to survive.

She accepted Roberto's offer of a glass of grappa and sat down near Frank. It wouldn't be long before Clario brought out his accordion to start the dancing, but now was the time for politics, relaxation, and gossip, lulled by the singing cicadas and the distant call of the cuckoo. There was much talk of the new atomic bomb the Americans had dropped on Hiroshima earlier that week. A Zampollo cousin, a church caretaker in Arquà Petrarca, the one who was always drunk, told how in the middle of one night during the war some Nazis had opened Petrarch's stone tomb. "I swear on my mother's grave," he said, his words slurring. "I saw them do it. They took our poet's skull away!"

"Sounds like you've been making your wine out of moldy grapes again," Roberto joked, and they all roared at the cousin's protests.

Graziella was explaining to Frank who Petrarch was but barely got past the part of Laura being his great unrequited love before Frank was dragged away by the *Our Gang* boys. They had bragged to their cousins all morning about playing baseball with "their" American soldier and were anxious to show him off. They made their diamond between the tables and the shade, setting out tin plates for bases. A ball and Clario's bat emerged from Frank's pack as Roberto explained to everyone what he knew of the rules.

Amid much arguing, everyone who wanted to play began dividing into teams, the Yankees and the Red Sox, with Frank as umpire. There was a show of tempers as Mario attempted to keep his sisters out of the game. *Girls can't play baseball* was his reasoning, although Graziella suspected it had more to do with competing for Frank's attention. Frank looked to Graziella with an exaggerated help-me-please expression on his face, and she went over to smooth things out, insisting that girls could indeed play baseball.

Finally, the game was under way. The men placed bets, the women cheered from the sidelines, and Lupo barked. All were having fun—until a cry of *Bonba! Bonba!* went up from second base. Everyone stopped what they were doing and rushed over to Salvatore, who was slowly backing away from something on the ground.

Graziella arrived at the same time as Frank, the guests parting to let them through, as if Frank would naturally know what to do. "What is it?" Frank asked. "I don't see anything."

"There. It's a bomb." Graziella pointed. It looked like a stick, about six inches long and red in color. She could hear the name *Pippo* echoing through the crowd, and Maria Serena took firm hold of Salvatore.

"That's a bomb?" Frank asked. "It doesn't look like one." He bent down to pick it up but a collective shrieking made him pull his hand away. Maria Serena's girls, no doubt seeing this as an opportunity not to be missed, each grabbed an arm and pulled him back.

"Good golly," he said to Graziella, extracting himself from the girls. "It's just a pen. Look, you can see the nib. God only knows what it's doing out here though."

"It's Pippo, the airplane. They said during the war he dropped exploding pens and toys, even poisoned candy."

"Pippo? That's a plane? I always meant to ask you what Pippo was. It dropped exploding pens—really? That seems pretty unlikely." Everyone listened to Frank, though they couldn't understand a word beyond *Pippo*.

"That's what the newspapers said. I've never actually heard of anyone finding one though." She looked down at the pen. It seemed innocent enough, but then she guessed that was probably the idea. Pick one up and *boom!* "Ugo said it was just Nazi propaganda to scare us and that nobody in Venice was afraid of Pippo." Everyone nodded as they caught Ugo's name, then the word *Nazi*.

"So Pippo was an Allied plane?"

"Maybe. Perhaps British. But we don't know for sure. There was even a story that he was Italian and came from Padua. Someone from Il Paesino said her cousin knew the pilot. Anyway, whoever Pippo was, he would fly over and bomb wherever there was light—although he bombed Maria Serena's barn in January and there was no light there. At first we used to go into the cellar when we heard him, but he would fly all night. So after a while everyone would just stay in bed and listen. After Giovanni's stroke, he became petrified of Pippo, convinced he was after him personally, and there were some nights he'd still make me take him down to the cellar. But even if Pippo didn't drop pens, maybe the Nazis dropped them and blamed it on Pippo."

Frank looked at the pen again, then back to Graziella. "I don't know, but in this case I'd bet anything one of the kids took it from the school and threw it here so he wouldn't have to do any work." He looked over at Mario and Gaspare standing next to where Salvatore still struggled in his mother's grip. Gaspare was looking a little odd, seemingly trying to twist his face into an expression of innocence. "And I think I know who it was."

"What is it?" Maria Serena said, one hand flying up to cover her birthmark as they looked her way.

As Graziella told her to wait, Frank smiled. "It's really funny, isn't it? We could be saying anything to each other right now, and everybody would just think we're talking about the bomb."

"Like what?" she said, her mind still on the potential bomb.

"Like I think you're the most beautiful woman I've ever seen, especially in that dress. And I wish we were in the barn right now taking off all our clothes—"

"Frank, stop!" she blurted out, looking around

wildly, sure everyone understood. She could feel her cheeks flushing, not for the first time that day, as everyone stared. Then she couldn't help it. She started to laugh.

"This is not a laughing matter!" Maria Serena said crossly, and Frank used the moment to evade her girls, swoop down, and pick up the pen. A moment of absolute silence and shock held the guests. Then, as Frank held it up for them to see, they burst into relieved laughter and applause.

"Sorry about that," he said, laughing as he turned back to Graziella. "I just needed a distraction. Not that I didn't mean it. The look on your face . . . Well, I'd really like to kiss you now, but I have a baseball game to umpire. See if you can get Gaspare to confess. Promise not to tell his mother."

"Well, after that, Frank Austen, I may never kiss you again." Still laughing, she took the pen over to Father Paolo.

"Yes, dear," Father Paolo said uncertainly, as if still expecting it to blow up at any moment. "It *looks* like a pen from the church." He was holding out a tentative hand to take it when Gaspare let out a yelp from second base. They looked up just in time to see Maria Serena swat him across the top of the head.

"He took it from the church to scare the girls with," she called out to Father Paolo before smacking Gaspare again.

Roberto was on the scene in a second, demanding answers, and Graziella found herself again playing interference, pleading that it was only a harmless prank and that Gaspare should be allowed to stay and play with the others. Roberto finally relented, admitting he'd played far worse jokes in his time, and the game was soon under way again with the Red Sox in the lead.

The spectators returned to the shade, while Graziella went to help the sisters clear the tables and wash the dishes. She only half listened to the Marias' conversation as she watched the game. It was a noisy and chaotic adaptation of the rules, and she smiled when Frank scooped Emilia into his arms and ran with her to first base. Tazio had taken off his jacket and shirt and was playing in his undershirt while Rosanna rooted from the sidelines in her ivory gown. Even Father Paolo joined in, standing gamely in the outfield, Maria Teresa beside him as if he needed support from the religious community. In their black frocks, with Maria Teresa in her wimple and Father Paolo in his broad-brimmed parson's hat, they looked more like pieces on Giovanni's chessboard than baseball players. Frank gave continuous commentary in English, which no one really understood but everyone enjoyed all the same.

It was when Frank pulled Enza into the game that everything went wrong. Enza had been standing on the sidelines, watching blankly, not out of any apparent interest but more as if her feet had taken her to this spot and simply stopped. She didn't resist when Frank took her hand and led her over to home plate. He showed her how to hold the bat, standing behind her and placing his hands over hers, coaxing her softly. "Keep your eye on the ball," he said, motioning to where Clario stood ready to pitch, and obediently she looked up from the bat to her uncle.

Everyone knew the story of Enza, and so they watched with interest, smoking their cigarettes and sipping their grappa. Behind Graziella, the Marias had fallen quiet. Only the children continued to shout: "Come on, Enza, hit the ball!"

There was the smallest crack as bat and ball connected. Frank took Enza's hand and walked with her to first base while Clario deliberately fumbled the ball until she was safe. Much cheering ensued, but Enza didn't acknowledge any of it, instead wandering off past Father Paolo and Maria Teresa to sit in the long grass.

"Enza is turning Frank's head," Maria Serena said to Maria Valentina as they returned to their work. "It's only a matter of time now before he asks for her hand. She can go to America with him and send money home. It would be so good for the family."

Maria Valentina, tying an apron over her belly, nodded, but Graziella knew she would be happier if Frank took one of her own older daughters off her hands, no doubt thinking either of them would make a much better wife than her strange niece.

"But," Maria Serena declared darkly, "that is if *someone* doesn't ruin it for her. God knows she's done enough already. I wouldn't be surprised if Ugo hasn't found himself a new wife by now."

The words hit Graziella like a blow to the stomach. She was used to the snide looks and comments, but this was a new level of cruelty, even for Maria Serena, and she threw her dish towel on the ground. "That's enough! I've had enough from you! It's not my fault Ugo isn't here. It's not my fault Ugo didn't marry the twins. And how do you think I feel about him not being home anyway? As much as all of you wish it wasn't true, Ugo was my husband. I loved him and yes, he loved me too. He'd never leave me for another woman, and if he was here right now . . ."

She broke off, taking in the malicious smiles of victory on the faces of Maria Serena and Maria Valentina. Maria Benedetta, who had been consolidating the leftovers, stood frozen with fear and cowardice. *The least she could do is come to my defense,* Graziella thought. *God, how I hate them all.* She wasn't thinking now. She only wanted to wipe those smirks from their faces, and so she spoke the only words she knew would hurt them for sure. She didn't care that around them people were staring. She barely saw them, her eyes blurring with angry tears. "Ugo is never coming back," she said coldly. "He's dead. Ask Tazio. He told me last week. He was killed in the Dolomites at the end of the war. We decided not to tell you so you could enjoy the wedding." The last part wasn't exactly true—she'd told Tazio she needed time—but that didn't matter to her right now. "I wanted to be considerate. Why, I don't know. It's not like you've ever been considerate to me."

Maria Serena dropped the plate she was washing and screamed, and for one moment Graziella thought she was going to lunge at her. Now all eyes were on them, the nearest people pressing closer in order to see what was going on. Those who hadn't caught the shouting would certainly have heard Maria Serena scream, and already Graziella could hear *Ugo is dead, Ugo is dead* rippling through the crowd until one by one they'd all stopped, with sharp intakes of breath crying *Oh, no!* until even the baseball game came to a standstill, the little boys standing with their arms hanging at their sides. She could only imagine their thoughts. Their uncle Ugo, the name they'd repeated in their prayers ever since they could remember. *Baby Jesus, please keep Zio Ugo safe.* Though sometimes without thinking they would reverse the order of the names. *Zio Ugo, please keep Baby Jesus safe.*

Maria Serena shouted for Tazio, and he came running from the field, pulling on his shirt, Rosanna trailing behind him. *Oh God!* Graziella backed away from the sisters. *What've I done?*

"It's not true," Maria Serena sobbed, clinging to Tazio. "Tell me that little bitch is making this up!"

"I'm so sorry, Tazio," Graziella said, Maria Serena's insult ringing in her ears. "I've ruined your wedding!"

Tazio held his mother. "No, she's not lying, Mama. Ugo really is dead, and no one is sorrier than I am. And you knew. You knew in your heart that if Ugo were alive he'd be here. We've talked about this." The crowd gathered around them, watching in stunned silence. Nino edged closer, looking torn as to whom he should comfort, his wife or Graziella, while Maria Benedetta and Maria Valentina clung to each other, tears flowing down their stricken faces.

Graziella sank to the ground, covering her ears with her hands to blot out Maria Serena's grief. "It's not true, it's not true," Maria Serena kept repeating. *"No xe vero, no xe vero."*

Through tear-filled eyes, Graziella could see only the skirt of her own dress, like looking into the sun. She picked up a handful of the soft fabric and buried her face in it. All those tears she hadn't shed when Tazio had first told her the news came pouring out now, soaking the yellow dress. She heard Rosanna's gentle voice at her side, felt her hand on her shoulder, and now Graziella was apologizing to her, over and over again. "I'm so sorry I spoiled your wedding."

And then it wasn't Rosanna's hand on her. It was Frank's. He bent down beside her and took her in his arms to help her up. Not caring who was watching, she buried her face in the front of his uniform, and he wrapped his arms around her. "What's going on?" he said, clearly unable to understand the conversation beyond Ugo's name.

Now she was apologizing to him too, bursts of explanation between her sobs. "I'm so sorry, Frank. . . . I couldn't stand it. . . . Maria Serena kept going on how it was my fault that Ugo wasn't here. . . . And then she told me I'd better not take you from Enza, that I'd done enough to this family and that Ugo had run off with another woman to get away from me. . . . And then she called me a bitch."

Frank held her tightly and stroked her hair, making soothing sounds. "It's okay, it's okay. You know what they're like." He handed her his handkerchief, and she wiped her face, catching the stares of the guests, who averted their eyes quickly. They wouldn't understand what she and Frank had said to each other, but she was sure they'd understand what they were seeing. They'd just learned Ugo was dead, and now here was his wife in the American soldier's arms.

"Let me take you home, Grace," Frank said, and he started to pull her away. She looked over to Tazio and Rosanna and apologized again, bringing on more tears.

196

"It's okay," Tazio said, coming over and kissing her wet cheek. There was no sign of the three Marias, and she assumed they'd been led off by their respective husbands. Only Maria Teresa was nearby, clutching Father Paolo's arm, her eyes under her wimple wide like a lost child's. Tazio looked at Frank and managed a weak smile. "Let Frank take you home and look after you. Zia Maria Teresa and Emilia can stay with us tonight. We'll take Nono back with us too. At least he slept through all this. I don't think I could've handled both him and Mama." He sighed. "I'm sorry she called you that name."

Graziella shook her head, but she couldn't speak again. Every attempt made her cry.

Tazio grasped Frank's shoulder, and his voice was heavy with emotion as he picked out the words in English. "Very happy . . . Graziella and you." He released Frank's shoulder. "Thank you."

Frank led Graziella away, his arm around her, and she leaned on him heavily. Behind them came the murmur of subdued voices. There wouldn't be any dancing tonight. They would finish clearing away the tables, mothers would take the younger children home to bed, but the rest would stay, finishing the grappa, talking into the night about Ugo and the war that had killed him. By nightfall, Ugo's place among the saints would be established.

"I want to go, Frank," Graziella said as they

approached the house. "I can't stay here. Please take me home with you." His boat was leaving in just a few weeks, but he had yet to ask her if she would leave with him.

"Of course, Grace," he said, holding her more tightly.

Although the house was empty, they went instinctively to the barn, as if knowing this wasn't a time to be in the bed she'd once shared with Ugo. They undressed, and her dress fell to the wooden floorboards like crumpled sunshine. But they didn't make love. They only lay on the mattress in the dusky coolness, looking up into the shadows where a dove cooed softly. Narrow beams of dusty sunshine seeping through the cracks of the walls made warm trails of light across their bare skin.

Frank held a hand above them, intercepting one of the beams, then closing his hand as if he could catch it. "If only we could keep this, put it in a bottle and pull it out on a cold winter's night. A little bit of Italian sun . . ." Turning his head to one side, he looked at her. She took his hand still warm from the sunbeam and pressed it to her face. He caressed it, his fingers tracing the contours of her cheek.

"I know why Ugo's sisters don't like you," he said, suddenly playful, punctuating the change in mood with a quick kiss. "And it isn't because you were married to Ugo."

She didn't want to talk about her sisters-in-law, just wanted to put the day behind her, but she could see he was trying to make her feel better and so she played along. "Why then?" she asked, pulling a piece of straw from his hair.

"It's because they're all a little in love with you." She looked at him blankly and he laughed. "Not the sisters—their husbands. Nino, Roberto, Clario. I see the way they look at you. You've stolen their hearts, and their wives are jealous."

She laughed. "Stop teasing me. Although I have to say Nino has been acting strangely lately. I actually wondered if he was a little jealous of you."

"You see. I don't even think they realize it. But I do know they think I'm one lucky devil." He propped himself up on one elbow and looked down at her. "You have to feel sorry for them. They probably thought they had a good deal. Marry the sisters and double their property. Yes, their wives aren't the most charming and beautiful—it would seem Ugo took the family's share in those departments—but they're strong and hardworking and, except for Maria Benedetta, they've produced lots of children. So I don't think the men are missing out in the bedroom."

She put her hands over her ears. "Stop. I don't even want to think about that."

He pulled away one hand to kiss her ear. "And then you came along. The beautiful, foreign, exotic Grace."

"I think you've got me mixed up with someone else," she said, laughing again.

He shook his head. "No one else in the world has eyes that color—like the light in the evening over the Alps. . . . No, I can't describe them. It just sounds stupid. All I can say is that it's a good thing Petrarch had Laura as his muse, because if it'd been you, he would've been so dumbstruck by your beauty he never would've written a single poem. I can picture it now," he said with a sweeping gesture. "You arrived here for the first time in that yellow dress—"

"No, you're wrong. Ugo bought that dress for me after we went to Venice. When I first arrived here, I was wearing an old blue polka-dotted dress Maria Teresa had given me. On our way from Spain, we stopped in Padua to see her. Ugo hadn't prepared me. I don't think he really notices . . . noticed," she corrected herself, "his sister's peculiarities. But Maria Teresa recruited help from the other nuns and found me some clothes. Mine were in rags, we'd been traveling for so long. Maria Teresa was very proud of the dress. She handed it to me saying, 'Here you are. A dress with twelve red buttons. It's good there aren't thirteen as that would make it a blasphemous dress.' I was just beginning to learn the language, and I had to ask Ugo if I'd heard her correctly."

"Yellow dress, blue dress." Frank waved it off with a grin. "One look in those eyes and you ruined those men's lives. How could they ever be content again, now that they knew what it was like to fall in love with a beautiful woman they could admire only from afar?"

"You're being ridiculous," she protested, trying to push him away, but he grasped her hands in his, pinning them down.

"And there's more," he said. "There's something I haven't told you."

"What?" she said, smiling. "That all of my sisters-in-law are in love with you? That's no secret."

"Not that." He looked very serious all of a sudden.

"What then?"

"You won't be shocked? You promise not to be mad at me?"

She shook her head vigorously, still thinking this was part of the game. "I could never be mad at you."

He took a deep breath. "I wasn't with the Eighty-eighth Division. I'm really a spy."

The laughter bubbled up again, but there was something in his eyes that made her stop. She struggled to sit up, and he released her hands, looking at her expectantly.

"You're not serious, are you? A spy? With who?"

"With the Americans of course."

"You must still be joking."

"I really am serious. I'm with the OSS. The Office of Strategic Services."

It sounded ridiculous, though why, she really didn't know. She knew there were spies on all sides. Germans, Italians, Americans, British: Italy had been crawling with them. Ugo had told her he had worked with Allied spies in Venice. Critical liaisons between the Resistance and the Allied command, they provided arms and supplies, sent codes through Radio London, and tried to predict German troop movements. The Americans had even recruited Italian-Americans, sending them back to their ancestral towns, where they fought alongside the Resistance or infiltrated the highest levels of Fascist command. At the same time, the Resistance worried about Fascists penetrating their own networks. Sometimes it seemed there were more spies than partisans or soldiers. So why couldn't Frank be one too? "But you don't speak Italian," she said. Unless, all this time . . . He was a spy after all, gifted at—she rejected the word *lying*—at subterfuge.

"Better than Italian. I speak German. I learned it from my grandparents. I told you about my grandfather who was senile. He and my grandmother came from Germany. They're the ones who started our family's farm. Everybody was suspicious of our family because we're Krauts, even though my dad's actually of English descent. Anyway, I wanted to prove we were as patriotic as everyone else. Since our farm got me out of the draft—providing food for the war effort and all that—I decided to enlist, assuming I'd go straight to infantry. But the recruitment office told the OSS I spoke fluent German. So they made me a spy." He brushed the hair away from her eyes. "I'm so sorry. I know I've been lying to you all this time, but that's what I had to do. You can't go up to someone you've just met and say 'Hi, I'm a spy.' You have to have a story. And mine was the Eighty-eighth Division."

"So the mountain river near Cassino?" she asked, trying to make sense of it all. "That never happened?" She remembered the night of the storm when he'd talked about being taken prisoner. He'd told it in such detail before brushing it off. She remembered his words: *Forget it. Forget what I just said.* That story had been bothering her ever since.

"Got it out of one of my boys' adventure magazines," he said sheepishly.

"But the war's over," she said. "What are you doing here in Italy?"

"This is my last assignment. Then it's home for me."

"You're on assignment?"

"Yes, I am," he said. "Or was. I was sent from Switzerland to Lake Garda to collect some documents left behind by the Nazis. We thought it would take a month or so, but I wrapped it all up pretty quickly. I'm not due back in Switzerland until the end of the month—and now I've met you."

"So there's no boat?"

He shook his head.

"I always thought there was something strange about your boat story," she said slowly. "But I got it wrong. I thought maybe you were ashamed to go home. I wish you'd told me the truth though. You could've trusted me."

"Not even my parents know," he said. "I'm sworn to secrecy. I'm not supposed to tell anyone. Ever. I'm sorry. I can't give you any more details."

"Then I can live with that," she said, pausing as a dove, startled from the rafters, beat its wings before settling again. "But there's nothing else I should know, is there?"

"Only that I love you," he said. And that's when he asked her to marry him.

8

She awoke as the first rays of light filtered through the leaves of the chestnut tree. Frank's arm was still over her, and she lifted it carefully, hoping to slip out of his embrace without waking him. It didn't work, and he opened his eyes.

"Don't go yet," he said, pulling her back into his arms.

"I have to. It's Sunday. I have to get ready for Mass." She sat beside him on the mattress and, feeling a little self-conscious, pulled the blanket up around her.

"But it's still so early." He propped himself up on one elbow. "And you're so beautiful, soon-to-be Mrs. Austen."

It was so tempting to stay. She leaned over and kissed him. "I don't want to go. But I'm afraid someone will come. And I don't want them catching me here with nothing to wear but yesterday's dress. They'll know. And after yesterday . . . well, I just want as few complications as possible. So go back to sleep."

He agreed, but it was at least another hour before she was in her room, trading the yellow dress for the brown-flowered one, the one that had become her everyday dress since Frank's arrival.

She only just had time to pour a bowl of milk for Emilia's kitten when she heard voices on the path.

She went out the back door and it wasn't without some trepidation that she greeted Father Paolo, Nino, and Maria Serena, who were coming from the direction of the church. It was Father Paolo who did the talking while Nino twisted his cap in his hands and Maria Serena stared at the ground. "We thought it best to see you before Mass, dear, so we can make an announcement in church," Father Paolo said gently. "Ugo must have a funeral, of course, and we think it should be Tuesday, before Maria Teresa returns to the convent. Everyone who came for the wedding would like to attend as well."

Graziella agreed, saying she could see no reason to delay it. She looked at Maria Serena, a little surprised and almost pleased that her sister-in-law had asked her opinion. "I'm sorry you had to find out like that. I was upset, but it still wasn't right of me."

Father Paolo seemed relieved and Nino nodded, still twisting his cap in his hands. They both looked terrible, and she had to remember they'd only just learned the truth. Even if they'd sus- pected it, it was still a devastating blow. But while Nino and Father Paolo looked bad, it was Maria Serena's appearance that shocked her the most. It was obvious she hadn't slept at all, purple circles ringing her reddened eyes, the birthmark the only color on her otherwise pale cheek. Her clothes—she was still wearing her mother-of-the-groom dress—were wrinkled, and her hair was still up in the same bun as the day before, leaking strands of graying hair down her back.

"I've come to apologize," Maria Serena said, addressing her own shoes. "I'm sorry. I shouldn't have called you that bad word." Graziella apologized again for the way she'd behaved, but Maria Serena didn't seem to hear. It was as if she'd come to say her piece, and it took all her concentration to do so. "Nino is very angry with me," she said, still looking at her feet, not seeming to care her husband was right beside her. "You know Nino. He doesn't say much. But he does say you're a good woman and that you've been very good to Papà." Maria Serena cleared her throat. "And he said you were a good wife to Ugo. And that Ugo would be angry with me." She started to cry. Not the wailing of the day before, just quiet tears that dripped down her face onto her dress. "I want Ugo back," she said with a whisper. "It was enough with Dario dying in Russia, then Maria Lisabetta and all the children in the fire, and Lorenzo. . . . And I don't know what we're going to do about Papà and Enza. . . . You'd think with the war over . . . But we'll never be the same."

And then Maria Serena did the strangest thing. She stepped closer and placed her forehead on Graziella's shoulder, her arms hanging at her sides as the tears flowed more freely. Graziella put her arms around her and patted her back, feeling awkward but also something close to sympathy. For all Maria Serena's faults, she had practically raised her little brother and loved him with the ferocity of a mother bear. Had she been beside Ugo on that mountain, she would have thrown herself in front of him without hesitation, taking the bullet herself rather than let anything happen to him. And Graziella thought she had probably stayed awake all night regretting she hadn't been there to do just that.

After they left, Graziella went to her room to get her sewing basket and the yellow dress, now wrinkled and dusty from lying on the barn floor. She rummaged through the basket until she found what she was looking for, a small cake of black dye. She stirred the dress into the tub with a wooden spoon, crying as sunshine turned to night.

This was not the way these things were supposed to go. It should have been a series of steps, a process, emotions that followed some predictable order. Bury one's husband, mourn for a year or more, then maybe meet someone new and remarry. But it hadn't gone that way. Had Frank arrived on her doorstep in six months, the timing might have been more appropriate, but he was here right now and she'd agreed to marry him the night before making her husband's funeral arrangements.

Later, when she took the dress off the clothes-line, she saw the dye had been too weak, turning it to the color of mud, its once soft fibers now hardened. She would wear it to the funeral, then never again.

The day of Ugo's funeral dawned with the threat of rain. *Alba rossa, o vento o giozza. Red dawn, either wind or rain,* she told Frank as he cleaned up their breakfast. He was still repeating the words when she returned to the kitchen wearing her now mud-colored dress. "When we get to America," he said, kissing her, "I'll buy you a new dress. Violet, like your eyes. We'll go to the top of the Empire State Building and then we'll hear Benny Goodman play and dance all night."

She left the house on her own, Nino having picked up Giovanni with his cart, and climbed the hill toward the Church of Santa Maria. Frank was to stay behind—less confusing for Giovanni, or at least that was the hope. Father Paolo had suggested it, and Frank had agreed. *As long as I'm there, Giovanni will insist on sitting next to me. And I don't know how he'll accept Ugo is in heaven if he thinks he's still beside him.* Nino had thanked him and said he regretted Frank couldn't be there since he was like family now.

The church was packed for the second time in less than a week. Only this time there was silence.

The younger children did not fidget or fight. Maria Serena's middle girls, sitting next to the Zampollo twins, did not giggle. In one half of the front row, the three Marias sat next to their husbands, while in the other half Graziella was squeezed between Maria Teresa and Giovanni. It was hard to say how much he understood as he stared blankly ahead.

According to Maria Teresa, 191 people were in attendance, but it seemed like the entire population of the Euganean Hills was there. Dozens of partisans lined the back pews and spilled into the aisles, and even the Zizzos came, looking slightly uncomfortable. Graziella glanced at the blond-haired family, thinking how they'd never know the son they'd lost had left behind a daughter named Emilia.

Just then, clutching her doll, Emilia climbed into her lap and asked for Frank. She'd been staying with Maria Serena along with Maria Teresa since the wedding. "After the Mass," she whispered to the little girl, giving her a hug. It was going to be very difficult to leave Emilia behind. Graziella wondered if she would know when she herself became pregnant, given she could sense it so soon in other women. Could she be pregnant even now? It was possible as she'd done nothing to prevent it, something that may or may not have been an oversight on her part.

Father Paolo bowed his head, pleading with

God, asking Him to take Ugo home. "Ugo made the world a better place and now heaven can only be a better place with him there," he said. He delivered the service with quiet, sincere dignity, stopping many times to regain his composure as he gripped the sides of the lectern.

"If only Ugo were here to sing," Maria Teresa whispered, her eyes damp behind her wire-rimmed glasses, and Graziella could only nod. She would not be the only one to miss Ugo. She wondered when Ugo had last seen Maria Teresa. Had it been at Maria Lisabetta's funeral last fall? Or perhaps he had stopped by the convent on a trip through Padua sometime during the winter?

The last time she herself had seen Ugo was in January, not long after the start of the new year. Giovanni had been napping, and she'd been standing at the kitchen window, looking out on the gray afternoon. It should have been dreary, but it was instead beautiful. The icy rain coated the road, the grass, the branches of the chestnut tree, everything cocooned in sparkling crystal.

The ice also brought a sense of liberation. Not even the Germans could get a motorcycle or truck up that road, now transformed from the steepest hill in the Euganean Hills to the steepest skating rink. She hoped it would keep up all afternoon, all evening, all night—surely then not even Pippo could fly and maybe she could have one night of peace, no risk this would be one of the times

211

Giovanni insisted on going down into the cellar—just blissful, uninterrupted sleep.

The vision of Pippo plummeting to earth under the weight of the ice on his wings faded as she caught sight of something moving among the naked grapevines. She brought her face close to the glass as she strained to get a better look, impatiently wiping away the condensation that formed under her breath. *No Germans could get up that hill today,* she repeated to herself firmly. The figure was lost among the vines, but not for long as it reappeared moments later at the edge of the terrace.

It was Ugo, wearing the red cap of his brigade. She flew to the door, stepping out, trying to run, but instead falling, falling, skidding along the icy ground, laughing when he bent down and scooped her up in his arms. His clothes were soaked through, and glistening bits of ice hung from the thick beard that had grown in since his last trip home. She clung to him, her feet not touching the ground, her face buried in his wet jacket. He smelled of the woods and rain and cold.

Let me see you, he said, setting her back down and holding her at arm's length. *It has been too long.* She looked up into those dark eyes, and he smiled, that lovely smile that was only for her, gentle lines gathering at the corners of his eyes. *God, I think every day I remember how beautiful you are, and then I actually see you and . . .* He kissed her, and she thought it was all worth it. Everything. If she had to endure this terrible war forever, it would be worth it so long as Ugo came home and kissed her. *Let us go inside,* he said. *You are shivering.*

So as to not wake Giovanni, they crept through the kitchen and up the stairs to the bedroom, their clothes falling to the floor in a sodden mass.

Later, as darkness fell with the rain, he held her in his arms and sang for her. So softly, softer than the drizzle against the shutters. *I know I have said this before, but it will not be much longer now, I am sure of it. Has it been terrible for you these past few months?* It had been, but she shook her head. *Have my sisters been too horrible? Papà?*

She shook her head again. *I'm okay, Ugo.* And she was now but knew she wouldn't be as soon as he left. *How has it been for you?* It was her turn to ask though she knew he wouldn't say much. He always wanted to protect her—the less she knew, the less she could be harmed if the unthinkable happened. Still, she was hungry for anything he could tell her.

It has been . . . difficult. This is our worst winter. We had to suspend operations, German reprisals were too great. And the Allies, they want us to wait for them, but they are trapped below the Gothic Line. But now that the Fascists and Nazis go unopposed, it is worse. We have to wait though because we have so few guns and even less ammu-

nition—the weapons are going where the need is greater. Had she ever seen him so close to looking defeated? He was always so confident, and it was a shock to see him any other way. But he was tired, and he admitted this for the first time. She asked him when he thought things would change. *Soon, I pray. If I could do anything at all to make this war end this very day, I would. All I want is for us to be together again.*

That night, Pippo stayed away as she'd hoped, but the family came—*they will never forgive me if I leave without telling them I am here.* They came slipping and sliding their way into the kitchen, laughing and crying as they embraced Ugo. The children looked up to him, the awe apparent in their faces. He was taller than their fathers, mythical in his strength. Their uncle Ugo, who any moment now could and would singlehandedly win the war.

Out of Ugo's bag came coffee, chocolate, dried figs, sugared almonds. *Liberated,* Ugo said with a smile, *from a German officers' club by an Allied friend.* A fire roared in the hearth while the brothers lit the lamps with their bad, smoky oil, and Graziella lifted a floorboard to take out Ugo's violin. He kissed it before drawing his bow over the strings, improvising for them one of his beautiful melodies. Everyone was quiet as they listened, the children holding the pieces of chocolate in their mouths, letting them melt ever so slowly.

Tears ran down Giovanni's cheeks, and they ran down Graziella's too. To have Ugo here, to hear him play again—this was all she needed. In his music she heard the rain, the cold, the warmth of the fire. She heard her tears and his own desperate longing for home.

Ugo put the children to sleep, a long row of them stretched along the length of their bed, and played for them a lullaby, music to follow them into their dreams. When he came back down, they didn't talk of failures or deaths. The doubt she had seen shadow his face earlier was no longer evident. He was defiant again, sure of victory.

The Allies want us to wait for them. But we cannot wait and we do not want to wait—this is our fight. This is our time to show the world a new Italy. A strong one, an egalitarian one. And there is hope, for all of Venice is turning against the Germans. They are starting to see the need for resistance— now we only have to organize their anger.

The adults talked late into the night, and for once they didn't feel hungry or afraid. There was no shortage of laughter as they planned what they would do when the war ended. Every day would be a feast with huge plates of meat, milk for the children, white bread, pasta drowning in the best oil. They would drink real coffee thick with sugar, followed by jujube fruit in grappa, a dessert so sweet it was synonymous in the Venetian language with utter happiness: *'Ndare in brodo de giugiole.* And then, when they'd eaten so much they were ready to burst, they would throw the shutters wide open and turn the mountain into a beacon of light that could be seen from the moon.

At dawn, the family left, sleepy babies in their arms, older children slipping behind. A quiet straggling line of tired, strangely happy people. The sun rose, and the ice glittered on the trees.

Ugo had stayed all that day, talking with her, helping with Giovanni, doing the few odd chores their icy world would allow, going to the church to pray and light candles for Maria Lisabetta and her family. He had stayed that night too, playing his violin, making love to her, only slipping out of their bed in the early hours of morning while she still slept.

Would she have done anything differently if she had known that would be the last time she ever saw him? Sitting now on the bench in the church, she looked up at the statue of the Virgin with her blue robes and kind smile. No, she wouldn't have. She had given everything she could, and she'd taken everything he had to give. It had been war, and they were only too aware every meeting could be their last. And so every reunion contained not only the joy of seeing each other again but also the sorrow that this could be their last farewell. Remembering that made it almost bearable. For perhaps she had known all along he was only on loan to her from the gods.

• • •

Wearing his uniform, Frank was standing at the bottom of the steps when she came out of the church. Conscious they were being watched, she walked toward him. They hadn't told anyone of their engagement yet, but she was sure it wasn't just her brothers-in-law who suspected something was going on between them. If it flew in the face of decorum, they seemed willing to overlook it, if for no other reason than Frank was American, and Americans were more modern about these things. And she was Canadian. And while they really didn't know what being Canadian meant, they were sure it explained something.

"How are you doing?" Frank asked. He took her arm and led her a few steps away from the others. The air was heavy and still as if holding its breath, while gray clouds had settled over the hills.

"I'm okay. A lot better now that you're here." She smiled. "Any luck with the trains to Switzerland?"

"Yes," he said, lighting a cigarette. "One leaves a week from tomorrow."

"That gives me time to say good-bye to everyone. I also need to decide what to do with Ugo's violin. I don't know if I should take it—it's so valuable. But I'd like to keep it because it was his. What do you think?"

Before he could answer, a shout came from the church steps. "Ugo? Is that you?" It was

Giovanni, of course. The close family members let out a collective sigh, while some of the more distant relatives and friends looked startled, as if really expecting to see Ugo in the crowd.

"Doesn't sound like Father Paolo's plan worked," Frank said, shaking his head as Nino and the priest led the old man down the steps and in their direction. "Maybe I shouldn't have come here after all."

"I really don't think it would've made any difference," she said. "Sooner or later he would've seen you."

"Where've you been, Ugo?" Giovanni demanded of Frank.

Father Paolo, obviously hoping to salvage his plan, tried to correct him. "You remember Frank, the American soldier, don't you, Giovanni?"

"American soldier? Holy Mother of God. You always were a bit of a fool, Paolo, but now you're just crazy." Leaning heavily on his cane, he beckoned to Frank with his free arm. "Get over here and put an end to all this nonsense. Those fool sisters of yours think you're dead. Dragged me here for your funeral." He turned to the Marias now and shook his cane at them. "You see? He's not dead." He stared at them fiercely through his dimmed eyes as if daring them to contradict him. "Idiots," he muttered.

The Marias looked to each other and their husbands, seeing in each other's faces tacit agreement. With that note of defeat that had crept into her voice ever since she'd shown up at Graziella's door to apologize, Maria Serena said, "You're right, Papà. We're all idiots."

Seemingly satisfied by this admission, Giovanni allowed Nino to walk him to the field next to the church, where Annunziata had set up the food on the same makeshift tables that had held the wedding feast only a few days before. Though the crowd was even larger, it was a much smaller spread this time, and Graziella knew that while the occasion called for restraint, their extravagance at the wedding had also seriously depleted their stores.

After the meal, the men drifted once more toward the trees, and again Frank passed out his Lucky Strikes. The women for once did not feel it necessary to immediately clear away the remains of the tables and so followed the men. There was grappa again, but the cups poured this time were much smaller. Nobody played baseball. No pranks either—the children seemed to realize the solemnity this occasion called for.

Graziella sat on the grass next to Enza, a little apart from the others. She couldn't get near Frank, the space around him occupied by the *Our Gang* boys and Maria Serena's middle girls while he held Emilia in his arms, her head resting against his chest. Rosanna sat next to Tazio, her arm linked through his. Graziella had no doubt now

Rosanna was pregnant, and she wondered if they themselves yet knew or if this was why Tazio had said they had their own reasons for wanting the wedding to go forward.

Clario brought out his accordion and sang the opening bars of *"Fischia Il Vento."* A song to inspire the Resistance, taught to them by Ugo. *The wind whistles, the storm rages. Our shoes are broken, yet we must go on.* . . . Everyone joined in the singing, only too aware of the final lines that promised the proud partisan's return home. From pockets, some men pulled out caps and bandanas, the colors of their partisan brigades shown with pride. Others hadn't been so supportive of the Resistance, and they sang louder than the others as if to show that while their courage may have failed them, their hearts at least had been in the right place. She looked around for the Zizzo family, wondering what they thought about this celebration of the Resistance, but she didn't see them and could only assume they'd left right after Mass.

It was Tazio who broke through the silence that followed the song, and Graziella was struck again by how much he looked like Ugo. If she stayed here, would she watch Tazio age, wondering if this was how Ugo would've looked at forty, fifty, sixty? They all listened to Tazio tell the story of that last hard winter in Venice, the Resistance driven underground as they tried to find a way to rid themselves of the enemy. Ugo's position had been that only a united Venice would overcome the Nazis. And so, in the early weeks of March, Ugo and several others evaded the Fascist guards and took the stage of the Goldoni Theater, where they issued a bold proclamation, asking the audience to join with the Resistance, the poor, the students, and the workers. Until then, the middle class had been largely ambivalent, giving their occupiers a sense of safety and complacency. The theater audience pledged their allegiance that night. The next day, the proclamation was the talk of the city, and while the Germans and Fascists attempted to terrorize the citizens back into submission, it was the turning point in Venice.

As Tazio told the story, Ugo was the hero, though Graziella knew Ugo would have told it a very different way, with himself as just one small part of a much greater movement. *There were never more heroes in the history of the world than one can find in Italy during these dark times,* he'd told her. He saw in the men he fought with not just the means to rid his country of its occupiers but the start of something new—an Italy built on principles of freedom and equality. *It must be new or the foundations remain for us to repeat it again,* he'd said. Still, as Tazio brought his story to a rousing end, she felt a surge of pride for Ugo. With tears in her eyes, she joined the others as they cheered and applauded.

Once again Clario picked up his accordion. This time, though, his song was not mournful but a spirited rendition of *"Bella Ciao*—Good-bye Sweetheart," the story of a partisan whose mountainside grave was marked by a beautiful flower, as she hoped Ugo's was.

This is the flower of the partisan.
O bella, ciao! Bella, ciao! Bella, ciao,
  ciao, ciao!
Who died for liberty.
O bella, ciao! Bella, ciao! Bella, ciao,
  ciao, ciao!

They all sang the chorus, the children shouting out the lines, the Marias weeping as they clapped their hands in time. Maria Valentina, her expanding belly seeming to diminish the frail Maria Benedetta even further, sat with her arm around her sister's shoulder, while Maria Serena and Maria Teresa stood close together. Only Enza, sitting beside Graziella, remained her usual detached self, while Giovanni had long ago fallen asleep and was snoring loudly in his chair despite the noise surrounding him. The song ended with more cheers, and Clario was on to the next, the mood having shifted in the course of the verses from mourning to one of almost celebration.

As Clario sang, Graziella watched the faces around her, thinking how everyone looked almost strangely happy. Even Maria Serena smiled as she wiped away her tears. This might have been the happiest she'd seen them since the ice storm when they'd danced in the kitchen to Ugo's violin playing. They had sung *"Bella Ciao"* that night too. There wasn't a person here who hadn't loved and admired him. Ugo would live on in their memories, becoming more mythical with every passing year. He was part of them, part of who they were. And he was part of who she was. She would carry his memory with her as she did those of her mother, father, Westley, everyone she'd loved and lost.

Frank had listened to Tazio's story with his head bowed, not understanding anything of course but likely able to surmise the sentiment, and his cheers at the end had been subdued, as if he didn't know what kind of balance to strike. How strange this must have been for him. How many men attended the funeral of their fiancée's husband? But through the singing he seemed more relaxed. He had placed Emilia on the ground and was showing her how to play patty-cake.

Graziella was smiling when she felt the tiniest tug on her sleeve. She looked down at the hand on her arm and then in surprise at its owner's face. Enza. Enza, trying to get her attention. Under her thick lashes her big dark eyes were almost frightening in their intensity. "He was my lover, you know."

Graziella barely heard the words and was tempted to ask her to repeat them. It had been so long since she'd heard Enza speak she'd forgotten what her voice sounded like. She was sure it had been different before, higher and lighter, while now it was lower, faded as if from disuse.

And then there were the words themselves. As shocking as hearing her speak. But then Enza's first words after so long could hardly be mundane. They would have to be important enough to break through her fog. *He was my lover, you know.*

Who? She glanced at Frank playing with Emilia. He'd told her there was nothing between him and Enza, that he was only trying to be nice to her, and she'd believed him.

Everyone continued to sing and clap as Clario led them in a long and bawdy ballad making fun of the King of Italy. Nobody was looking their way.

"Frank?" she asked finally, her voice as muted as Enza's.

"Not Frank. No. The German soldier. Hans. His name was Hans. There was no funeral for him. He's buried up near Brigand's Den. Papà took him there. I didn't know before where they buried him, but I heard Papà tell Mama last night. They were talking about Zio Ugo's funeral, and he said there should have been one for the German boy instead of taking him to Brigand's Den. But Mama got angry with him." Enza's voice gathered strength as she talked, still low but steadier and faster now, as if she was desperate to get this story out.

Graziella was still confused. A German soldier named Hans? "The deserter Father Paolo helped at the beginning of the war? He died?" Father Paolo had hidden the young man in the tunnel until the false papers had arrived from the photographer in Este. She thought he had joined up with the Resistance.

"No. Not him. Hans hadn't deserted yet. He was afraid. But he was planning on it. He caught me delivering food to the partisans hiding up in Brigand's Den. He was guarding the path because the Germans knew someone would come with supplies. He should have shot me right then, but I started to cry and then he started to cry. He was young, like me. He spoke a little Italian. He let me warn the partisans. We met after that whenever we could, in secret. Until Papà found us together in the barn." Shivering, Enza ran her hands along her arms as if hugging herself to keep warm, and Graziella noticed how thin she was, almost skeletal. Was she eating anything at all? Enza had been such a beautiful, spirited girl, but now she was sick with grief.

That's when it sunk in—the *grief*—and she stared at Enza with horror. Enza was mourning this young man. "Then it wasn't rape," she whispered.

The girl shook her head.

"You were in love with him?"

Enza nodded.

There was a fresh round of cheers as Clario ended his ballad and started another. Enza sat silently as Graziella looked to Nino, cheering along with everyone else. What had really happened there? She imagined Nino finding Enza and Hans together, his anger, not easily stoked, rising to the boiling point. Did he think at first it was a boy from the village? God knows enough of them had been in love with the beautiful Enza, and he had chased off more than one who'd thrown stones at her window in the night. But if it had been a boy from the village, a sound beating would have been warranted, maybe a hasty wedding, but not this.

She imagined him pulling the boy off his daughter, Enza screaming as Hans tried to explain himself, his native German breaking through the imperfect Italian. And Nino, comprehending but not comprehending. Rapes had happened before. Far too many. To wives and sisters and daughters. She remembered the night the Fascist had turned up at the farm with the two Nazis. To make them leave, Giovanni had told them she had a disease. Nino wouldn't have thought. He would have assumed. Any German on top of his daughter. The quiet, gentle Nino driven to rage by what he thought he saw.

"I was screaming for Papà to stop, but he

wouldn't," Enza said evenly, as if she'd rehearsed what she wanted to say. Graziella pictured her weeping over the body, the pistol Ugo had given Nino for protection still in his hand. Ugo would have been heartbroken to learn the gun had been used against an innocent boy. "He and Mama forbade me ever to tell anyone. He was German, and the whole family could be killed now. He'd raped me and deserved what he got. When I tried to tell them differently, they wouldn't listen. Papà doesn't know about Hans catching me at Brigand's Den. He doesn't know that Hans could've killed me or that the partisans got away because of Hans. He doesn't know I became pregnant either and what Mama made me do. I wanted to tell Papà everything, but in the end I couldn't. I knew he wouldn't be able to live with himself. And so I had two choices—make him listen to the truth and destroy him or just let him believe he'd saved me. So that's what I did. He thinks he saved me, though sometimes when he looks at me, I see the doubt there."

And so Enza had never told. Not a word to anyone. No one knew the real story. Everyone approved of what Nino had done—a father saving his daughter. What any one of them would have done, even though to be found out meant certain death.

Enza had remained silent when Maria Serena brought her to Graziella late last summer.

Graziella remembered Maria Serena's anger when she'd asked Enza what she wanted. *What are you asking her for?* she'd said. *Do you think she can look after a child? You expect me to look after some German soldier's bastard? She'll never get a husband!* And so Graziella had given her the *Aristolochia*. This poor girl.

"Oh, Enza," she said. "What did I do? I took his baby from you. I'm so sorry. If I'd only known."

Enza looked at her with those huge eyes, not a tear in them. "It's okay," she said. "Mama was right. There was nothing else to do. I only wish there'd been enough to kill me too." She said this last part with a conviction that frightened Graziella. "I don't want to talk about this any-more. I just wanted you to know. Somebody should know."

"But if you'd had his baby, you'd at least . . ."

Enza put her hands over her ears, shaking her head violently as she turned away, and Graziella knew it had not been okay. She placed her hand on Enza's shoulder, but there was no response. Enza had retreated back within herself.

Graziella got up and walked numbly to the road, the sound of Clario's accordion following her. She heard Frank calling after her, but she couldn't answer him.

Frank caught up to her where the road met the path behind the house. She just shook her head. "Grace, it's okay. I know this is hard for you."

"It's not Ugo. Oh, Frank, I can't tell you. You'll hate me. It's Enza. I only wanted to help, but I made things worse. . . ."

"What is it? You know I could never hate you." He tried to take her into his arms. She struggled to get away from him, but he only held her harder, and she gave in, crying into the front of his uniform. She knew he wouldn't hate her, but she didn't deserve forgiveness. She'd helped ruin Enza's life.

Big drops of rain began to fall, and Clario's accordion faltered in the distance. Frank led her inside the house, sat her down at the table, and brought her a cup of wine, but she didn't drink it. Instead, she buried her head in her arms and told him everything. He listened in silence, stroking her hair as it splayed out on the table around her head.

"My God, Grace. You did what you thought best, and maybe it still is. You don't know if Enza could've raised a baby. Maybe it would've been worse to have it. Please don't be so hard on yourself. You have to forgive yourself. Look, it's been a long week."

"How can you say that?" She was angry now. "It isn't right. I helped ruin a girl's life. Why do I deserve to feel better about that?"

Frank pulled out a chair and sat down. "Listen to me. It's really terrible about Enza, but everything about this story is terrible. What were the chances of that boy and Enza living happily ever after? What makes you think he could've deserted and not been caught and killed for it?"

"But Father Paolo would've helped."

"But could he? Would he even have had the chance? You just don't know how these things are going to end. For all you know, the Nazis could've caught up with him and killed all of you—Enza and yourself included—for harboring him. Things happened the way they did. They're tragic, I agree. But if Nino hadn't killed him, things could've taken an even more tragic turn. You were doing what you thought was right at the time, and there's no way of knowing it wasn't right after all. If it wasn't for this damned war, you'd never have been put in this position. Jesus Christ, Grace! Blame Mussolini, Hitler, the King, the Allies for putting those two kids in such an impossible position—anybody but yourself."

The rain was picking up, and as she watched it through the open doorway she imagined everyone fleeing to the shelter of the church. She hoped Nino would take Giovanni back to his house, that Giovanni wouldn't insist on coming back here. She couldn't bear him right now, and the thought of seeing Nino was just too much.

"I understand about regret, Grace," Frank said a little wearily. "Yes, I was a spy and in considerable danger, but I got off easy. No nights in icy rivers, no losing toes to frostbite, no one shooting at me. My assignment was what many would call cushy, dining with Nazi officers, smoking cigars, drinking wine stolen from poor farmers like Clario. Pretending to be sympathetic to the Nazi cause wasn't too hard to pull off when I had a warm bed and plenty of food." His hands tightened until the knuckles turned white. "Until I had to watch people get tortured and killed and there wasn't a goddamn thing I could do about it. What was a life or two sacrificed along the way if I could get key information that could help the Allies win this thing? So I had to keep my mouth shut and hope these men weren't dying for nothing."

He got up abruptly and went to stand at the open door, looking up the hill toward the church. There was a crack of thunder and the rain became torrential, streaming down from the eaves and forming a curtain of water over the open door. "There was this one time. We were at a fancy hotel. I was attending a ball there, an elaborate birthday party for one of the officer's mistresses. The officer invited me and a few others to a back room for a glass of champagne. And for some entertainment. I was expecting an exotic dancer. But it wasn't. It was four young men." He spoke quietly now, and she strained to hear him over the downpour. "They'd been captured the night before. The Nazis tore their fingernails off one by one. It was the most horrific thing I'd ever seen. Or heard—

you can't even begin to imagine the screams. It went on for hours. None of them would talk though, so then they were burned with cigarettes. Again and again and again. I don't think any part of them was left untouched. Finally, when the Nazis realized they would never give up any information, they shot them between the eyes, point-blank. Laughing." He turned to her now, his face contorted with disgust and shame. "They were laughing, Grace, and I had to laugh too.

"And I knew them, Grace. I knew those men. Our eyes met, and they recognized me. And I knew if they talked, they would give me away. That it would be me getting tortured next." He clenched and unclenched his fists. "It's a pretty sick feeling to realize I was more afraid for myself than for them."

She went over to him, wanting to comfort him in some way, but he waved her away. "Just like you, I don't know if I can ever forgive myself," he said. "When I think about it logically, I guess I did the right thing. What could I have done? Just gotten us all killed and then I couldn't have helped anyone. But in my heart, I know there's no way it was right. There's just no goddamn way to justify it. I was a coward."

He stopped there, his final words almost lost in the sound of the rain. She reached for him again, and this time he didn't pull away. She held him in the open doorway, her cheek pressed against his shirt. Water splashed over the sill, soaking the hem of her dress and pooling around their feet.

You'd think with the war over . . . But we'll never be the same, Maria Serena had said only the other morning. However, when Graziella finally spoke, it wasn't Maria Serena's words she used but Ugo's, hoping Frank would find comfort in them as Ugo had, as she wanted to. "There were only bad choices to make, Frank. . . . Those men, they're with God now. That's all we can ask for."

9

Graziella was washing Frank's shirt, day-dreaming about America as she absently scrubbed at a grape stain that refused to budge from the collar. They were to leave the very next morning. They'd have an autumn wedding at Frank's family farm, when the leaves were yellow and red. Then they'd take the train to New York for their honeymoon, see the Empire State Building, buy that violet dress, dance to Benny Goodman. She could already feel the soft violet silk swirling around her legs. She would need a new wool coat and shoes too, and they would run through the leaves in Central Park in the golden light of the afternoon. And maybe, just maybe, she was already pregnant now, and by then she'd feel the baby move inside her. She almost laughed aloud at the thought of it all, a bubble of soap making her sneeze instead.

This was how they'd been talking this past week, making plans, thinking of the future. Until they figured out where to live, they would stay with his family. *Her* family now. His father, Henry, his mother, Greta, his little sister, Clara. This morning Frank had gone to Il Paesino to put Maria Teresa on her train back to the convent and to send two telegrams, one to a former OSS colleague at the American embassy in Switzerland who Frank said would help arrange her travel documents, no questions asked, and another to his family: *Home in September with fiancée STOP Plan for October wedding STOP Love Frank STOP.* She already knew she'd like them, imagining them to have all the warmth of her own family.

If she felt any sadness, it was because she wished her own family could be at the wedding, or even Emilia—although, when she thought about it, as she had many times before, had her parents been alive to invite, she'd never have met Emilia or Frank. Or Ugo. None of this would've happened. It was strange to think how things turned out. What unpredictable twists and turns life takes, one thing leading to another. Who would've thought too, that first day when Frank appeared on his motorcycle and showed her his photo of Clara, only five weeks later she'd be on her way to America with him? Certainly not her.

She pushed back her hair with a soapy hand. Only just last month, she'd still been convinced Ugo was coming back. But she'd been wrong. Perhaps she should just give up on this whole idea that she could sometimes sense things other people couldn't. Instead, she could follow in her father's footsteps and pick up a specialty of no particular interest to anyone other than a handful of other botanists. She could obtain her doctorate and even continue her father's research. Write another book on the spruce budworm, *Further Studies Regarding the Eastern Spruce Budworm: Population Oscillations and Effectuations on the Canadian Forestry Industry: A Paleoecological Study by Dr. Graziella* . . . no, not Graziella anymore . . . by Dr. Grace Austen. It was a liberating idea, and she found herself humming as she dipped the shirt back into the water.

She didn't know the melody at first, and so she repeated it. The notes hung on the air, and finally she recognized them, the cadenza at the end of the first movement of Beethoven's Violin Concerto. Ugo's improvised cadenza, more beautiful and melodious than anyone else's, and she remembered it now with utter clarity. It took her away from thoughts of America and Frank and back to a crowded concert hall in Venice. Ugo was on the stage, playing with his eyes closed, putting everything into those phrases. *I will play for you alone,* he'd said. *I always play better when I play for you.* And when he finished, there was complete silence, as if the audience had forgotten how to breathe. Finally, as the last echo of music died away, he lowered his violin, opened his eyes, and smiled right at her. The audience jumped to their feet, cheering, and she was standing too, wearing her yellow dress, saying to the man beside her, *That's my husband.*

She looked down at Frank's shirt between her hands, stared at the grape stain, bright as ever, and knew everything was about to change. She knew it with a kind of certainty she'd never felt before. Just as she'd made her peace with the past, it was coming back and everything was about to be plunged into chaos once more. She knew this even before she heard the voice coming from the open doorway behind her, knew she'd been terribly, terribly right all along.

"Graziella?"

She'd been right, and yet she didn't want to believe it.

He repeated her name, ever so softly. "Graziella?"

Slowly, she turned to face him, still holding the shirt, water streaming down the front of her dress and making puddles around her feet. Her lips formed his name but no sound emerged.

How was it that seeing him now, framed in the light from the open door, he looked less real than in her dreams? Was it because he was thinner? Or was it that he looked so much older? In the stoop of his shoulders was a foreshadowing of himself as an old man. His skin was pale, those dark eyes that usually held so much conviction uncertain. His hair was long, almost to his shoulders, and under his beard his cheeks were hollow. Him, but not him. She should've known he'd return from heaven or hell to be with her again. How could she ever have doubted him?

But she had doubted him. She'd thought he was dead and so was making her life with another man. And here now was the husband she'd loved so much standing before her like some sort of apparition. She should be running to him, crying out with joy and relief.

And yet she didn't move, the kitchen floor like an ocean between them. "Where have you been? Do you know how much I missed you?"

A bee lazily circled the room before making its exit, while the kitchen curtains fluttered in the hot afternoon breeze. How could everything be so ordinary in the face of such upheaval?

"I am so sorry, Graziella . . . ," he said finally, his voice fading away. He sounded as tired as he looked. "I am so happy to see you. I have dreamed of this moment for so long."

He took a step toward her just as Emilia ran through the doorway behind him, her arms full of struggling kitten. "Zia Graziella, Lupo keeps chasing Daisy!" She stopped, her eyes flitting between them as she edged closer to her aunt. She clearly didn't remember him. He'd changed so much since the last time she'd seen him, the last time they'd all seen him. *What happened to you?*

She gathered Emilia and Daisy in her arms along with the wet shirt. "It's okay," she said, trying to sound reassuring, though her voice trembled as she said the words she thought she'd never say again. "Zio Ugo is home."

But there was no time for the little girl to absorb this as Lupo and Gaspare came skidding through the door, followed by Maria Benedetta. Emilia, her uncle forgotten, shrieked as Daisy leaped from her arms, scratching the little girl's face as she bolted for the stairs. Emilia struggled out of Graziella's grip. "Tell Lupo to leave Daisy alone!" she shouted at Gaspare before running up the stairs after the barking dog.

But Gaspare and Maria Benedetta didn't seem to hear. Instead, they stood staring up at Ugo. Gaspare was old enough to understand what the funeral had meant, and he looked at Ugo as if a ghost had suddenly appeared. But Maria Benedetta saw it differently, her hand freezing in midair as she attempted to cross herself, falling forward into Ugo's arms as she gasped out the words: "A miracle! A miracle! Ugo has risen from the dead!"

Her words startled Gaspare into action. He yelled for Lupo before backing off through the open door, tearing down the path through the woods to where his father and uncles and cousins were starting work on Tazio's new house, echoing his mother's words while Lupo bounded after him. "A miracle! A miracle! Zio Ugo has risen from the dead!"

Graziella dropped Frank's shirt into the sink before leaning against it. She heard Emilia still upstairs cajoling her kitten to come out of hiding.

She listened to Gaspare's shouts, Lupo's barks, Maria Benedetta's wails, and yet she stood silent.

Ugo, arms around his sister, looked at Graziella, his words lost in Maria Benedetta's sobs. It should be herself in his arms. She imagined them around her now. She had dreamed of this meeting for so long, and yet now, when his eyes sought hers, she looked away, wishing Frank were here beside her, yet knowing Frank was what was keeping her from running to him. For so long Ugo had come between her and Frank, and now it was Frank who was keeping her from Ugo. *Oh Ugo, what have I done?*

She closed her eyes and there was Frank. *Are you happy?* he'd asked only that morning, the sun through the leaves of the chestnut tree playing across his skin. *I love you,* she'd answered without hesitation.

She opened her eyes just as the train whistle sounded from the valley. She pictured Frank waving good-bye to Maria Teresa, starting the climb back up the hill, whistling, oblivious to the fact everything had changed.

But there was no time to think, even if she could. Already she could hear Maria Serena breathlessly threatening Gaspare with the thrashing of a lifetime if he was lying. "It's true, it's true!" Gaspare shouted over and over as they all came pouring into the room: Nino, Roberto, Clario, and the *Our Gang* boys, then Maria Serena and Maria Valentina. And then it was Maria Serena who was gasping: "It is true! It is true!"

Salvatore took one look and was out the door again, shouting as he ran to the church. "Ring the bell! Zio Ugo is home!"

The Marias pried each other off him, covering him with kisses, and the men reached over their wives to kiss him on both cheeks, tears in all their eyes. Down Ugo's face they ran freely.

And then into the middle of all this chaos: Giovanni, leaning on his cane, having managed somehow to get out of bed on his own. "What's the meaning of this racket?" he shouted. "Where's Ugo?" His words silenced the room, and Graziella knew they were all remembering there was another Ugo now. Even the Marias stepped back, clearing a space between their brother and father.

"Papà, it is so good to see you." Ugo held out his arms, the pleasure of seeing his father evident in his tired smile.

Graziella felt the tension in them all, a collective holding of breaths as they waited for Giovanni's reaction. It didn't take long, but the vehemence of his response surprised them. They expected confusion. They expected disbelief, incomprehension, but not this.

"Get away! Get away!" he shouted. "You're not my son!" Giovanni lashed at him with his cane as he backed up through the bedroom door, stumbling against the frame. Ugo rushed forward, ready to catch him, but Roberto put out a hand to stop him while Nino went and helped the old man, urging him back inside his room, calling out to Graziella to bring some wine.

"He's forgotten me," Ugo said dazedly as Graziella poured the wine. At the bottom of the sink, Frank's shirt sat in a soapy heap. What had she been daydreaming of while she washed that shirt? A violet dress and the Empire State Building and dancing to Benny Goodman . . .

Cup in hand, she went to the door, looking out on the brilliance of the morning without really seeing it. She should go and wait by the road for Frank. She heard the church bell, hesitant at first, but picking up momentum. She imagined Salvatore, all his weight hanging from the rope, swinging the bell into action, sending out the news, and she pictured everywhere on the mountain and in the valley people putting down their rakes and their hoes, their sewing and their babies, looking up and wondering what had happened that the bell should ring like this.

Just then, Father Paolo and Annunziata came tearing down the hill. The priest held up his robes with one hand while he waved wildly at her with the other, the cross of his rosary bouncing on his chest, while Annunziata in her apron brandished a wooden spoon, her lunch preparations obviously interrupted, both of them shouting: "Is it true? Is it true?" They swept Graziella back into the room without even seeming to see her, and now it was Father Paolo who wept into the front of Ugo's shirt.

"Can I take that to Papà?" Clario asked, and she realized she was still holding the wine.

She shook her head. "No, let me, please," she said, and she nearly staggered into Giovanni's room, closing the door behind her before sinking onto the bed next to Nino.

"He wants Frank," Nino said, taking the cup. He had a sip himself before holding it up for the old man beside him who, quiet now, drank obediently.

"I know," she said wearily. Giovanni was trembling, and she reached across Nino to pat his thin hand.

Maria Serena's voice carried through the door. "It's okay, Ugo. He's very confused. He'll get better now that you're home." There was a murmur of agreement.

"Oh, Nino, what am I going to do?" she asked.

Nino looked down at the cup in his hand. "You're happy Ugo is home, yes?"

"Yes, of course," she said, the conviction in her voice sounding forced even to her own ears. "It's just that it doesn't seem real. It's such a shock. All these months trying to accept he wasn't coming back . . ." Nino's face was full of sympathy. She didn't know whether Nino and his brothers were, as Frank had said, "a little bit in love with her," but she knew Nino cared, that he wanted her to be happy and understood why she couldn't be. "And there's Frank," she said, just as a new thought occurred to her. What if she and Frank had already left? What if Ugo had come home tomorrow instead of today and the family had to tell him she'd gone just that morning with another man? What if she arrived in America and learned Ugo was still alive?

Fresh shouts reached her ears through the door, along with Tazio and Rosanna's voices. Tazio's especially, his absolute joy evident as he greeted the man he loved as a brother.

All the times she imagined Ugo's homecoming, all the times she wished to look up from drawing water or hanging laundry to see him standing there, and now all she could do was hide in Giovanni's room. If Frank's motorcycle hadn't broken down on the hill a month ago, this would've been the happiest day of her life. *What do you do when the thing you want most comes true—just when you've come to want something else even more?*

Nino timidly touched her arm. "What are you going to tell Ugo?"

I thought you were dead. I fell in love with another man. But now that you're home . . . "I don't know."

She heard snippets of conversation from the other room. *Mountains . . . You walked all the way from where . . . ? Stand back and give him some air. . . . We held your funeral last week. . . . Father Paolo, can a funeral be reversed? . . . You're so thin. . . . We'll make all your favorite food. . . . Someone get Ugo some wine. . . .* No one mentioned Frank.

She took a deep breath before slowly getting to her feet. "Will you stay with Papà, Nino? Frank will be back any minute, and I think I should meet him, not let him walk in on this."

"Of course," he said. "And Graziella?" She nodded, her hand on the door. "I think Ugo will understand. He's a good man."

Graziella felt a wave of gratitude, and she went to put her arms around him. "I know, Nino. That's what makes all this so hard."

She slipped back into the room unnoticed, all eyes still on Ugo. Tazio stood next to him with his arm around his shoulders. He'd always been a slighter version of Ugo, but now that Ugo was so thin, it was the other way around, Ugo a slighter version of Tazio. Ugo caught her eye over Rosanna's head. She saw the worry there, the incomprehension. Lines that had never been there creased his forehead. She turned away quickly, trying to make it to the door, only her way was blocked as more nephews and nieces and cousins and neighbors arrived. There were at least thirty people in the room now, with another two dozen gathered at both doors, hoping to catch a glimpse of Ugo. She tried to listen to what they said, to

245

what Ugo was saying, but except for the echo of *Ugo, Ugo, Ugo* through the crowd, she could hear nothing. He kept looking at her as if wondering what was wrong, but she still couldn't meet his eyes. She desperately wanted to intercept Frank on the hill and prepare him, imagining him wondering the reason for the church bell, but now Emilia was back downstairs and she wanted Frank as well. "Gaspare will do what he says," she was saying to whoever would listen. "Lupo chased Daisy to the top of the wardrobe, and now she won't come down."

"Please, not now," Graziella pleaded with Emilia. "I have to go." Only when she looked up, Frank was already beside her.

"Hey, what's all the fuss about?" he asked with a smile as he bent down to hug Emilia. "Are you having a party and didn't invite me? And why's the bell ringing?" She didn't answer. Couldn't answer. Too aware of the silence that had fallen over the crowd, all eyes on herself and Frank. What was she going to tell him anyway? *Ugo is home. Ugo is alive.* He looked at her with alarm now, his hand reaching out to take hers. "Is something wrong? Is it Giovanni?"

She shook her head, wanting to prepare him but not knowing how. He looked from her to the family, and everyone backed away until she and Frank were left facing Ugo across the room. Frank dropped her hand as he took a step back, the shock of recognition evident on his face, and she could only conclude he already knew there was only one man who could receive such a homecoming. Emilia clung to Graziella, burying her face in her dress, her frightened whimper the only sound in the room.

"My God," Ugo said in English. "Frank? What are you doing here?"

Graziella looked from one man to the other in disbelief, pushing Emilia away.

"I was just about to ask you the same thing, Ugo," Frank said. "We thought you were dead!"

"You know each other?" she asked, although she already could see the answer. *Frank and Ugo knew each other.* She looked at Frank. He nodded, confirming the impossible. "All this time and you didn't tell me?"

Frank reached for her but she pulled away, her hand finding Rosanna's sleeve. She clung to it, her mind seeking to make sense of what was happening, the past five weeks flashing before her. Frank appearing on his motorcycle. *Ugo's your husband then?* he'd asked. All the times he listened as she poured out her grief, never telling her. *There's nothing else I should know, is there?* she'd asked when he'd confessed to being a spy. *Only that I love you,* he'd said before asking her to marry him. And she'd said *yes.*

She looked back at the floor, but not without catching the family's stares, Maria Benedetta making the sign of the cross, Father Paolo moving his lips as if he might be whispering a prayer. They might not understand English, but they would understand this much: Ugo and Frank knew each other. She wished they'd all go—she needed quiet, she needed to think. But she didn't have the strength to say anything. Everything was changing, and she didn't know what to do about it.

It was Giovanni who broke the silence, his voice coming from his bedroom. "Ugo? Is that you?" he called.

Ugo looked to the door, but before he could respond, Frank answered, his eyes on Ugo, his troubled expression contradicting the reassuring tone of his voice. "It's okay, Papà. I'm here." He turned to Graziella. "Please tell him I'll be there in a minute."

"Well, be quick about it," Giovanni said after Graziella had translated. "I don't like this. I won't have strangers in my house."

"Papà? Mary, Mother of God!" Ugo said, meeting Graziella's eyes again, looking to her for answers. "What is happening?"

Graziella could see that Father Paolo was discreetly trying to herd the family toward the door, but they ignored him, holding their ground. Even if they couldn't understand what was being said, they weren't about to miss a thing. Ugo backed up Father Paolo's request with a fervent *par piazere* and at last they obeyed, slowly moving toward the doors, joining the people gathered outside the house.

In the empty room, the gulf between them seemed even wider, she and Frank near the door, Ugo by the table. Frank shifted uncomfortably. "Your father thinks I'm you. We thought you were dead, so we let him think it. It made him happy. We didn't see any harm in it."

Ugo looked at them both, standing side by side, and Graziella could see him putting the pieces together. She found herself stepping away from Frank as if that would keep the truth from him.

"I think you should just tell me," Ugo said. "From the beginning." He pulled out a chair and sank into it heavily. He grimaced with pain, and she felt his pain too, close to her heart. If she could feel this, why couldn't she have felt that he was alive out there somewhere? Or maybe she had. Maybe that was why it had been so hard for her to accept he was dead. She wanted a chair herself, but she couldn't cross the floor, and so she leaned back against the sink, already feeling as if the wet shirt on the bottom belonged to another lifetime.

"I came here last month," Frank said finally. "It's true, Grace, that I was sent to Lake Garda to go through some papers the Nazis had left behind. But I was also sent here to check on Ugo. The Allies wanted to know whether he'd turned up after the war ended. They're keeping tabs on all the Resistance leaders, especially the Communists. They're afraid the Communists will come to power here.

"But when I arrived," Frank said, turning to Ugo, "you weren't here, and Grace was barely hanging on. All she wanted was for you to come home. How could I tell her that even if you weren't dead, you *still* weren't coming home? I really did expect to see you here. I really did think you'd come to your senses. That is, if you hadn't been killed in the meantime. Because God knows you seemed hell-bent on making that happen." Frank spoke quickly, angrily even, his eyes flickering between the two of them, and she listened to him as if in a dream. This couldn't be real, this couldn't be about her life.

"The very first night I arrived," Frank continued, "I found Grace standing at the edge of the cliff. God knows what would've happened if I hadn't been here. She was desperately missing you, and you were too full of wounded pride and self-pity. . . ." He broke off, shaking his head as he turned to look at her. "Anyway, maybe if I hadn't fallen in love with you, I'd have done it all differently."

"I still don't understand," she said weakly.

"My God, Grace, I'm trying to explain!" The frustration was evident in his voice. "It's because either Ugo was dead or he really had left you! He *wanted* you to think he was dead. He wasn't coming back. He told me himself that he planned to never come back, that he could never face you again. How was I supposed to tell you that?"

"It's not true," she cried. "Ugo would never leave me!" But Ugo wouldn't meet her eyes, looking instead to where the book Frank had given her lay on the table. She could hear Giovanni whimpering in the other room, followed by Nino's reassuring whispers, while outside there was a renewed murmur.

"I'm sorry," Frank was saying, softer now. "I shouldn't have gotten angry. I think I should go now. This isn't the time . . . all these people. Your family, Ugo, they think of you as a god. Ask him, Grace, why I didn't tell you. He knows." Frank turned to go as Giovanni called out Ugo's name again. "Get Nino to take Giovanni to his house. Tell him I'll see him later. I just can't go in there now."

He went to the door, but he didn't leave yet, instead turning around and coming back. "Grace," he said, his voice breaking. "Every day I tried to tell you, but I couldn't think how. I didn't want to hurt you and the more I fell in love with you, the more afraid I became. I was afraid you'd be angry with me for not telling you in the first place. And I wasn't even sure myself what had happened to Ugo, what he was going to do or not do, so how could I explain it all to you? And then when Tazio told you Ugo had died fighting in the mountains,

I thought it was better never to say anything, to just let you believe Ugo had died a hero and to leave you with your memories. Do you understand now?"

Feeling almost sick to her stomach, she shook her head. How could she understand? She had no idea what he was talking about. She looked at Ugo sitting hunched over the table, not interrupting, not protesting, defeat etched into his face.

"I'll come back later tonight." Frank was whispering now. "We can talk then. If you want." He reached out to touch her cheek, but she turned away and Frank let his hand drop to his side. "I love you," he said, his voice barely audible. "This doesn't change that. I wish I could be happy for you right now. I wish I could be happy to see Ugo—he was my friend. I should be happy to know he's alive. But all I can think is that I'm losing you, so maybe it's just best I go for now."

She followed him out the door and around the house to the motorcycle, barely noticing the people who parted to let them through. She wanted to say she loved him too, but the words that had come out so easily that morning wouldn't come out now. Nothing would. All she could do was stand there with her hands at her side, watching as he got on the motorcycle. "I'll come back tonight, I promise," he said as it roared to life. Not broken after all. *I think I was waiting for a beautiful damsel in distress. And luckily my motorcycle broke down at her door.* Five weeks ago she had stood in this very spot, watching the same motorcycle labor up the hill, wishing it was Ugo coming home to her. How long ago that was.

The family and neighbors fanned out across the road, watching as Frank rode down the dusty hill toward the village. The *Our Gang* boys stayed still, their fathers' hands on their shoulders. Emilia held onto her doll and cried, refusing Maria Benedetta's efforts to comfort her with promises of bread and honey. Only Lupo ran after him.

Finally everyone was gone, even Giovanni, who'd left with Nino. Ugo watched from Giovanni's chair in the yard as Graziella drew water from the well, filled the tin tub, and placed it over the fire. She went into the house and brought out some herbs, adding them to the water. Rosemary for pain, witch hazel for strength, lavender for peace. Ugo handed her his clothes, ragged, caked with dust, smelling of sweat and sleepless nights, and said nothing as she impulsively threw them on the fire and stirred them into the flames.

Silently she poured the fragrant water over his head, touching him for the first time as she massaged the soap into his scalp, feeling him relax under her hands. She left him as she went to find some clothes. A pair of pants that were Giovanni's and his own shirt, the one she'd worn over her nightdress for so long, the one she'd pulled on the night she'd stood at the edge of the cliff in the mist. When she came back, he was holding a razor, but his hand shook as he held it to his beard, and so she took it from him, carefully following the lines of his cheek.

They didn't speak until he'd eaten the eggs she prepared for him. "Is it finished?" he asked in English, the language they'd always used between themselves. She turned from the door and sat down across from him at the table. It was hard to believe the world was still the same place as when she was washing Frank's shirt. She wondered where he was now. Would he come back tonight as he said he would?

"I don't know," she said. "I'm sorry I didn't give you a better homecoming. I spent so long wishing you were back and then just when I thought I could accept you weren't—you're here. It's not that I'm not happy you're alive. It's just that it's a shock. We held your funeral last week, you know."

"I know," Ugo said. "But what about Frank? If you missed me so much, how did you fall in love with him so quickly?"

"That's not fair, Ugo, and you know it," she said, her whole body stiffening. "You don't know what I was going through. I don't even think I knew. What was I doing standing out there on the edge of the cliff? It was because of you—because I couldn't see going on without you. And besides, what do you care if you were going to leave me? Because it's true, isn't it? I could tell by your reaction—Frank was telling the truth."

He let out a long breath. "I am tempted to lie to you and say it is not true. But it is. All I can say is that I did not mean to leave you. But in the end it was the same thing." He rose slowly from his chair and went to stand at the open door. "Wounded pride and self-pity. Frank was right about that." He stood on the threshold, his back to her, leaning heavily against the door frame, the late afternoon sun wreathing him in light. "I tried to kill myself. Or at least get myself killed. But it was not meant to be."

These were not words she ever would've expected from him. She would've expected him to return with his head held high. "Please Ugo, you have to tell me what happened to you. Help me understand. But first come and sit down. You look so tired. Have more wine. It'll make you stronger."

He slowly walked back to his chair and sat down obediently. "Where do I start, Graziella?"

"You knew Frank," she said as she refilled his cup. "Start there. I thought he was in Germany at first, and then he mentioned Switzerland. But obviously if he knew you, it was Venice all along."

Ugo nodded. "He has a great-aunt living there. She is German but hated Hitler. She did not let the

Germans know this of course, and she was very useful to the Allies, the OSS, and Frank in particular. Through her, Frank had access to the entire German command in Venice. He pretended to be a rich German-American, avoiding the draft and sympathetic to the Nazis. It did not take him long to befriend them. At the same time, he worked with me, keeping me informed of Allied plans and warning me when he could about German strategy. It was a dangerous game for him to play, and I worried about trusting him, but as it turned out," he added, taking a hard swallow of wine, "he was wrong to trust me."

"No, Ugo, that's not true," she protested, but he raised his hand and cut off her words.

"Let me finish," he said. "After the manifesto at the Goldoni Theater in March, there was a real sense of hope in the city. Everyone was united, the Germans were on the defensive, the Allies were so close—but we were so pitifully armed. Frank kept telling me to wait. It would not be long. But I was so impatient. I was beside myself with the inaction. I could sense victory and I wanted it all over." She remembered his trip home during the ice storm, how defeated he'd seemed, how desperate for the war to end.

"Then one night we were at his aunt's palazzo. Frank brought out some brandy and cigars, and we began making toasts. To our families, to our countries, to the end of the war." Without seeming to notice what he was doing, Ugo pulled the copy of *Glengarry School Days* toward him, opening and closing the cover as he spoke, his hands that had held a violin bow, a rifle, her own hand with such steadiness now nervous and shaky. "We both became more than a little drunk. I know I talked about you, though it was not the first time. We had become good friends by then." The ironic tone wasn't lost on her. She watched as he opened and closed the book. Frank didn't just know Ugo—he knew her too. He'd introduced himself and she'd told him her name and all the while he'd known about her. What she looked like, how she and Ugo met, how much they loved each other. . . .

Ugo pushed the book away. "And then Frank let slip that the Germans had just received a new shipment of guns and ammunition at their main storehouse near the Church of the Angelo Raffaele. Close to where we used to live. I knew this was the chance we were looking for. We could finally arm the people, rise up, and drive the Nazis out of our city once and for all. We could do it ourselves. We did not need to wait for the Allies and risk them destroying the city with their bombs. And then you could come home. Back to our little apartment, back to the way things were. There was nothing I wanted more.

"I guess Frank saw the hope in my eye, for he immediately told me to forget it. It was foolhardy to even think about it, and besides, any such action could blow his cover and get him killed or at least disrupt our network. But he was so drunk, I was not even sure he would remember our conversation in the morning." Ugo picked up his cup and took another large gulp of wine before continuing. "But I remembered. And I was convinced this was just what we needed. So I quickly organized a plan. Too quickly. Baldassare, Vincenzo, Biagio, and Donato were to carry it out. Good men, every one of them, and Baldassare and Donato with wives and children too. And . . . I got them killed, Graziella! As surely as if I had pulled the trigger myself."

He pounded his fist on the table, spilling the last of the wine. She watched it run down the table, staining the edge of the book. She didn't move, just stared at Ugo, sitting now with his face in his hands. She knew how this story ended. She knew these men had been tortured, and once she'd worried Ugo had been among them. And she knew something else. That Frank had been there too. That these same men had known him and could have given him away. *It's a pretty sick feeling to realize I was more afraid for myself than for them,* he'd said. And it had happened all because Ugo had used bad judgment and acted rashly.

"Frank was right—it was foolhardy. It was very stupid," Ugo said, setting the now-empty cup upright and dabbing at the spill with a dishtowel.

"There was no way to penetrate the storehouse. Too many guards and not enough of us. I had not planned enough. I had been too hasty, too convinced by my previous successes. I was beginning to think I was invincible, that I would never be caught. I thought I could do it—they could do it—but it was impossible. I was never more wrong in my life. And these men were killed. Because of me. They were tortured at one of the hotels where the Nazis had their headquarters."

"Don't, Ugo. I know, please don't—" She stopped, realizing she was about to say *torture yourself*.

But Ugo shook his head and went on, his voice barely a whisper. "Their fingernails torn out. Their bodies burned with cigarettes.The most brutal things one could imagine. And none of them breathed a word. Not one. They protected me, they protected Frank, they protected everyone. And they died for me," he said, starting to cry. "I let them down. All because of my own pride." She reached out to touch his arm, but he flinched and pulled away. "Frank came to me the next day. He had been there, seen everything. He was furious, demanding to know what the hell I had done. I should have discussed this with him, he said. Maybe he could have found better information. Or, better yet, maybe he could have talked me out of it. The men had not said a thing, but he knew it was only a matter of time before the Nazis figured out he was the link. He would have to leave the city.

"I was wild then. Four good men died because of me. I had potentially risked our entire Venetian partisan network. I had ruined the relationship with our best Allied contact and put my friend in danger. I was too ashamed. I asked God to strike me down then, but He did not answer. And I hated Him for it, Graziella! I hated Him. And as I could not face God, I could not face you either. It is true what Frank said. I could never come back to you, and I told him so." He looked at her then, his eyes wet with tears, and she knew he didn't think he deserved her forgiveness or her love.

"Oh Ugo, stop, please." She reached across the table to take his hands in hers. "Remember when I blamed myself for Maria Lisabetta's death? You told me it wasn't my fault, that there was no knowing what would happen. There were only bad choices to make. You were only doing your best. You said yourself just this last January that the Resistance in Venice needed weapons and ammunition. So you were doing something you thought would help the effort. You took a chance because chances were all you had."

He didn't answer her then, just pulled his hands out of her grip, and she knew he didn't believe her. Knowing Ugo's convictions, it was no wonder he'd had such a deep crisis of faith. Not just religious faith but the very faith of getting up every day in the world and knowing everything was all right, that the war would indeed end, that he could put one foot in front of the other, that his wife would be waiting for him with open arms.

Daisy came down the stairs and rubbed against Ugo's legs. He bent down to pick her up. "You have a kitten now," he said.

"It's Emilia's. Frank rescued her."

"Frank again," Ugo said with a slight shake of his head. "He has become very good at rescuing things." Daisy curled up on Ugo's lap, and he stroked her ears. "I do not blame him for coming here to spy on me. He is just a pawn in all this too. We were all pawns."

Daisy's purring could be heard over Ugo's words as he went on. "After I left the city, I went to the mountains. Not long after my arrival, I ran into someone I knew from Venice, Michele Corinaldi." She nodded at the name, remembering this was the same man Tazio had spoken to, the man who'd thought he'd seen Ugo die. "I was not happy to see him. I did not want to be where anyone knew me. And Michele kept telling the other Resistance fighters I was *Il Monaco,* hero of Venice. I almost took a gun to my head on more than one occasion. I was on a suicide mission. I fought hard, hoping every day to be killed, hoping to be put out of my misery. And finally I was shot, on the very last day of fighting. The bullet nearly hit my heart, but I did not die. I could not even do that right." The sudden anger in his voice startled the kitten, and she jumped from his lap and ran out the open door.

"I lay there staring up into the darkness, pretending to be dead, hoping I looked mangled enough to be mistaken as so. Eventually, the monks from the local monastery came to bury the bodies, and one of them realized I was still alive. He took me to the abbey and looked after me, but I did not feel any better."

"I would've come for you, you know, if you had sent word," she said. "I wouldn't have left you there. I would've helped you. I would've done anything for you. I loved . . . love you so much." She wondered at this correction, which was the truth now, and there was a flash of those faraway mornings in Venice, learning Italian and Venetian, conjugating verbs to the sound of bells. *I love you. I loved you. I have always loved you. I will always love you.*

"I should have known, Graziella. But I was not in my right mind. That is the only way I can explain it. Even now I am not sure my mind is fully right. I do not know if it ever will be. All I can say is that I am so very sorry."

"What made you finally change your mind? What made you decide to come back?"

"You," he said simply. "I tried to fall back into monastery life, tried to find comfort in the rhythms of work and prayers. I did not want to think, I just wanted to follow everyone else, forget I was ever in a war, or try to at least. The monks saw I was not unfamiliar with abbey life, and a few weeks ago the abbot approached me to see if I was willing to join them. I of course had to tell him in good conscience that I was married. He did not seem surprised to hear so and asked me to tell him about you. I told him you were a good wife and that I loved you very much. That every night I saw your face in my dreams, but I could not come back to you after what I had done. And then he reminded me of our marital vows and that my redemption would be found not in a mountaintop abbey but with you. It was as if I came out of my fog then. What had I been doing all this time? Why should you suffer for my sins? I knew then I had to come home. I tried to write first, but I did not know what to say, so I just started walking."

The room was becoming darker, the shadows outside lengthening as the sun set. The crickets had begun their singing, and through the open door she saw the first of the fireflies.

"I want to go back to Venice with you," he said. "Go back to our old apartment. We could build a greenhouse on the roof, like the one in your garden in Toronto. There is my music too, though at times it is hard for me to hear." He shook his head. "That is what I think I want, but then I will see the families of those men and I will have to tell them what happened."

"You can go back, but you don't have to tell those families anything," she said, her voice gentle but firm. "It might very well be kinder to let them go on believing their men died as heroes, that they didn't die needlessly. Make your confession to Father Paolo, not to those grieving families. Let them keep their stories and memories." It struck her then how this was what Frank had tried to do for her, protect her from the truth.

She took Ugo's hand in hers again and held it between her palms, curling her fingers around his. This time he didn't pull away. "You're not the only person to make mistakes, Ugo," she said after a long pause, and she told him then about her own shame, that of Enza and the baby. He listened with his head bowed. She didn't tell him Nino had used the gun Ugo had given him, and it occurred to her for the first time that the boy would possibly still be alive except for that gun.

"Do you remember the day not long after we arrived in Venice when we borrowed Baldassare's boat?" she asked softly. "We rowed out to San Lazzaro because we wanted to see the room where Byron had studied. They asked you to stay and sing the vespers with them. They knew of your singing and were so honored when you agreed. But they couldn't keep singing, and one by one their voices dropped away until only your voice filled the chapel. It was as if the very stones held their breath to listen. Afterward, when we rowed back, the lagoon was so still. We stopped to watch the shooting stars, hundreds of them, it seemed. I think it was the closest I'd ever come to truly believing the way you believe, Ugo. And I couldn't fathom how I was there at that moment with you beside me. What had I done to merit such complete happiness?"

"You remember it perfectly," he said. "I am sorry I let you down. More than anything, I am sorry for that."

She wasn't sure what else to say, and so she led him upstairs. They removed each other's clothing, and she felt the ridges of his spine, each rib protruding from his chest, his legs and arms nothing but hard muscle and sinew. She touched his wounds. The scars from Spain that had robbed them of children and now this new one, only inches from his heart. She traced the ragged outline, imagined the suffering, and under her touch she felt his pain dissolving.

Ugo kissed her then, and she returned it. But in this kiss she remembered another, from only that morning as sun flooded through the loft window. Frank said he'd be back tonight, but she had yet to hear the click of the barn door. And so as once she'd held Frank and cried for Ugo, now she held Ugo and cried for Frank.

"I am so sorry, Graziella," Ugo said, as if he knew her tears were not for him. "Maybe it would have been better for you if I had never come home."

She shushed him. "Go to sleep, Ugo. No more of that. You're alive, and for that I'm grateful."

And he did fall asleep while she lay there for what seemed like hours, thinking about Frank and Ugo, about everything that had happened this day, about all they had told her. But the only thing she knew for certain was that she wasn't pregnant. She would know if she were, and the sureness wasn't there. It had simply been wishful thinking.

With a sigh, she slipped down the stairs, lit the lantern on the table, and went to the barn. It was empty, but Frank's things were still strewn about. An untidy pile of blankets lay on the mattress, two dirty coffee cups beside it, the remnants of their early morning breakfast.

She set the lantern down next to the mattress, stood at the window, and through the leaves caught a glimpse of stars. Her stars. There was the one for Ugo, no longer needed. Somewhere up there were her parents' stars too, and Westley's. She wished she could ask them for some sort of guidance. She almost wished for the buzz of Pippo—hearing that would be easier to deal with than this. At least then she would know what to do—close the shutters, run to the cellar, and shut the trapdoor tight.

She turned from the window and sat down on the mattress, pressing the rough blanket against her cheek. Then she pulled Frank's saddlebags toward her, though what she was looking for she couldn't say. Perhaps something important enough for him to come back for. She lifted one flap and saw the clothing that was now so familiar. Socks, T-shirts, a khaki green collared shirt, a white one, his uniform. On the other side was a shaving kit, a mess tin, a leather pouch containing matches, two unopened cartons of cigarettes, and an empty flask that smelled of whiskey. The pack contained another carton of cigarettes, several packets of chewing gum, two Hershey's bars, an Italian phrasebook, the baseball, and a book of quotations. On impulse, she opened it and turned to Shakespeare, the lines he'd quoted her in the kitchen the night of the storm looking back at her.

How could this day end so differently than it had begun? This morning had started with so much possibility—she and Frank ready to go to America and get married. And then Ugo had returned, but it hadn't been the joyous reunion she'd always envisioned. Instead, he was a broken man who'd let her believe he was dead and then returned just when she was moving on with her life. And Frank had lied and then he'd left, not even giving her a chance to say good-bye. And she wasn't pregnant. And she didn't know what she wanted anyway, except to not feel any of this.

10

It was music as only Ugo could create it. She heard it first in her dreams. *This is a good place for the greenhouse,* her father was saying. It was her childhood greenhouse, the one in their back garden in Toronto, now on the rooftop terrace of the apartment in Venice. The sun was setting and the sky above them was bathed in the deepest shades of pink and violet. Her father wore an orchid of matching hues in the buttonhole of his old tweed jacket. *Yes, definitely a good place for the greenhouse. You did well, Grace.* She laid her head against the worn softness of his sleeve while around them condensation rained down gently from the glass ceiling. Her mother was there too in her favorite burgundy dress, Emilia in her arms. *It's so good to see you both again,* Graziella told them against the plaintive notes from Ugo's violin. Below them the city glowed with the colors of sunset, and they could see the domes of San Marco and Santa Maria della Salute. And then there was Westley, who had brought the snow with him, great iridescent flakes the size of Christmas tree stars. *We'll make angels in the snow and watch them take flight with the winged lions,* he said, and then bells tolled, and then she was awake, her father's soft sleeve really just Frank's scratchy blanket.

She turned onto her back and sighed, a ribbon of light through a crack in the wall falling across her eyes. She closed them again, feeling the warmth on her face, the dream fading as she remembered where she was and everything that had transpired. *If only we could keep this, put it in a bottle and pull it out on a cold winter's night. A little bit of Italian sun . . .*

The crowing of the rooster in the yard was echoed by the strings, and for a moment she heard Ugo's joy at being home, a tumbling of notes like the rush of a waterfall, but falling short of their destination as uncertainty returned. It was all there: the regret, the despair, the pain, the long journey home. She heard the voices of their lost comrades, saw the jagged peaks of the mountains to the north, felt the cold wind, the sadness of the nights, and the love for her that had brought him home, back to the wife who no longer waited. And although the music knew she was in love with someone else, she felt it drawing her back toward its creator and her own desire to follow.

But then there was another sound. Closer. She opened her eyes again and turned to it, pulling the blanket around her as she looked at Frank across the loft. He sat on the dusty floor, leaning against the wall, his knees drawn up in front of him. "So now I've heard it," he said quietly. "I've finally heard Ugo play. Someday I'll tell people what I've heard, but I won't find the words to describe it."

"No one can," she said. "How long have you been sitting there?"

"Before the sun. Before the music started. I watched you sleep." He paused. "Were you here all night?"

She knew what he meant. He was asking if she'd spent the night alone. "No," she answered. "Not the whole night. I'm sorry."

"I wonder if I've always known I can't compete with Ugo."

She shook her head. "I don't think Ugo can compete with Ugo."

He came over and sat down beside her on the mattress, looking at his things on the floor. Picking up the book of quotations, he flipped through the pages.

"I looked at the lines from Macbeth," she said. "Did you really remember them from school?"

"Not really. Just the vaguest memory of having read them. I did remember the witches though. I liked them, and they really are like your sisters-in-law." He set the book down again with a brief smile. "We used this book for code for a while."

He was so close, and even as Ugo's music called her away, she wanted to move closer and rest her head against his thigh. She caught his scent, mixed with that of fresh-cut hay and the warm breezes of night. He picked up a new packet of cigarettes and ripped off the top before shaking one out. But he didn't light it, only tamped it against his palm before placing it on the floor next to the packet.

"Where did you go yesterday?" she asked.

"I rode for a while, then circled back. I ran out of gasoline around Clario's. I slept in his barn. Or tried to."

"The motorcycle was never broken, was it?"

He shook his head. "Just overheated. It only needed to cool down."

"You knew that all along, didn't you? From the beginning."

"I wasn't sure at first, but I figured it out soon enough. By then, though, I think we both wanted me to stay."

There was a long moment while she tried to decide if she'd always known this. "Tell me something that's really true, Frank," she said finally.

He kissed her forehead. "That I love you. That I want you to come home with me. That's all true."

Ugo's music faded away, the final cadence left unresolved. A question waiting for her answer. She sat up, still holding the blanket around her. "How could you spy on your friend?" In the music's wake was quiet. Not even the doves in the rafters stirred.

"The Allies aren't finished here. The last thing they want in Italy is a Communist government, and in Ugo they saw a leader. It doesn't matter that Ugo thinks Stalin's got it all wrong. It's all the same to them. Besides, I wanted to see for myself if he was still alive and whether he'd come home. I was only supposed to find out what Ugo was up to. But then, it was like I said yesterday . . . I fell in love with you and was afraid to tell you the truth. Anyway, they think he's dead. I sent a telegram after Tazio said he'd died fighting in the Dolomites."

"And now?"

"I suppose they'll find out eventually."

"What will they do to him?"

He shrugged. "I don't know. Maybe offer him a position in the new government as a reward for his service, hoping it'll make him see things differently. That tends to work."

"And if it doesn't?" she asked. "Because Ugo won't be bought off."

"I know that. Don't worry. Rumor is the OSS is on its way out, and who knows what will take its place. If he lays low for a while, they'll forget. They'll find other people to keep files on. Everything is such a mess right now. Big things fall through even bigger cracks."

"And if I don't go with you, you wouldn't . . ." She wasn't even sure what she was asking. "You wouldn't make things . . . difficult for him?"

"I'm surprised you'd even think that. I'd never do that."

She believed him, and although his answer was

the best she could hope for, she couldn't quite bring herself to say *thank you*. "You know, I kept hoping these last few days I was pregnant. But now I know I'm not." It came out sounding a bit like an accusation. They looked at each other, and she knew he was thinking the same thing: *Would that have made this easier?* Could she stay with Ugo if she was carrying Frank's child?

"It can still happen," he said. "As many as you'd like. You know that."

"Is it going to come down to that? Two lists, one for the reasons I should stay with Ugo, another for the reasons to go with you, and see which one is longer?" Why did it have to be like this? Last night she assumed—knew everyone assumed—that with Ugo back, this was all behind her. Frank would go, and they would all kindly forget. But it wasn't so simple. There was a choice to be made, and she wasn't sure she could make it. "Don't go yet, please."

"I came back, didn't I? I won't go until you tell me to."

She was about to say something, although she wasn't quite sure what, when a shout came from the yard. Nino calling her name. Once, twice. Then: "Ugo? Frank? Anybody?"

It was Ugo who answered. "What is it, Nino?" The men's voices carried through the open window.

They couldn't make out Nino's words, but they

273

caught the urgency in them, and she sat up straight, knowing her own worries were about to take second place to another's. She was still wearing her old white nightgown, and she picked up one of Frank's shirts from the pile she'd made on the floor, slipping it on as she had so many other mornings. "Something's wrong," she said, more resignation than worry in her voice. "We'd better go."

"Christ," he said, getting up and following her. "More wrong than this?"

Ugo's eyes gave nothing away as they walked into the kitchen together, only nodding toward Nino sitting in the other chair, wringing his cap in his hands, his face contorted into deep lines of worry. "It is Enza," Ugo explained. "She is gone. Salvatore said she went out in the middle of the night. Apparently she does this often but always returns. That is why he did not tell anyone until this morning."

"Do you know where she went?" she asked Nino, knowing even as the words came out this was a stupid question. He wouldn't be here if he knew. He wouldn't be here unless he thought something was terribly wrong.

Nino shook his head. "Maria Serena thought she might have gone to find Frank."

She translated for Frank, almost hearing as she did so the wheels turning in Maria Serena's mind. With Ugo back, Frank would honorably step

274

aside. He was free again, and Maria Serena could get on with her plan to marry Enza off to him. What did she say at Tazio's wedding? *She can go to America with him and send money home. It would be so good for the family.*

But Enza wouldn't look for Frank. It wasn't Frank she loved but Hans, the German soldier, buried up near Brigand's Den, far enough away from the family that his murder would not be linked to them. She pictured Nino carrying the boy's body up the steep path, over the treacherous rocks, laying him out in a shallow grave. *I only wish there'd been enough to kill me too,* Enza had told her only last week. It was inevitable, Graziella thought. From the day it happened, this was to be the result. And now Ugo was back, and Enza saw herself forced into a marriage she didn't want. In Enza's unhappy mind, this was the only way out.

Graziella could see they were waiting for her answer. Frank, Nino, Ugo, all looking at her expectantly. "I think she's gone to Brigand's Den," she said.

Looking startled, Nino opened his mouth as if to ask why, but nothing came out. Clearly Enza was right. Nino knew. He knew but couldn't bring himself to acknowledge it. He got up from his chair, and Ugo followed, a little slower than Nino, pain flashing in his eyes. He closed them for just a moment, and when he opened them again, they were clear. "I think we'd better get Father Paolo," Ugo said, his words causing Nino to make a sound like a small animal in distress.

Graziella went up to her room and pulled on her plain brown dress. She threw the nightgown and Frank's shirt onto the unmade bed, seeing the indentation in the pillow where Ugo had rested his head. It caught her by surprise, making her catch her breath sharply, this everyday little thing missed for so long, now there. She turned away and hurried down the stairs. The book Frank had given her was still on the table, a ribbon marking her place, the edges stained from when Ugo had spilled his wine. It seemed impossible to think she could simply pick up where she'd left off, that all the characters would be unaffected by the events of the last day. Frank's shirt still sat in the bottom of the sink, hardened into a mass of wrinkles. Expecting Enza to be in a state of shock at the very least, she took down a vial of *Arnica* from the kitchen cupboard and slipped it into her pocket. Then, taking a deep breath, she went to the path where Maria Serena and Tazio had since joined the others.

Maria Serena was visibly shaken to discover Frank hadn't seen Enza. "Why Brigand's Den?" she asked Graziella. "They tell me you think she's at Brigand's Den." Graziella could see she didn't share Nino's doubts. To Maria Serena, the story remained the official version—her daughter had been raped by a German soldier. She was genuinely perplexed as to why Enza would climb all the way to Brigand's Den in the night.

"It was something she said to me," Graziella said quietly.

And now Maria Serena was even more confused. "Said? Said? When did Enza say anything?"

Graziella didn't answer, telling her instead they should get Father Paolo. Maria Serena took a step back, suddenly unsteady, and Tazio took her arm. Graziella could see the incomprehension and worry in Tazio's eyes, but he didn't question her. "Let's go then" was all he said.

It was Graziella who spoke to Father Paolo. She stepped into the dim coolness of his house, whispering so as to not let Annunziata hear. She didn't tell him everything though. Only that she feared Enza might have harmed herself, that it might already be too late. Silently, he fingered the cross of his rosary and took his black hat from the peg.

They followed the road into Il Paesino, more running than walking down the steep hill, startling the small iridescent lizards sunning themselves on the roadside and sending them scurrying. They were a good hour's walk from Brigand's Den, and she feared for Ugo's strength. But when she questioned him, he protested, insisting he was already much better. "Thanks to you," he said with a strained smile, his eyes traveling to Frank's back.

In Il Paesino, about twenty men and women and at least as many children had gathered in the square in front of the village church to discuss yet again the news of Ugo's homecoming. Overjoyed to see him now, they crossed themselves and cried, embracing him, holding out their babies to be kissed. Children clung to his legs and begged to be picked up. Frank stood back, the man they'd once regarded with such curiosity now invisible in Ugo's presence. Graziella caught his eye before looking away again.

Ugo greeted them all hurriedly, making excuses. He was very sorry, he said, but he could not stay and talk right now. He promised to be at church on Sunday to sing, but could they please excuse him as the family had matters to attend to. Still, the villagers were reluctant to let him go, and they followed him up the steps behind the village church, past the post office, only dropping away at the entrance of the path that led through the woods up to Brigand's Den.

It was a steep climb. They were out of the sun now, but the air was hot and close, and Graziella felt the sweat trickle down her back. She lifted her hair from the nape of her neck as she watched Ugo just in front of her. He kept up, but his breathing was heavy. She was just hoping he'd had something to eat for breakfast when he pulled a piece of bread wrapped in cloth from his pocket. He turned and offered it to her. "Here. I don't think you had anything to eat this morning."

"You have it. You need it more."

"I ate this morning. Please, take it." She did, but he didn't leave her side. "Did you . . . ," and he nodded in Frank's direction. "Did you stay with him? You were not there when I woke up. I missed you." He spoke in Venetian. There was no accusation in his voice, only sadness. Frank, walking behind Tazio, turned at the sound of their voices. She held up the bread to him, but he shook his head, looking from her to Ugo, as if knowing their conversation had nothing to do with bread before turning his attention back to the path.

"No," she told Ugo. "I went there to think. He came back this morning, just before Nino arrived." Not exactly the truth. *Before the sun,* Frank had said to her. *Before the music started.*

Behind her she could hear Maria Serena talking in urgent, hushed tones to Nino, who kept repeating, "We'll find her, we'll find her. I'm sorry, I'm sorry." Every once in a while Maria Serena called out Enza's name but received only an echo in reply.

Bringing up the rear was Father Paolo, who murmured Hail Marys in between his attempts to soothe Maria Serena. "I don't know, dear," Graziella heard him say. "But Graziella, well, she sometimes knows things."

Sometimes is right, Graziella thought as she

glanced at Ugo. *Why didn't I know he was still alive?* she asked herself for what seemed like the thousandth time. *Or maybe I did, but there was Frank. Dad was wrong about me being a healer. I may know the properties of plants, but when it comes to people, I'm hopeless.* She hadn't known Ugo was alive, she hadn't known Frank was lying, she couldn't do anything about Giovanni's dementia, and she had failed Enza as well as Maria Lisabetta and her family before that. She'd even failed to save her own brother.

She tried to divert these thoughts by concentrating on the undergrowth. There was *pungitopo,* or "prick the mouse" in English, with its razor-sharp leaves that grew in impenetrable clumps. A lone foxglove with dusky pink petals beside a clump of wolf's mouth, no longer flowering. Goat's beard, or wild asparagus, gone to seed now. *Lamium maculatum* too, at the base of every mauve flower a drop of sweet nectar, prized by the children. And out of a fallen log, the mushroom *Phallus impudicus,* literally "impudent phallus" after its shameless shape.

Then she stopped naming them, listing their medicinal uses instead. Soothes sore throats. Sedative. Diuretic. Digestive aid. Anesthetic. Antiseptic. Aphrodisiac. Dewormer. For boils, cankers, ulcers, eczema, rashes. Use with caution. Overdose induces vomiting, delirium, cardiac arrest, certain death.

The higher they went, the more distraught Maria Serena became, and Tazio dropped back to walk with her. He touched Graziella's arm as he passed, and she murmured her thanks for this small sign of support. "Someone else better go first," she heard Frank say. "I don't know the way." He dropped behind as Ugo took the lead. If Ugo was tired he didn't complain, moving doggedly on. She remembered those winter nights over the Pyrenees as they fled Spain. The steps that never tired or faltered despite his injury and hunger. *The Bolsheviks,* he had told her as they trudged through the snow, *spelled out alphabets on signs and carried them on their backs as they marched to save their revolution. Everything was against them, and yet they wanted to learn how to read. A real revolutionary,* he added, *is motivated by love.* Why should she think of these things now? Because that was the Ugo she knew.

They stopped at the fork in the path, one way leading down over the rocks and into Brigand's Den and the other taking them higher, to the clearing above. Graziella told them all to wait, saying it was best she go alone.

"You cannot go alone," Ugo said in English, breathing hard. "It is too dangerous. One slip of the foot and you could go over the edge." He sat down heavily on a fallen log. "But I am too weak right now. Frank, you must go with her."

Graziella looked from Ugo to Frank, wondering

what it must have cost Ugo to send Frank in his place but doing it anyway because he trusted Frank most among everyone there to keep her safe.

Frank went in front of her, and they grasped at the roots and branches as they descended over the smooth mossy rocks, their feet searching for grip among the crevices. A fluorescent green lizard shot out from under her foot, and Frank swore as he grasped the sharp leaves of *pungitopo*. It was only a matter of minutes before they emerged at Brigand's Den, a rock with an opening that went all the way through like the keyhole of a giant's door. They stepped into the opening, and it felt safe inside this rock, clinging to the side of the mountain.

Around them was scattered the debris of the men who'd found refuge here during the war: rusty tin cans, bits of rag that had once been clothing or bandages, the remains of a campfire, burned at a terrible risk of detection. And on the rocks, charcoaled messages, fading now: *A longo vive la rivoluzion! Viva l'Italia! Carlo ama Julia—bella ciao.*

They stepped through to the other side. Frank, startled by the suddenness with which the rock ended, put out an arm as if to keep her from plummeting to the plain below. Graziella stared down through the trees growing out of the mountainside and wondered how far it was to the bottom, should one take that step. She saw herself for a moment standing at the edge of a different cliff in her nightgown, called back by Frank. But there hadn't been anyone up here for Enza. She could still hear Maria Serena frantically calling for her daughter. Frank at Graziella's side followed her gaze down the mountainside. "Do you think . . . ?" he started to ask before breaking off.

"I don't know. I hope not. Now that we're here, I don't feel she has." She looked to Frank, and for a moment her thoughts were not on Enza but on the many ways he was still a stranger to her. All this time, listening, knowing, and not saying anything. *Why didn't you just tell me?* she thought once more, and yet right now, she couldn't have said what difference it would've made.

She heard the sound of someone sliding down the rock behind them, and they looked back to see Nino. "It wasn't down here," he said, pointing upwards. "I didn't come down here. I took the path to the clearing. Maybe she's there. Maybe she didn't come down here." Nino started back up now, not the way they'd come but behind Brigand's Den, grasping hold of branches and rocks as he climbed.

She and Frank exchanged glances before following him. She slipped near the top, and Frank caught her, holding her hand until she regained her footing, pulling her over the edge and into the clearing. It was a flat grassy area encircled by low scrubby bushes, and they saw nothing until a hedgehog emerged from behind what looked more like a small pile of dirty laundry than a girl. Nino let out a cry and was beside her in an instant, gathering the limp figure into his arms, crying into her neck.

Graziella and Frank ran over to them as Tazio, Father Paolo, and Maria Serena arrived at the clearing. Enza's eyes were closed, her skin cold despite the heat, her arms and legs scratched and bleeding from brambles and *pungitopo*. Graziella picked up her arm, her own heart resuming its beat only after finding a pulse, weak as it was. The climb, the night spent on the mountain—in Enza's frail, half-starved state, it had all been too much for her. No, she hadn't jumped, but Graziella knew the girl had no will to live either, that to die here by her lover's grave was the best she could hope for. Graziella looked up into anxious faces. "She's in shock, but she's alive" was all she said.

There was a murmur of relief and a brief prayer of thanks from Father Paolo as Graziella took the *Arnica* from her pocket and poured a little between Enza's parted lips. Enza grimaced but didn't open her eyes. "We need to get her home," Graziella said.

Holding Enza tightly against his chest, Nino struggled to his feet. He moved across the grassy clearing toward the steep path that took them back down. Graziella again pictured Nino with the boy's body draped over his shoulder, the long terrible climb in the night. The boy must have been far heavier than Enza, and yet Nino could hardly carry her. The fear for his daughter that had given him strength then had taken everything from him now, and his steps trembled.

"Let me, Nino," Frank said, and Nino nodded as Frank took the limp girl.

Tazio put his arm around his father. "Let's go, Papà. She's going to be okay."

Graziella looked back at the clearing, peaceful in the sun, a bright blue butterfly skimming over the grass. No outward signs of the secret it kept. When she turned, it was to see Father Paolo looking from Enza to Nino, those dark eyes usually so full of good humor now serious and troubled. *He knows too,* Graziella thought. Nino would have made his confession, though he would have told the official version, the one he forced himself to believe in, not the real story, that his daughter was in love with the man he'd killed. But Father Paolo was clearly putting the pieces together, realizing what had been missing from Nino's confession was destroying both father and daughter.

Ugo was waiting for them at the fork in the path. He embraced Maria Serena as she threw herself tearfully into his arms, reassuring her as he watched Frank walk by with the barely conscious

Enza. The two men exchanged brief nods, their expressions inscrutable.

Graziella would've liked to walk alone, but she soon found herself alongside Father Paolo. Trickles of sweat ran out from under his black hat and down his forehead. "Another happy ending. First Ugo and now this." He dabbed at his brow with his handkerchief as he spoke. If he'd been troubled earlier, he now covered it with his usual layer of cheer.

"I don't know how happy it is," she said. "Enza's a very desperate girl. But you're right. I feared the worst, and thankfully that didn't happen."

"Thanks be to God for that!"

Ahead of them Maria Serena walked beside Ugo, her arm tucked through his. "You talk to Enza," she was telling him. "I know she'll listen to you. Tell her you think it would be a good idea if she went back to America with Frank. He would make a good husband for her. I just know she's been better since he was here. It was just that Frank and Graziella . . . and I think she was upset about that."

Ugo looked over his shoulder at Graziella, but she pretended to be interested again in the plants along the side of the path.

"I do not think that is the problem," Ugo said to Maria Serena. "I do not think she wants to marry Frank and go to America. That may be why she ran away. It is time to accept Enza is very sick. I think it is best if she goes to stay with Maria Teresa. She will be safe there, and with the grace of God perhaps she will find some peace. Perhaps if she were there now, this could have been avoided." He said it gently, but there was a hint of reprimand in his voice. Maria Serena, suddenly contrite, mumbled her agreement.

It will finally happen now, Graziella thought. *She'll listen to Ugo.*

Father Paolo touched Graziella's arm. "I know this is difficult for you, but I think under the circumstances God will be very understanding. I don't mean to rush you, but whenever you're ready to make your confession, I'd be happy to hear you."

She looked at Father Paolo, not understanding at first until she followed his gaze to Frank's back. She felt slightly irritated with his implication of adultery, but she knew he meant well and was only trying to be helpful. Their eternal souls were his ultimate concern after all. Of course he'd assume she'd return to Ugo. She did her best to smile. "The first thing I'd have to confess is that I'm not Catholic."

Father Paolo laughed lightly. "I know, my dear Graziella. I knew from the first day I met you. Everyone noticed. You cross yourself in all the wrong directions. Up, down, and every which way. You look like you're shooing flies."

Back in the village, the crowd had grown. Everyone seemed to be there, and Graziella glimpsed a BACK SOON sign on the door of the post office as they passed. The news of Enza's disappearance had reached everyone, and they were ready to organize a massive search party if Ugo returned without his niece. They told Ugo this as they pressed around him again. *Thanks be to the Virgin that you and now Enza have been found!* Graziella saw fatigue fighting for precedence over his smile. He was trying so hard to match the enthusiasm of their welcomes, but exhaustion was winning out.

The baker, a man who had lost two sons to the Germans, offered his delivery cart and donkey. "Get Ugo to ride in the cart with her," Frank said to Graziella, laying Enza down gently inside.

She agreed, extracting Ugo from the crowd with apologies. "I'm sorry. Ugo is still very tired from his long journey." She couldn't quite bring herself to say *my husband*. "He'll be at the church on Sunday to sing, as he promised."

She followed along behind the cart, Nino leading the baker's donkey with the promise to send it back with Salvatore as soon as they got Enza home. "There's no hurry, my friend," the baker said. "Today, everyone's here and has already taken their bread." With the exception of a couple of dogs, the crowd was left behind again at the base of the mountain. While the baker's donkey was younger and stronger than Nino's old one, it still needed help to get the cart up the hill.

They stopped to let Ugo out at the house, and Nino took his place on the cart. "I'll be back soon," Graziella told Ugo as Father Paolo led the donkey away. "Get some rest." She looked to Frank, not sure what he intended on doing, not sure if she could ask him to stay with Ugo. It wasn't like they could sit down to a friendly game of chess together.

"I'll stay here," Frank said, resting a hand briefly on her arm. "I'll make sure Ugo gets something to eat."

She nodded her thanks before catching up with the cart and taking Tazio by the arm. "I didn't think Frank would leave for good yesterday," he said.

"I really didn't know," she said. "Maybe it would've been better if he had."

"It's difficult for you, but him too. He's in love with you."

Tell me something that's really true, Frank, she'd said that morning.

That I love you.

They dropped behind the cart, keeping their voices lowered as she related everything Ugo had told her the day before. "I can't believe you didn't know Frank in Venice too."

"I knew Ugo was working with Allied spies, but

I had no idea who. No one person knew everyone in the network. It was supposed to be for our own safety."

She picked up a daisy head that was lying on the path and plucked off the petals one by one. *He loves me, he loves me not. . . .* "Oh, Tazio. I don't know what to do."

"I won't lie to you," Tazio said. "I'm praying with all my might that you stay with Ugo, that you stay with us. But don't underestimate Ugo. He has his family, his faith, his music. He'll be impossibly sad, but he won't wither away. He'll be okay, I swear to you. He's not like Enza. He's stronger. That he walked most of the way home to be with you shows he's already getting better. He's just tired, and it was a huge shock for him to find Frank here."

"I don't know if you're making a case for me to stay or go," she said with a sigh. They emerged into the clearing, near Maria Lisabetta and Lorenzo's old place. Tazio had already pulled down a great deal of the house and had no doubt been working there that morning when he heard Enza was missing. There were no windows like empty eyes anymore, just a pile of rubble. Beside the road, a beehive-shaped shrine was beginning to take shape, an offering of flowers already placed across it.

She was about to comment on it, how it already felt happier there with the house down, when

Tazio whispered into her ear a little mischie-
vously. "If I show you something after you tend to
Enza, can you keep a secret?"

Tazio was waiting for her a couple of hours later,
the shrine having grown in her absence. "It's good
mortar," he said as he closed the sack. "It was on
its way to Verona, but the stationmaster thought a
few bags wouldn't be missed in the inventory." He
wiped his hands on his pants. "How's Enza
doing?"

"She was sleeping when I left," she said, setting
down the pail of food Maria Serena had sent along
for him. "She'll be okay though. At least physi-
cally."

"And Papà?" Tazio asked pointedly. He, like
Father Paolo, was clearly piecing the story
together.

"Your father is almost a greater concern. Enza
really is his favorite, and he's being torn apart by
guilt. He and Father Paolo are set for a long talk.
He needs to find forgiveness. But he's not the only
one." She told Tazio her own role in the mess.
"My mother used to say that good intentions pave
the pathway to hell. It seems to be the story of our
lives."

"Nonsense," he said, hugging her. "I'm sure
God would put in a very good word with the Devil
for us. We're doing pretty well, considering. And
a lot of that is thanks to you." He pulled back and

gave her a smile. "Do you still want to see my secret?"

She nodded and followed him to a small stone toolshed. The shed door creaked on rusted hinges, and she waited outside while Tazio kicked at the dirty straw on the floor until he found what he was looking for. "Do you see that?" he asked, and she peered into the gloom at a trapdoor. "I can't tell you how nervous I was to open it. I imagined Lorenzo burying an entire German regiment in here. I expected to find their bones, if I didn't find them still alive."

Graziella laughed a little nervously. Even though Tazio had already eliminated this as a possibility, she still half expected to see a wisp of something ghostlike escape from under the door.

"Ready?" Tazio said dramatically, giving a bad impression of a trumpet fanfare.

"I'm ready," she said, laughing in earnest now. "You can't make me wait any longer. It's not fair!" He was teasing her now, and she was grateful for the distraction. If she were to leave Italy, she would miss Tazio. Rosanna too, and she'd never know their child. But before the thought could become too sobering, Tazio swung open the trapdoor, and it hit the wall with a thud.

"I don't see anything," she said, moving closer. "It's just moldy old straw. You're not playing a joke on me, are you?"

"Don't be so impatient," he said, kneeling down

and pushing aside the straw. A moment later he held up a green glass bottle.

"It's wine," she exclaimed. "Lorenzo was hiding wine out here. God, what we wouldn't have given to know this was here last winter. I can't believe he was keeping it from his own family."

"Those were my thoughts entirely. But then I realized I didn't recognize the bottles. They aren't ours. They're thicker, more expensive. They're packed in two wooden cases." He pushed more of the hay aside.

"You think someone else hid them here? Maybe after the house was burned down?"

He shrugged. "Could be. Or Lorenzo stole it and kept it from us after all. We all knew he wasn't right in the end. And don't go beating yourself up over that now. You did what you could. Perfection is a trait God keeps for Himself."

"You sound like Father Paolo."

"Maybe I should've become a priest like Mama wanted. Although it would've made marrying Rosanna difficult." He held up a bottle with a yellowed and faded label. "Look, French brandy." He pulled out another. "And this is champagne. A few have lost their corks, but most of them look to be in good condition."

"What are you going to do with it all?"

"I don't know. That's what I was hoping you'd help me with. It would fetch a good price somewhere, but we could also have one really big party, which I'd love you to be here for. We could have a going-away party if you decide to leave, but I don't know if anyone would have the heart for that. Least of all me." He looked at her seriously. "So, what do you say we open the brandy now? I'm sure this is as good a time as any other."

She tried to find reasons to decline. She needed to get home, to see if Ugo was all right, to see if Frank was still there. To pack her bags or tell Frank to go without her. But she couldn't. She couldn't have turned her footsteps in the direction of home if she tried, and so she found herself agreeing, following Tazio out of the shed and into the dappled light beneath the poplars. She watched as he took out his pocketknife and drove it into the cork at an angle, working it out before holding it up to his nose and sniffing it. "Whew! Potent!" He took a cautious sip, then handed her the bottle. "That's powerful stuff. Careful now—we could get the whole mountain drunk on the cork alone!"

She sniffed at the bottle, the smell evoking the empty flask she'd found in Frank's bag, only more medicinal. But still, she wasn't prepared for just how strong it was. Burning its way down her throat and into her stomach, it took her breath away. Tears sprang to her eyes, and soon she was coughing and gasping for breath.

"You were only supposed to take a little sip!" Tazio said, rescuing the bottle from her hand as she tried to catch her breath. He patted her vigorously on the back, and now she was laughing.

"That's awful!" she gasped at last. She staggered over to a rock, sinking onto it and holding out her hand to Tazio. "Give it to me!"

"I don't know. Are you sure you're not drunk already?" he asked teasingly, holding the bottle against his chest.

"No. But I think it would be a very good idea." She made room for him on the rock, and he sat down next to her. He took a swig before passing it to her, and she sipped at it again, much more cautiously this time. "I remember my father drinking brandy with guests after dinner. He'd give me a sip, but I don't remember it being this strong. Do you think it gets stronger with age?"

"If it does, it must've been here since Napoleon invaded Italy. Maybe *he* buried it in the shed."

She laughed again before stopping abruptly and looking down at the bottle in her lap. "Oh, what am I going to do, Tazio?"

"Well, I'd say right now you're getting drunk."

"You know what I'm talking about."

He took the bottle back. "Well, there's always a third option."

"And that is?"

"You could run away with me," he said with a smile. "We could become pirates. Sail the seven seas. Take over French ships, steal their brandy, and stay drunk all the time."

She really couldn't have expected Tazio to solve this for her. Still, she appreciated his efforts to cheer her up, and so she played along. "I think Rosanna might have something to say about that."

"Oh, Rosanna can come too. I don't have any objections to having two beautiful wives. I think it's expected of pirates. Maybe I'll get a wife from every country." He took another sip and held out the bottle to her again. She shook her head, and he jammed the cork into the neck of the bottle and put it on the ground beside him. "I have another secret," he said, his voice serious now. "Rosanna thinks she might be pregnant."

Graziella could hear the hope in his voice, the pride of parenthood already there. "She is," she said. "I knew at the funeral. I think I knew at the wedding, but I confused it with her happiness at finally marrying you. My guess is a girl and that she's going to arrive a little shy of nine months from your wedding date. Congratulations, you're very lucky."

He put his arm around her and hugged her. "I know. Whatever you do, don't tell my mother about the 'little shy of nine months' part. I was counting on you to tell her the baby was early. I'm sorry you might not be here to deliver her. Maybe we'll call her Graziella. Or your Canadian name— Grace. If you decide to stay with us, we'd like you and Ugo to be the godparents.

"I know it has to be your choice, and I want you to do what will make you happy. But still, I'd . . . no, not just me. I think it's pretty safe to say, we'd *all* like you to stay." He picked up the bottle again. "Another sip for courage?"

11

They sat in the shade of the chestnut tree, so engrossed in conversation they didn't see her as she came around the corner of the barn. Between them an upturned log held a wine bottle and a packet of Frank's Lucky Strikes. Graziella paused, looking from one to the other, thinking how there was nothing in this scene to indicate these men were anything other than two old friends escaping the afternoon heat together.

"It's up to the courts now," Frank was saying as he poured more wine for himself. He held up the bottle questioningly, and Ugo placed his cup next to Frank's to be refilled as well. "They'll be brought to trial. Justice and all that."

"You Americans have a lot of faith in your system of justice," Ugo replied wearily. "It is not so easy here."

"Which is why the revenge killings are happening, I know," Frank said. "But innocent people have been killed too and—"

"I don't think he's trying to justify them, Frank," Graziella interjected, the sound of her voice causing them both to turn.

Ugo was the first to recover. "Frank knows I would not do that," he said, his smile erasing some of the fatigue from his face. "But where have you been? We were about to send out a search party."

"You don't look like you're about to send a search party," she said, wondering if she didn't feel a little resentful of the two of them talking so easily together while she tore herself apart over them. If Tazio's brandy had given her any courage, she didn't feel it now. She just felt terribly tired and a little weak. She hadn't eaten anything since Ugo had given her the piece of bread on the way to Brigand's Den, and it was so very hot. She leaned against the rough bark of the old chestnut for support.

"How's Enza doing?" Ugo asked. Sparrows flitted at his feet as if expecting that he, like Giovanni, would shower them with crumbs.

"A little better," she said. "She's sleeping—something you're supposed to be doing right now."

Ugo opened his mouth to speak but was interrupted by Frank's somewhat strained laughter. "There are a few people I'd like to tell that to. The great *Il Monaco*'s wife telling him to take a nap! It sure would get some laughs."

"I am sure it would," Ugo said without smiling, still addressing Graziella. Now that she was here, it wasn't quite so easy between the two men. "You look a little strange. Are you sure you are all right?" He stood up slowly, and the sparrows retreated slightly to the stones edging the fire pit. "Would you like some wine? Or maybe some water?"

She waved him off, thinking she probably owed Ugo an apology for being so short with him. "I'm okay, thanks. Just a little too much to drink. I should probably have a nap myself."

"You're drunk?" Frank said incredulously. "What've you been drinking?"

"French brandy." She wiped the sweat from her forehead with her sleeve. "Tazio found some in Lorenzo's shed. It's a long story."

"It can wait," Ugo said. "You should come inside with me. You need your rest too." He spoke in Venetian, excluding Frank from the conversation.

She looked from Ugo to Frank and back, feeling if she were to follow Ugo into the house now it would seem like her decision was made. "I don't know, Ugo," she said in English, stepping away from him. "I just don't know what to do."

He looked at her, the realization of just how difficult this was for her clearly written on his face. She saw the fear there and knew she couldn't put off this decision any longer. He didn't have the physical or mental strength to keep wondering whether she was going to stay or go. And if he didn't have the strength to cope with this level of uncertainty, how could he cope with the reality of her actually leaving?

Tazio had said she should follow her heart. Ugo, he'd said, would be all right. He had his music, his faith, his family. But she knew those things weren't enough. His fall from grace had been a hard one, and he was only too aware of those who'd suffered as a result. And as once she'd known she was stronger than Westley, she knew now she was stronger than Ugo and the only person who could help him. She couldn't leave him any more than he could have left her in a burned-out field hospital in Spain all those years ago. As he had once saved her, it was now her turn to save him. It wasn't because she was his wife but because it was the right thing to do.

At the same time, she knew Frank would be okay without her. He would be sad, certainly, his love maybe even turning to anger, but he would ultimately find happiness. He had that easy way about him. He would never be alone, never be lonely. She pictured Frank dancing with another woman. They were both laughing, and his laughter was genuine. Someday he might tell this woman about the war, but he wouldn't tell it all— not about the time Ugo's men were tortured, not about Ugo, not about herself, though sometimes in the night she knew he would remember.

It was true she had come to long for the escape Frank could provide. An easier life, away from this country ravaged by war. She had dreamed of his children, of a violet dress, of going dancing.

And probably it would've worked, probably they would've been happy together—had Ugo not come back.

But Ugo had come back. She could still go to New York with Frank, put on that dress and dance all night, but when the music stopped and she dropped into a chair with breathless laughter, she would envision Ugo here, sitting in Giovanni's chair, the sparrows at his feet, his violin on his lap, looking out over the valley, alone.

During her silence nobody spoke or dared look at each other. Finally, Ugo turned and without a word walked slowly toward the house. She took a few steps after him, only getting as far as his chair, leaning on the back for support as she watched him go inside.

Frank stood up and held out his hands to her, but she shook her head, and he lowered them. "I'm so sorry, Frank," she said, gripping the chair for strength. She couldn't have it both ways, be both Grace in love with Frank and Graziella in love with Ugo. She was Graziella now and had been ever since she'd met Ugo. It had been so nice to be Grace again, but she couldn't go back in time. She could only go forward, having hopefully learned something along the way. "I have to stay."

"I said I wouldn't go until you told me to. Are you telling me now?"

"I don't think I can tell you that. But this is what I have to do. This one I can't get wrong."

"It's because I lied to you, isn't it?"

"No. I've forgiven you for that. I understand why you did it. And what's done is done. It's what happens next. It's what I do now that's important. I have to get this right."

"But what about you?" he asked, pleading with her now, as if knowing this was his last chance. "Is it right for you?"

She nodded slowly. "Yes. If only because I couldn't live with anything else."

"And me?"

She pictured him again dancing with the woman who wasn't her and saw the contentment in his eyes. "You'll be all right, Frank. I know you'll be."

"How can you know that?" he asked almost angrily.

She could only shake her head. "I don't know, Frank. I just do. You'll remember that when you get back, won't you?"

He didn't answer her, just stood there as she walked a little unsteadily into the house. Ugo wasn't in the kitchen, but she could hear his footsteps on the floor above. His violin sat in the open case on the kitchen table. She took a plum from the counter and forced herself to eat it before pulling down a bottle of alcohol infused with lavender and pouring a generous amount into a bowl of water. Taking a cloth, she dropped it into the bowl and took it upstairs.

Ugo was lying on his side, staring at the wall. She placed the lavender water on the chair beside the bed before going to the window and closing the shutters, leaving just a narrow beam of light.

He turned to her as she sat down on the bed beside him. She wrung out the cool, fragrant cloth and placed it on his forehead. Then she unbuttoned his shirt and pressed her palm over the wound by his heart, feeling no infection, the tissue healing. *That was the easy part,* she thought.

"I am sorry," he said, staring at the ceiling now. "I should not have acted like that out there. I do not think I realized until now how close I am to losing you."

She took the cloth from his forehead, put it back in the water, wrung it out, and replaced it. "You're not going to lose me, Ugo," she said quietly. "Not now, not ever."

"Are you sure of that?" he asked. "He could give you children. He could take you away from all this."

"Do you remember when you proposed and I told you that you were enough for me? I meant it then, and I mean it now. When I thought you were gone, I wished we had a child together so I could have someone who reminded me of you, someone who would've loved you as much as I did. That was my only regret, but now you're back and so it's gone. Anyway, it's impossible to compare the children I can't have with you with the ones I could have with Frank. I don't know if that makes any sense, but I just don't know how else to describe it."

"But I cannot ask you to stay out of pity for me," Ugo said. "I do not think I could live with myself if I thought you were doing that. Sacrificing yourself for me. There are enough things I have to live with. If the right thing for you to do is go with Frank, I will have to live with that too. As much as I want you to stay, to have you here with me and know you would rather be with Frank . . ." He broke off with a shake of his head.

She placed her fingers over his lips. "I've made up my mind, Ugo, and I'm not going to change it." She put as much conviction into her words as possible, and if she was scared, she wasn't going to let it show in her voice. "I promise. Everything is going to be okay."

"How do you know that?" he asked, almost echoing Frank's words to her earlier.

She lay down beside him, her cheek against his arm, and told him about her dream from that morning. The greenhouse on the roof, the rose-colored sky, her mother and father, his music, the feeling of home, of peace. Somewhere in the telling he fell asleep, but she told him about Westley and the snowflakes and the winged lions anyway, listening to him sleep, hoping it was all true, until sometime in the early evening just as dusk began to fall, she too finally slept.

• • •

When she awoke, it was dark and her throat was painfully dry. She sat up on the edge of the bed, her feet on the cool wood floor, aware now of a dull pounding in her head. She sat still for a moment, pressing her hand over her hot forehead. Tazio's French brandy, no doubt. She'd had nothing to drink since then. She didn't even know how long she'd been asleep, if it was still the same day or not. She still wore her dress, and her unplaited hair was tangled around her shoulders. Beside her Ugo's breathing was deep and calm.

She stood up, the pounding in her head becoming more pronounced, and went down the stairs, feeling her way through the darkness of the kitchen to the sink, almost crying out when she stubbed her toe against a table leg. The water pail was on the counter next to the sink, and she scooped out cup after cup of the oaky-tasting water, stopping only to catch her breath.

She heard a distant rumble of thunder as she replaced the cup on the counter. She thought of Giovanni over at Nino's, wondering if he'd feel the storm's arrival, if it would wake him, if he'd start calling for Ugo. How grateful she'd been to Frank that night so many weeks ago, holding Giovanni in his arms. *Now I lay me down to sleep,* he'd prayed with him. After it had stopped raining, they'd gone outside and he'd made the bark boats and they'd run down the muddy hill.

It's good luck to see a rabbit at dawn, he'd said, about to kiss her, and she'd wanted him to but was so afraid. *Maybe Ugo will come home today!* And then she'd been sorry when he'd turned away.

She lit the lantern on the table, turning down the wick to lower the flame, then picked it up and went to the door. She'd forgotten to feed her hens that evening and couldn't remember if she'd fed them in the morning before they'd set out to find Enza.

The scent of rain hung in the air, and the thunder rumbled closer now. Above her the clouds parted and the moon, bright and full, hung briefly over the valley before another bank of clouds closed over it. This was an end-of-summer storm, a harbinger of autumn, one that would bring a cool morning and talk of the impending grape harvest.

She went into the barn to get the grain, pausing at the bottom of the loft steps, wondering if Frank was up there staring into the darkness, listening to her footsteps. She would do the right thing and stay with Ugo but not if she had to say good-bye to Frank in the stillness of the night. In all likelihood, however, Frank had already left. She imagined him stretched on a bench outside the dark station in Il Paesino, waiting for the dawn and a train. The train that would've taken them to Switzerland had already left earlier that day and who knew where the next one would go, but he wouldn't care. Any train, anything, just to leave.

Holding a scoop of grain, she closed the barn door and let herself into the henhouse, the door creaking ever so slightly on its rusty hinges. The hens stirred on their roosts, cocking their heads toward the lantern before settling again, seemingly unperturbed by her neglect. She returned to the yard and poured the grain into the trough. After dumping the remains of their water pan, she went to refill it at the well.

She left the lantern hanging outside the henhouse door and walked over to the bench by the cliff just as the first drops began to fall. Hesitant at first, the rain soon gathered strength, becoming torrential in a matter of seconds, soaking her dress and hair. She heard the thunder again, even deeper now, and she wondered if Ugo would awaken, if he would reach for her and wonder if she'd already broken her promise to him.

She closed her eyes and raised her face to the rain, feeling it hard and cool against her skin. She held out her arms and let the rain fall between her fingers. Five weeks ago, clouds had filled the valley and she'd stood here at the cliff's edge and felt its pull. She'd been dreaming of Ugo, had felt him kiss her, and had woken to find it wasn't real. If only the rain could wash it all away, everything that kept her from being anything but happy he was here now.

A sound behind her made her open her eyes. She turned away from the cliff, her arms dropping back to her sides. The lantern, protected under the roof overhang, was still burning feebly where she'd left it, a small beacon among the rain-soaked sumacs. She could see nothing that would've made her turn until she noticed the door to the barn was open. She had closed it after she'd gone for the grain and before she'd entered the henhouse—she was sure of that.

The lantern flared briefly, and she caught sight of a figure among the shadows. It was so dark and she was beyond the reach of the lantern's light, yet he would know she was out here. She stood still, the rain almost icy now as it ran down her face.

He struck a match, shielding it with his hand as he bent over it to light his cigarette. She caught for a moment the downcast eyes, the shock of blond hair, then the match was out and there was only the red glow of his cigarette. She was shivering now, gripping the back of the bench. He had run to her once. Only that time, he'd been here by the bench and she up there in the window of the room where Ugo now slept.

There was a sudden gust of wind, sweeping the rain up with it. The lantern on the side of the barn swayed and went out as the barn door closed. She didn't know if it was the fault of the wind or if he'd closed it himself. But if it had been him, he didn't open it again either, and so she wrapped her arms around herself and made her way through the blackness back to the house.

• • •

It was the sound of the motorcycle that woke her as the morning light slipped through the shutters. She heard Lupo's bark and voices too. The *Our Gang* kids. Frank must've found gas somewhere and gone to pick up the motorcycle from Clario's. She imagined the children running behind it. No, he would let them ride, each taking turns sitting behind him, their little arms clutched around his waist, holding on with perhaps a tinge of terror but surely sheer joy.

Ugo stirred beside her but didn't wake, his breathing peaceful. *Sleep that knit up the raveled sleeve of care.* He had slept all that previous afternoon, that evening, not noticing when she'd stepped out of her wet dress and climbed back in beside him, her hair still soaked from the rain. Shivering, she'd pulled a blanket over them both, and with his body warming hers, she'd fallen asleep again, though it was the shadow of Frank standing in the door of the barn that crept at the edges of her dreams.

She turned over now, thinking how she would stay here, wait until the motorcycle pulled away, and spare herself the painful good-bye. But she couldn't, if only because she didn't want her last memory of Frank to be of him wordlessly shutting the barn door in the rainy night, knowing she was out there.

Her dress still lay where she'd dropped it, damp

and wrinkled, and so she pulled on her brown-flowered Sunday dress and quickly combed out her tangled hair in front of the mirror. *No one else in the world has eyes that color—like the light in the evening over the Alps.* How long would it be before Frank's words stopped coming back to her? She looked at Ugo once again and went downstairs.

Outside, the air was crisp. As she had predicted, the rain brought the first hint of autumn. The *Our Gang* kids were gathered around Frank, watching as he secured his saddlebags, desperate to help. Excited by the motorcycle, they had yet to grasp he was leaving for good.

"I know you shouldn't eat chocolate before breakfast," Frank was saying. "But I think we can make an exception today." He opened his pack and took out the two remaining Hershey's bars. He unwrapped them, broke them in half, and passed them around, laughing as the children stuffed them into their mouths. The first time he'd met them, he'd given them gum and she'd told them to say thank you. They didn't remember any better now, but this time she didn't remind them.

Frank stood when he saw her, and Emilia ran over, wanting to be picked up, her doll under her arm, nearly tripping over the long dress she was wearing as she launched herself into Graziella's arms. Graziella clung to her. *Another good reason to stay,* she told herself.

311

Frank picked up the saddlebags and draped them over the motorcycle. "I went down to the village last night to get some gasoline," he said lightly. "Your stationmaster's going to be a rich man soon, the way he keeps skimming off the shipments."

It was just something to say, she knew that. She watched him tie the bags, his hair falling over his forehead. She couldn't see his eyes, only the curve of his nose that had always seemed so perfect to her.

"Did you say good-bye to the rest of the family?" she asked, desperate herself for something to say. "I know they'd want to say good-bye."

"I don't think they'll be all that sorry to see me go. They're uncomfortable around me now that Ugo's home." Frank shrugged on his pack. "Still, you'll say good-bye for me?"

"Of course."

"And Ugo too?"

She nodded.

"I have to go now," Frank said to the boys. "When you're grown up, you come and see me in America, okay? We'll go to a real baseball game. Look after your aunt here, and Emilia too." He spoke with forced cheerfulness, ruffling all their hair in turn. Graziella did her best to keep her voice bright as she translated what Frank had said.

"Is Frank going back to America on his motorcycle?" Mario wanted to know.

"A baseball game in America!" Salvatore shouted.

And then there was just Emilia to say good-bye to, and Graziella couldn't let her go. Frank told her, as he had the boys, to look after her aunt. Seeming to understand better what was really happening, she threw her arms around him and hugged him fiercely, her little face pressed against his T-shirt, her arms encircling his neck. When it became clear she wasn't letting go, Frank gently pulled her hands away. *"Ciao, bella,"* he whispered, and then it was Graziella's neck she was clinging to.

Frank reached over Emilia and stroked Graziella's cheek. She tried to imagine what it would be like to look back through the years and remember this as the last time he touched her. She took his hand and held it hard for a moment before letting go.

"I saw you last night." It was almost a question. She wanted to know what had happened, if only so she wouldn't wonder for the rest of her life.

"I saw you too," he said quietly.

"Then why didn't you say something?"

"Would you've changed your mind if I had?" He held her gaze and, not trusting herself to speak, she nodded. "Then I guess I did the right thing," he said sadly. He climbed on the motorcycle and started it up with a roar.

She didn't move as he pulled onto the path. He

waved and all five of them waved back, and then he was on his way, along the path, past the barn, and into the tunnel of trees. The boys yelled, "Good-bye, Frank! Good-bye! *Ciao! Ciao!*" Emilia struggled to be put down, and then she and Lupo and the boys were all running after him, calling *"Ciao! Ciao!"* as the motorcycle disappeared.

And then Graziella was running too, catching up with the children, then passing them. She ran as fast as she could, past the new shrine, past the field where the Judas tree once stood, past Nino's, then Clario's, and finally Roberto's. The motorcycle was long gone, the children had long given up, but she kept running and running until she couldn't run any longer.

Feet stinging from the stony path, lungs burning, she stumbled down the embankment to where a spring bubbled among the ferns. She sank to her knees and, after drinking deeply of the earthy water, splashed some on her face. Her feet were cut from the path, and she washed them in the spring before grasping the hem of her dress and tearing it away. Carefully, she wound the cloth around her feet before climbing back up the embankment toward the path. Well beyond the farms, the path went through the thick woods before descending into the valley and meeting the main road out of Il Paesino, the road Frank was now taking toward the Swiss border.

Somewhere a woodlark sang, and above her the sky through the dense canopy of leaves was like shattered pieces of sapphire.

It had been over a year since she'd been so far. Ugo had sent a message through the stationmaster, asking her to meet here instead of at the house. There had been too many patrols, and he was afraid of putting her in danger. So she'd made the long walk carrying a basket of food—chestnut flour bread, a stewed chicken, a couple of bottles of wine, the first cherries.

The stationmaster's instructions had been to wait by the spring, and so she'd stood in the middle of the path, peering through the ivy-wrapped trunks, afraid to call out, spinning around when a branch cracked behind her only to discover it was a hare. It had been May, and the air had been heavy with the scent of *Acacia*. The white blossoms of the *Sambucus* tree had floated down, and the forest floor had been covered with flowers like a dusting of snow.

The hare looked up at her without fear before turning and bounding away into the underbrush. But there was no Ugo. She felt a mounting dread that Ugo and his comrades had been caught by the patrols after all, their bodies already hanging in the square in Il Paesino as an example for all who thought they could resist.

She had waited and waited, watching the petals of the *Sambucus* drift down. The hare came back and sat on its haunches, watching her with curiosity as it nibbled at some young shoots before moving on again. Minutes became hours, and every horrible thing she could imagine became more possible.

As the light through the leaves began to fade, she gave up and was about to return home when all of a sudden around her the forest started to move. Dark shapes flitted among the trees, closer and closer, until the trunks seemed to split almost in two as first one man appeared, then another, and another, at least a dozen of them, so quietly, so smoothly they seemed born of the trees. She had turned around as they came out and surrounded her, and still she hadn't known if they were friends or not.

And then, finally, Ugo, smiling, his arms around her, her body flooding with relief and joy in knowing he was safe. The same Ugo who waited for her back at the house. She pictured him there, sitting at the kitchen table, head in his hands, imagining her on the back of Frank's motorcycle, racing out of the Hills.

She was out of the forest now, past the farmhouses and fields, every aching step taking her closer to home, to Ugo. Nothing had been more terrible or more beautiful than this summer. This summer of Frank and this summer of Ugo, of Grace and of Graziella. Her final farewell to what had been and what might have been, and her return to the reality of what was. Her choice, for better or for worse. And as she stepped closer and closer, she started to cry all over again.

She heard the music as she approached the house. But it wasn't Ugo playing. It was someone new to the violin. A note played hesitantly at first, slightly off-key, sliding higher, then lower, the perfect pitch played more confidently, though the bow scratched slightly. She paused, listening a little longer, the notes now making more sense—the opening bars of *"Bella Ciao." Come take me with you. . . . Good-bye sweetheart, bella ciao, bella ciao* . . . She bit her lip to keep from crying again.

The door to the kitchen was open, and there was Emilia. She stood on one of the kitchen chairs, Ugo's violin held under her chin. Ugo was beside her, supporting the instrument with one hand while the other helped her guide the bow. Emilia did not look at her fingers on the strings. She was watching Ugo's face as he murmured encouragement.

Her fingers found the notes confidently now, and instinctively she discovered vibrato, her little finger quivering on the string, the bow drawing out the note. She smiled at Ugo, pleased with this breakthrough. *"Belissima!"* he said. So great was their concentration they didn't see her standing there.

It was Emilia who noticed her first. "Zia Graziella! I'm playing the violin like Zio Ugo!"

"Yes, you are," she whispered. She couldn't tell who was smiling more widely. Ugo's face showed no trace of fatigue. There was only excitement, his eyes sparkling.

"She is amazing, is she not?" he asked.

"She's like you, isn't she?"

"She has a gift for certain." He smiled at Emilia, and she beamed back.

"Will you put down your violin like your first teacher and never play again?" Graziella asked.

"Better. I will play with her. But we have to find her another violin. A small one—this one is too big. I will write to the conservatory in Venice. I am sure they can find her one. She can come to Venice with us. She needs good teachers, not just me. . . ." He broke off, and the expression on his face changed, worry and uncertainty returning again.

But that smile! It had been there while he talked about Emilia. A violin. And going to Venice. There would be a greenhouse on the roof. There would be music again. In that brief smile, in those few words, she glimpsed the Ugo she had always known. And she felt something tremendously uncomplicated. Relief? But more than that even. Hope.

He took the violin from Emilia and placed it on the table. Then he lifted her down and kissed the top of her head. "Go see Daisy now. We will play later, I promise."

"I am sorry," he said after Emilia had left. He put his arms around Graziella. "I was not thinking. Frank is gone, is he not?"

She nodded, her eyes filling with tears again. It would be that way for a while. But she was grateful for his arms around her. For the end of this summer, for the escape autumn would provide, for the promise of Venice, and the hope of their finding something beautiful again.

And then there was Giovanni, standing at the door, Nino supporting him. "I heard music," Giovanni said. He looked at them through his dimmed eyes, taking a step in their direction. "Oh, it's you, Ugo. It's about time you came home."

Epilogue

Fifty Years Later

The letter made its way up the hill on a warm spring afternoon. Graziella put on her reading glasses and opened it in the kitchen doorway. It was the latest of many letters postmarked from the far corners of the globe. Containing messages of sympathy, they came from friends, neighbors, old comrades, distant strangers. From those who loved Ugo's music or had simply loved him. Graziella had pasted them all into a bulging scrapbook to give to Emilia one day. But this one was different.

Dear Grace,

How to begin a letter that's fifty years overdue? I hope for starters it finds you well and that you remember me and that summer at least a little. Please accept my sincerest condolences on Ugo's passing. I know it was over a year ago, but I've made so many false starts on this letter.

She had long ago stopped thinking she would ever hear from Frank again. It had been, as he'd said, almost fifty years. There had been a time when she couldn't sort through a pile of letters without a stomach-churning mixture of dread and hope. She'd made her decision, and it was the right one, but it was not so easy to forget that summer. And somehow it was good to know now it hadn't been easy for him either. That after all these years, it still meant something to him.

The hardest thing I've ever done in my life was go back to America without you. I went home to Vermont, but I was restless there. It was the same as I'd hoped it would be, but I was different. I missed you, and I couldn't seem to tell my family any of that. All they knew was I'd come home without my girl.

That fall I bought a motorcycle, went to California, and got a job in a vineyard. I can't tell you how often I'd look up from my work and see you standing there among the vines in your bare feet and that old brown flowered dress. I can't tell you either how many letters I wrote but never sent.

She pictured him as she read, hearing the cadence of his voice in the words. His hair would no longer be blond, but his nose would still be crooked, and somehow she knew he would still be handsome.

321

Eventually, I did go home and later to college on the GI Bill. I lived in Boston and became an engineer, building bridges in New England. And I married too. I resisted for so long, sure I didn't want anyone but you. I remember you telling me I'd be all right, but no one was more surprised than I was when Heather came into my life. We had five children and twelve grandchildren, and since Heather passed away six years ago, two great-grandchildren. I don't know why, but I never could tell her about that summer.

She had been so close to going with him. If he'd come out to her that night in the rain, it might have been her with all those children and grandchildren. Thinking how strange that seemed now, she looked up from the letter and out the door, the landscape a blur of green hills and blue skies through her reading glasses.

She took the letter upstairs and slipped it between the pages of *Glengarry School Days,* the book he'd given her all those years ago, its edges still stained red from where Ugo had spilled his wine. Setting it back, she looked at the framed photos that lined the top of the dresser. A few of Emilia as a child, a large one of Ugo giving Emilia away on her wedding day, snapshots of Emilia's daughters on the days they were born, and one taken on her own fifty-fifth wedding anniversary, when Ugo had played in Paris. They were atop the Eiffel Tower, his arm around her shoulder, and she thought they still made a handsome couple, though she was always surprised to see how much she'd aged. Ugo showed no sign he had only three months to live.

Is it true, so many reporters and fans had asked after he died, *about his improvisations? Or are they only a myth?* She always smiled and answered evasively, making them more curious than ever. His improvisations had been reserved for his closest friends and family, and he still played them in her dreams.

Even though they'd made it to fifty-five years, at first it hadn't been so easy. Those initial few months together back in Venice as she dealt with her decision and Ugo's slow recovery were among the most difficult. But slowly they slipped into the rhythms of life until finally there was the day Graziella could say with confidence, *I did the right thing. I made the right choice. Not just for Ugo, but for me.*

Soon after their arrival, Ugo built the greenhouse and Graziella opened a flower shop with the plants she grew there. Orchids were what she became famous for, but for those who knew to ask there were also her remedies. Blessed thistle to stimulate breast milk, yarrow for colds, and pots of jasmine mixed with lemon balm for love. *Aristolochia* she never prescribed.

Emilia was with them too, every day more their daughter, making them a family, more healing than any cure Graziella could have concocted. Emilia knew of course the sad story of Lorenzo and Maria Lisabetta. Knew too of the man who'd given her the hair that wreathed her face in golden curls. But it was Ugo and Graziella who'd really been her parents, and she was proud to call herself their daughter.

In later years, as Ugo retired from concert life, he spent more and more of his time in the reading room of the Party offices near the Arsenale. There, over an espresso and the left-wing newspapers, he argued the political topics of the day with old comrades, reviewing past battles and the growing list of obituaries of those who'd fought alongside them. *We won the war,* they still said in wonder, and it was good for Ugo to be reminded of that. No one ever learned what really happened the night of the storehouse raid, just as no one ever knew who paid for the educations of the children of the men who'd lost their lives.

Turning from the photos, Graziella went downstairs again, just in time to see Emilia come through the door, carrying in one hand the case that held Ugo's Stradivarius and in the other a bag of groceries. "How you still climb that hill at your age is amazing," Emilia said, out of breath. "I'm afraid it's just me today. The girls are doing teenager things with their friends, and my darling husband has decided to spend the weekend working. I, on the other hand, am happy to escape. Venice is sweltering, and it's only May. You're smart to spend so much time here in the Hills. . . ." She broke off, looking at Graziella with curiosity. "What's going on? You look like the cat that ate the canary."

I saw you, you know, when Ugo played Carnegie Hall. I came all the way from Boston, hoping you'd be there, and you were, along with Emilia. I was so proud when she played with Ugo for his encore. I wanted to say hello but I lost my courage.

On that trip, the three of them had gone to the top of the Empire State Building, and she of course had thought of Frank. How they were to go up there together on their honeymoon. He was going to buy her a violet dress. *Like your eyes.* She wondered if he remembered that too.

"Your lightness of spirit, that's what Frank gave you," Graziella said after she read the letter to Emilia. Emilia knew about Frank, about how close Graziella had been to leaving with him, but all Emilia could remember was his smile as he swung her through the air.

After dinner, Emilia took out the violin, and Graziella walked to Tazio and Rosanna's to tell them about the letter, soaring arpeggios following her down the wooded path. She found them sitting outside at their garden table, glasses of Rosanna's homemade limoncello between them.

"After all this time," Tazio said, handing her a glass. Tazio had retired a few years back, the management of the vineyard now in the hands of his and Rosanna's two sons and Mario. Clario had died long ago but not before seeing his prosecco make its way into the best restaurants of America, just as he had once dreamed aloud to Frank.

It was Rosanna's idea to bring out the wedding photograph. She dusted off the glass with her apron and set it down on the table between them. There was a time Graziella had avoided looking at this picture. It was supposed to be of the bride and groom surrounded by guests, but Frank was the one front and center, surrounded by adoring children and their equally adoring mothers while Giovanni clung to his arm. Frank seemed oblivious to it all, his smile only for Graziella, who looked up at him from the bottom of the steps.

So many people in the picture were gone now. Giovanni had died only a few months after it was taken, his mind and body slipping away together. He had remembered Ugo to the end, but his final words had been for Frank. *What was the name of that American soldier, the one with the motorcycle? He caught Pippo, you know. Bravest man I ever met.* Enza sitting in the grass with her back to the camera had gone to the convent in October but, despite all their prayers, had faded away to nothingness by the next spring, a heartbroken Nino following her a few years later.

During the long recession that followed the war, one by one almost all the children of the Marias had left, moving to the cities or immigrating to Britain, Canada, America, or Brazil. Indeed, only four stayed: Tazio, Gaspare, Salvatore, and Mario. They rode out the lean years, taking over their fathers' farms, marrying, raising families, becoming more prosperous with every decade, passing on the land to their own children, as Giovanni would've wanted. Gaspare had even converted his childhood home to a bed-and-breakfast for the tourists who came now to hike the trails that crisscrossed the Hills.

"My father and uncles were all a little in love with you," Tazio said, still studying the photo.

"And you weren't, Tazio?" Rosanna asked with a wink at Graziella. Tazio kissed Rosanna and told her she was the love of his life, and Rosanna told him not to forget it unless he wanted to find himself alone in his old age.

I'm thinking of coming to Italy for a visit, to see Venice and your beautiful Hills again. Grace, I remember everything about that summer as if it were yesterday. We were so young then, weren't we? I was foolish, I know,

but I did love you very much, and I've often
thought about you through the years, hoping
always you were happy.
Is it too late for us to be friends?
Yours,
Frank

Graziella found the *Our Gang* boys, now stocky
and graying, on the church steps. They gathered
there on fine evenings to smoke cigars and trade
the day's news, and she joined them whenever she
could. The church had been closed since Father
Paolo's death fifteen years ago. Now the exterior
was lit by floodlights for the tourists, and the bell
was rung only for special occasions, the latest
being the baptism of Tazio's youngest grandchild.
Salvatore, Mario, and Gaspare had never forgotten "their" American soldier and had passed
down their stories of him, just as they'd passed
down the story of Pippo.

"He was the one who gave us the name *Our
Gang,*" Salvatore said. "And here we still are. You
think he'll play baseball with us again?" They
laughed at this idea, and Mario held up the cane he
used when his knee was acting up and swung it
like a bat.

"You remember, Gaspare," Graziella asked,
"when you stole the pen from the church and pretended Pippo dropped it?"

"I didn't steal it," Gaspare said, blowing fragrant smoke rings. "It really was a bomb. Frank was just lucky it didn't blow up in his hand."

"*Vero?*" Salvatore said.

"Of course it's true," Gaspare was saying as the sound of a plane flying high overhead interrupted their laughter.

"Hey Salvatore, maybe that's Pippo now, coming to get you!" Mario said. They all looked up into the dusky sky, searching for the plane that would be taking people to Venice or beyond.

"Could be. Mama always used to tell me to behave or Pippo would get me," Salvatore said. "Scared me half to death. Anyway, just wait until I tell Mama Frank is coming. The phone lines are going to hum tonight!"

Graziella didn't doubt this for a moment. While the Marias had long ago made their peace with her, they were still incurable gossips. At ninety-one, Maria Serena still lived in the home she once shared with Nino and their twelve children and liked to be seen driven around in Salvatore's Alfa Romeo. Maria Valentina now lived in Monselice with one of her daughters. She'd gone on to have ten girls in all, Mario remaining her only son. Maria Benedetta, having grown quite plump in her old age, lived in Milan with her own daughter, a famous soap opera star named Miracola. And Miracola was indeed a miracle, the child Maria Benedetta had conceived that same summer all those years ago. Sadly, there was no telling Maria

Teresa. Two years earlier, she'd died peacefully at the convent where she'd spent most of her life, no doubt counting the angels who'd come to take her to heaven.

"What a summer," Salvatore concluded with a sigh. "The war was over, and we were still young enough to get away with everything."

Back at the house, Emilia was reading in her room. Wishing her a good night, Graziella took a blank sheet of paper and a pen and went to sit outside on the bench by the cliff. Not the old wooden one, the one they'd always called "the soldier's bench," but a stone one Ugo had bought to replace it after it had rotted away. Soon the fireflies would come out, and the evening air was full of the fragrance of spring: *Sambucus, Acacia,* wisteria, roses.

Dear Frank,

How wonderful to hear from you after all these years, and thank you very much for your kind words and condolences.

Of course I remember that summer. How could I forget it? It was the best and worst of my life. And you're right—we were so very young and . . .

She was about to write the word *foolish,* as Frank had, but couldn't. Putting the pen down, she looked out over the valley, the sky and hills taking on the rich colors of evening. She remembered that very last night when she'd stood here by the bench, shivering as rain streamed down her old dress. She remembered too the lantern swaying in the darkness among the sumacs and Frank in the open doorway. If he'd called to her, she would've gone to him.

Would you've changed your mind if I had? he'd asked the next morning as he prepared to leave. She had nodded, not trusting herself to speak. *Then I guess I did the right thing,* he'd said sadly. And then he had climbed on his motorcycle and ridden away.

She picked up her pen again.

Yes, we were young, but no, in the end, you weren't foolish. The times demanded us to be wiser than anyone ever should have to be. You did the right thing, Frank, and I thank you for that with all my heart.

And no, it isn't too late to be friends, nor for you to visit. I would like that very much.
With fondness,
Grace

Finis

ACKNOWLEDGMENTS

As always, thank you to our agent, John Pearce, at Westwood Creative Artists and our editor, Peter Joseph, at St. Martin's Press/Thomas Dunne Books. Both your insightful input and good spirits are always very much appreciated.

We'd like to give special thanks to those who read drafts and provided comments and edits along the way (among other things): Mary Bird, Ivan (Bud) Caswell, Frances Daunt, Camille DeSimone, Erica Garrington, Theresa Lemieux, Rob Meddows-Taylor, Emily Neal, Susan Neal, Gail Pearce, Hannah Silverman, Jessica Tremblay, and Sunita Wiebe.

Thank you to Jessica Tremblay for making us look so good in our author photo and to Vicky Lipinski for our gorgeous Web site.

We are particularly grateful to the Ontario Arts Council for giving us the time to delve into the book for two months without the distractions of our regular day jobs.

To those who answered questions, provided help and advice, put us up for the night, or otherwise encouraged or inspired us: Purang Abolmaesumi and Sharon Hanna, Ajay and Amelia Agrawal, Christine and Krishna Agrawal, Aneil Agrawal and Kris Quinlan, Anurag Agrawal and Jennifer Thaler for the spruce budworms, Jasmine Baetz, Randy Beleza Tony, Lydia, and Andy Buonaguro, Mary Cameron, Nicole Campbell, Teresa Carrere, Chris Casuccio, David Caswell and Trish Wigand, Christian Catalini, Michele Chandler, David Chown, Stephen Colbert and Jon Stewart for making us laugh when we wanted to cry, Westley and Austin Côté, Frances Daunt (who sadly passed away in 2008—we miss you and thank you for The Imperial Order of the Daughters of the Empire), Paula Davidson, Carla Douglas, Peter du Chemin, Mike Filey, Anna Friedenberg, Ellen George, Leopoldo Giro and Graziella Rizzolo, Elizabeth Greene, James Gregor, Keyvan and Bahareh Hastrudi-Zaad, Mary Huggard, Gaspare Ingoglia, Istituto di Venezia, Janice's colleagues in "Honolulu," Tara Kainer, Allen, Doris, and Lori Kirk, Gwendolyn Kirk, Jeanette Levy, Dr. David Loewen for the finer points of vasectomies by shrapnel, Lorrie Grace McCann, Lisa and John McHale, Shelley and Jim McKeen, Heather McMartin, Beth Megale, David Mills and Margie Anderson, Chris Miner, Pamela Neal, Novel Idea Bookstore in Kingston, Kathryn Parise, Pasta Genoa in Kingston (especially Mara) for keeping us fortified, Ann Patchett for writing *Bel Canto,* Rusty Percy, Cecil Perido, Susanne Peterson, Sean Purdy, Lino Ravarotto and family, June Richards, Alexander, Gail, Justine, and Clelia

Scala, Margaret Smith, Heather Spragins, the staff at St. Martin's Press and Westwood Creative Artists for all their support and hard work, Francis Thatcher, Jillian Tremblay, Lisa Witzig, WonderWorks Bookstore in Toronto, and others too numerous to list here—thank you.

Our greatest thanks go to Rosanna Zucaro, our friend and language teacher in Venice, whose knowledge of Venice, the Italian Resistance, and the Venetian language were invaluable. Please have a spritz for all of us in Campo Santa Margherita!

The epilogue is for Lino and Poldo: *Ve ringrasiemo par averne dà na man e ospità, e bevì un goto de Proseco par noaltri sora i scalini de la ciesa de Cornoleda! (E òcio a Pippo!)*

Center Point Publishing
600 Brooks Road ● PO Box 1
Thorndike ME 04986-0001 USA

(207) 568-3717

US & Canada:
1 800 929-9108
www.centerpointlargeprint.com